The Bidding

The Bidding

BILL HAUGLAND

Véhicule Press

Published with the generous assistance of The Canada Council for the Arts, the Book Publishing Industry Development Program of the Department of Canadian Heritage and the Société de développement des entreprises culturelles du Québec (SODEC).

The Bidding is strictly a work of fiction. Plot line and characters are a product of the author's imagination and in no way intended to reflect on individuals, living or deceased.

Cover design: David Drummond
Set in Adobe Minion by Simon Garamond
Printed by Marquis Book Printing Inc.

Dépôt légal, Bibliothèque nationale du Québec and
the National Library of Canada, second trimester 2011

LIBRARY AND ARCHIVES CANADA CATALOGUING IN PUBLICATION

Haugland, Bill
The bidding / Bill Haugland.

ISBN 978-1-55065-314-4

1. Title.

PS8615.A785B54 2011   C813'.6   C2011-901219-7

Published by Véhicule Press, Montréal, Québec, Canada
www.vehiculepress.com

Distribution in Canada by LitDistCo
www.litdistco.ca

Distribution in U.S. by Independent Publishers Group
www.ipgbook.com

Printed in Canada on 100% post-consumer recycled paper.

*To my son, Hugh, whose gentle spirit
enriched the lives of so many.*

He opened his eyes to darkness so absolute that the room had no discernable dimensions. He had no idea where he was. He couldn't tell, by staring into the satiny blackness, whether he was in fact in a room or in some sort of container.

Ty Davis took a deep breath. The air seemed clean enough, so it was probably not a closed container. He wracked his brain for answers. What was his last conscious memory? Had he been asleep or in some sort of coma? Had someone knocked him out?

He ran the fingers of both hands through his hair and across his forehead. There was no detectable injury; no lumps or lacerations. "Drugs," he thought. He had to have been drugged. An icy terror raced up his spine. The air he was breathing was no longer clean. Ty Davis smelled smoke.

Friday afternoons in the CKCF Television newsroom followed a pattern. T.G.I.F. fever raged. Everyone looked forward to handing off to the weekend team and heading home for two days of R & R. If there were no juicy local stories in the works, assignment-editors, lineup-editors, any reporters who weren't on the road, script-assistants and news-anchors sat at a boardroom table for the three o'clock production meeting. The object was to come up with a viable lead-story for the six o'clock show. An hour had to be filled and the day had been shaping up poorly. News-director Clyde Bertram presided.

"Ideas?" he asked, looking around the table. Bertram had the butt of a House of Lords cigar sticking out of his mouth. "C'mon, c'mon. This is why we pay you people the big bucks." He curled his thumbs around his suspenders, pulled on the elastic and snapped both strands into his considerable bulk.

Assignment editor Jason Moore was under the proverbial gun. His day-file had come up empty. Perspiration on the top of his balding head reflected the overhead lights. He pawed at a note-pad and addressed Bertram. "It's gotta be this mid-March snow, Clyde. I have footage of plows, slippery sidewalks, people stuck in traffic."

Bertram rolled his cigar to the opposite side of his mouth. "Every time it snows we run a piece. What'd we get? Two inches? That's a non-story in my book, Jason. Who gives a shit?"

Moore's face reddened. "The day-file was all but empty this morning," he replied sheepishly.

The news-director showed some teeth, more of a grimace than a grin. "All that proves is a lack of imagination on your part."

Reporter Ty Davis was seated at the opposite end of the board-room table. He decided to rescue Jason and pitch his own story as a possible lead. "The nurses' union is bitching again about overtime. I've got Suzanne Déry, the president, complaining about rank-and-file compensation."

Bertram raised an eyebrow. "Two things," he said. "One, it was front page in the *Star* yesterday. *We* don't follow *them*. We find an angle and the *Star* chases us. And two, there's a page three follow in this morning's paper. Nobody's talking strike. They're just blowing steam."

"What about a feature?" Moore wanted to know. "It's Friday the thirteenth. Ty could go out and do a *streeter*. Find out if people have triskaidekaphobia … you know … a morbid fear of the number 13."

"Jesus Christ!" Bertram exploded. "What is this, a news-op or a game-show? Fuck it. We go international."

Anchorman Art Bradley had kept his silence throughout the meeting so far. He wrote the international package for the six o'clock hour. It wasn't often he was called upon to come up with the top-story. "A mudslide in Guatemala," he piped-up. "Whole village wiped out. People trapped. Houses swept down a mountainside."

Bertram nodded. "That's it then. Follow it up with the latest out of Vietnam. Ty, you and Greg Peterson head out and do something on that Friday the thirteenth crap. And, Jason, we'll lead the second package with the goddamn snow." He pulled a Zippo lighter out of his shirt pocket, lit the cigar butt and blew out a cloud of blue smoke. The meeting was over.

Bradley was smirking. No one at the table had any confidence in his writing abilities. Most of the material he produced for the evening news had to be rewritten by one of the lineup-editors. Everyone, however, had been exposed, at one time or another, to his arrogance. The *Flash News* anchorman thought of himself as a star. He wanted to be treated like one. He turned a sarcastic smile on Moore. "Bicycle-thefts," he muttered.

The assignment-editor collected his notes from the table and stood up. "What?"

Bradley towered over Moore. He prided himself on his appearance and had little use for a balding, five-foot-five subordinate. "Nothing in those notes but bicycle-thefts. Cops and robbers. Night after night. Cops and robbers."

Moore's nose and ears were a bright pink. He knew that Bradley considered himself to be a brilliant internationalist. "We're a local newscast, Art. Maybe you should realize you're a local anchor. Besides," he made a popping noise with his tongue intentionally stifling an urge to tell Bradley to go fuck himself, "bicycle-thefts are about as profound as you get." He stalked away from the taller man and waved at Davis. "Got a sec', Ty? Clyde left a surprise for us in my office."

"Surprise?"

"Well, not the kind that comes wrapped."

Ty followed Moore into a glassed-in cubicle he called his office. Teletype machines, police radios and a dispatcher's two-way radio surrounded his desk. A clean-cut young man was seated in front and to the left of the desk.

"Ty," Moore said, "meet Jérôme Poirier. Jérôme, this is Ty Davis, our senior reporter."

Poirier rose from his chair and extended his hand. "I've seen you on the tube, many times. And, please, call me Jerry. It's a pleasure to meet you, Mr. Davis."

Ty winced. "*Mister!*" he screwed-up his face. "Let's agree on something real quick. If you want to be called Jerry, then I'm sure as hell not *mister*." Ty had noticed that Jérôme Poirier spoke with virtually no trace of a French accent. Their age difference had to be less than a decade.

"Sorry about that. Ty, then."

Davis nodded. "That's more like it." He turned his attention to Moore. "You said Clyde left a surprise in your office, Jason. I'm assuming Jerry, here, *is* that surprise."

Moore gestured at both of the men to take a seat. "Straight out of a broadcasting course at Ryerson Institute in Toronto."

"Great," Ty appeared puzzled, "so how is this a surprise for me?"

"Jerry joins the talent-pool as a junior reporter. Strictly on a probationary basis." Moore pointed at Ty, "And *you* get to show him the ropes."

Ty glanced at Poirier. The young man seated next to him had all the earmarks of a privileged background. Ty knew the history. Quebec's Francophone élite often left the province for their post-secondary education, returning with a degree and a flawless ability to function in the English language. Many went into politics. Others quickly found their way into the corporate halls of power. Jerry Poirier had a Mont Blanc pen in his shirt-pocket. Ty, whose Oxford Avenue address in NDG was already beyond his pay-scale, figured Jerry for an Outremont product. Private Schools. High-end all the way.

"Lucky me," he said.

Poirier shifted uneasily in his chair. "I promise a couple things," he said, self-consciously rubbing his hands together. "I promise not to call you *mister* and I'll stay out of your way. If you have the time to show me how to do things the *Flash News* way, I'll be very grateful."

"Deal," Ty replied. "I have to call my wife. Why don't you and Jason discuss how the assignment-reporter relationship works and I'll be right back." He stood up and walked out of the room.

Friday, March 13th, 1972 was turning out to be more of a frustration than a curse. The weather was cold and damp. The news mobile-units were snow-covered and needed to be cleaned off. There was little or nothing in the day-file that had presented a challenge.

Ty knew that producing a feature on triskaidekaphobia after the three-o'clock meeting would be hectic. He'd be under pressure to get the job done as quickly as possible, get it to the lab for processing, back to the station for editing and scripting and into lineup's hands *before* the 5:45 deadline. That would put him smack in the middle of the Friday evening rush hour. He'd have to let Elizabeth know not to hold supper. She and their seven-year-old daughter, Catherine, and five-year-old son, Robin, would have to eat without him. The kids would be ready for bath and bed before he even got home. Ty and Elizabeth had had their problems, not the least of which was his work-schedule. She'd recovered from the postpartum depression that followed Robin's birth. Alcohol abuse was no longer an issue, but she was still prone to mood swings. He couldn't have known, as he picked up the phone, that Liz's emotional peaks and valleys and rush hour traffic would become the least of his worries.

Greg Peterson was downing the day's sixth cup of coffee when word came down of the late-day assignment. He'd told his girlfriend, Susan Waldon, that he'd meet her train from Ottawa. They'd planned to spend the weekend at his photo-studio in Old Montreal.

The Suzie-Q Agency provided a welcome supplement to a cameraman's salary. Marg Peterson, his mother, was promising steak and potatoes for supper and Greg wasn't pleased with the idea of setting out on a new job. Time with Suzie was his most important priority, and she would have to return to Ottawa Sunday afternoon. He was looking forward to going home.

His twenty-seventh birthday had recently passed and Greg justi-fied living with his mother. Her retirement from a personnel position at the phone company left her with the means to pay the rent, with little left over. Marg Peterson had ignored an ever-present poverty that walked the streets of the Park-Extension district, refusing to acknowledge her own lack of funds. As a pensioner, she'd chosen to spend the rest of her life in the community. Greg's CKCF-TV paycheck was a vital part of her household income. He put his coffee cup down on the equipment shelf in the photo department, thinking about steak and potatoes. The Bell and Howell silent camera was already in the mobile. Greg needed a shoulder-harness for the sound camera and a battery-pack. He checked his watch. Nearly three-thirty. This was going to be quick and dirty.

Ty walked into the room, followed closely by Jérôme Poirier. He introduced the cameraman to the junior reporter and proceeded to brief Peterson on the job ahead. "Clyde figures just a bunch of talking heads. I'll keep the question as simple as possible. 'Are you superstitious about Friday the 13th?' Something like that. Archives can provide us with some stock-footage of black cats, maybe somebody walking under a ladder or spilling a salt-shaker. We'll run it as B-roll."

Greg shrugged. He wasn't looking happy. "Y'know, Suzie is coming in from Ottawa at six-thirty. Does this look like overtime?"

Ty grabbed the shoulder harness and handed it to Poirier. "Here. You'll soon find out that carrying stuff is part of the job. Hell, I don't know, Greg. What time are you off?"

The threesome walked toward the stairs to the rear parking lot. Greg held the sound camera under one arm. The battery-pack was slung over one shoulder. "Five o'clock," he replied. "I'm off at five. Where do you want to shoot this epic?"

"As close to the lab as possible. Maybe Ste. Catherine and St. Laurent?"

"You may have trouble finding anyone to speak English in that area."

"Yeah, you're probably right. Let's set up near the Sun Life building. We can hit Dorchester Boulevard and head to the lab from there. We'll have to wait for the film and rush it back to the station. Five o'clock might be pushing it, Greg."

The parking-lot at the rear of the CKCF building was covered in a slushy, mid-March snow. The temperature hovered around the freezing mark and Mobile 7 hadn't been off the lot since late morning. The windows were iced over. Greg unlocked the driver's side door and pulled the trunk-lever. "Might as well put the equipment in here," he told Poirier. "Since you're now officially part of the team, you can start with this." He handed Poirier a windshield scraper.

The call came into Jason Moore's office at 3:45. The assignment editor had been going over his day-file for the fourteenth. Clyde's reference to his lack of imagination pissed him off. He wasn't about to let another day go by without some original ideas.

"Jason?" It was Montreal Police Lieutenant Peter Loughlin.

"Hello, Peter. How're things in the glamorous world of police public relations?"

12

There was a pause on the line. Loughlin cleared his throat. "I can think of numerous adjectives to describe what I do. Glamorous isn't one of them. Look, Jason, I wanted to tip you off on something that's going down, right now."

Moore set his day-file aside. "I can use anything you got. It's been a shitty day."

"Saint-Sauveur," Loughlin replied. "We were investigating a possible child-abduction here in Montreal. Trail led to the Laurentians where a couple of bodies turned up. A man and woman. Looks, for all intents and purposes, like murder-suicide."

Moore scribbled the information on a notepad. "What about the kid?"

"No sign of anyone else. But they're searching the place, as we speak. The Quebec Provincial Police are involved but if the bodies are connected to a Montreal kidnapping it stays in our jurisdiction."

"Thanks, Peter. I've got a reporter-camera unit on the way." He hung up the phone.

A cold wind blew out of the northwest, as Ty Davis, Greg Peterson and Jérôme Poirier parked Mobile 7 at the corner of Metcalfe and Dorchester. Greg opened the trunk and retrieved the sound-camera and harness. "Maybe we'll catch some people going in or coming out of the Sun Life building," he told Ty. "Nobody's walking down Metcalfe unless they absolutely have to. Wind's too strong."

"Top of the stairs. Next to those pillars," Ty replied. "Good idea. We can knock this off quickly and get the hell out of here." He started up the stairs. "For an easy edit, I'll give the question to the people off-camera. Roll on the answers and we'll butt-cut them back at the station. That'll speed things up. Leave the mobile running. It's bloody freezing out here."

Poirier was climbing out of the car when Jason's voice blared on the two-way. "News to Mobile 7."

"What do I do?" Poirier shouted into the wind. "Want me to reply? It's assignment calling."

Ty waved at him and started back down the stairs. "Hold on. Hold on, Jerry. I'll talk to him." He opened the driver's side door and pulled the microphone off the dashboard-mount. "Mobile 7," he said. "What's up Jason?"

A squelch noise emitted from the radio. Moore's voice came back. "What's your 10-9, Ty?"

"Metcalfe and Dorchester. Sun Life building."

"Forget the feature," Moore replied. "I'm authorizing overtime. There's a police operation underway in the Laurentians. Saint-Sauveur. Looks like murder-suicide."

Ty cursed under his breath. "You realize it's four o'clock, Jason? Suzie's coming into Montreal from Ottawa. Greg's supposed to meet her train. I've told Liz I'd be late for supper, but Saint-Sauveur? With rush hour traffic heading up the Autoroute, it'll take us two hours just to get there."

There was a brief interval before Moore responded. "I know. I know, Ty. Either I send you guys, or I bring the night shift in early. By the time they get to the station, pack up the equipment and head north, this thing will be history. I've got no choice. You're it."

Ty hesitated before answering. "What about the six o'clock show? You can forget about anything from us."

"Just get up there, Mobile 7, I'll tell Bertram. 10-4?"

Ty exhaled. It was a sigh of resignation. "10-4. Mobile 7 is 10-30 en-route."

2

MONTREAL DETECTIVE-SERGEANT Alain Robichaud stopped his car outside the old farmhouse on Rue Principale. There were two other patrol cars in sight. One had preceded him from Montreal. The other was a Quebec Provincial Police cruiser. An older model Chevrolet station wagon was also parked in the long driveway.

He radioed into headquarters and climbed out of his car, silently wishing he'd listened to his wife and worn his heavy coat that morning. The Laurentian Mountains had borne the brunt of the March snowstorm. He'd passed numerous cars, equipped with ski-racks, on their way out of Montreal. The village of Saint-Sauveur would be teeming with spring skiers on the weekend.

Robichaud had anticipated a quiet Friday, pushing papers around his desk at the Saint-Urbain Street headquarters in Montreal. "*C'est la vie*," he thought, as he swung open an outer screen door and pushed through the front entrance of the house. He was greeted by Constable Richard Gaétan.

"Two bodies," Gaétan said. "Both in the living room."

Robichaud followed the Constable into a large room with beamed ceiling and an open-fireplace. Hot coals smoldered on the hearth. "Looks like this was very recent," he said.

"How'd they die?"

"Gunshot. The woman took one in the back of the head. The man appears to have shot himself."

"Caliber?" Robichaud asked.

"Vintage World War II .45 automatic. Gun's on the floor beside the male."

Robichaud crouched beside the bodies. Both were nude. "Looks like they were having a party," he said. "Where are their clothes?"

"That's the thing," Gaétan was pointing to a couch. "Plenty of clothes in the bedrooms but those cloaks, or whatever they are, seem to be what they'd been wearing."

Two full-length, hooded cloaks lay on the couch. One was bright red, the other blue.

"Something else," Gaétan said. "Look at the woman's hip."

Robichaud did. There was a recent wound on the right hip, circular in shape.

"Looks like some sort of puncture wound," he said. "So?"

"Yeah, well by itself it doesn't seem significant. He stooped down beside the man's body. "Look here." An identical mark appeared on the body's right hip.

Robichaud shook his head. "Don't ask me," he said. "This whole thing is turning out unusual. And what about the young girl who was snatched in Montreal?"

"We've been looking," Gaétan replied. "Sergeant Roger Tremblay of the QPP and I."

"And?"

"Nothing so far. Tremblay's in the basement right now. I was waiting for you. A witness claims to have seen *this* pair," he gestured with his chin at the bodies, "forcing a young girl out of that Chevy and into this house."

Robichaud wrinkled his forehead. "You responded to the initial call from Crémazie?"

"I was in the north end. Dispatch sent me right up here."

"And the QPP?"

"Heard our radio band. They sent Tremblay over immediately. He's the one who found the bodies."

"He get the witness, as well?"

"Apparently she flagged him down when he arrived. But no one has actually interviewed her." Gaétan raised his shoulders. "What can I say? So far, there's no sign of any kidnapped girl in this house."

"So, where's the witness now?"

"She owns a small antique store here. Right across the street beside the church. She told Tremblay she was shoveling snow on the sidewalk out front. She had a clear view of this driveway."

"I'll need to talk to her." Robichaud stood up. "You and Sergeant What's His Name keep looking." He headed for the door.

* * *

Greg Peterson drove Mobile 7 through the last toll gate before Saint-Sauveur and took exit 60 off the Laurentian Autoroute. He and Ty had used payphones in the lobby of the Sun Life building to notify Greg's mother and Ty's wife Elizabeth of their destination. Marg agreed to pick Suzie up at the train station. Liz had hung up on Ty after saying "Here we go again. So what's new?"

Jerry Poirier was full of questions. "What's the procedure when we get there?"

Ty was in no mood for questions and answers. He told Poirier to keep his eyes open and his mouth shut. As Greg swung on to Rue Principale, Ty apologized to the junior-reporter. "Just observe. We don't know what we're up against, here. Sorry about snapping at you."

"What's the address?" Greg asked.

Ty grabbed the radio mic'. "Mobile 7 to News."

Moore's voice came back. "Go ahead Mobile 7."

"What's the address up here, Jason?"

"Rue Principale, the main street through the village."

"That's where we are. It's a long street. Full of stores and such."

"Look for Avenue de l'Église. I just got off the phone with Peter Loughlin, the Montreal PR Officer. The guy in charge up there is a Detective-Sergeant Alain Robichaud. Loughlin talked to dispatch. Apparently you're looking for a very old house, off the main street. There's a driveway between the shops, right at the corner of de l'Église. And look for a huge church, on the corner."

"10-4."

"You got a tape-recorder, Ty?"

"Affirmative."

"See if you can get a clip from Robichaud and get it back to us by phone. Voice around it and we'll use a slide of you and plug a full report on the late news. It's a quarter to six. You've got fifteen minutes."

Ty waited a moment before responding. "I'll do my best, Jason. Fifteen minutes isn't much time."

"I know, Ty. If you can't find Robichaud, just give us a thirty-second voice report on whatever. Even a description of the house.

Here's what I know. Girl abducted on the corner of Crémazie and St. Laurent, seen by her young friend being dragged into a station wagon. Elementary school kids on their way back to school from home after lunch. Both the Montreal homicide division and the QPP are involved. There are two bodies up there. Both shot. Apparently a vehicle matching the friend's description, is parked near where you are now. 10-4?"

"Got it," Ty said. "Stop!" he told Greg. "There's Avenue de l'Église. "We're 10-40 on location, Jason. I'll get to a phone and call the recording-line. I don't think there's a snowball's chance in hell I'll have time to snag a clip from the cops. I'll just do the voicer."

"Understood, Ty. By the way. You're lead story at six."

Detective-Sergeant Robichaud emerged from the antique shop at the same moment Mobile 7 pulled into the driveway across the street. He stepped back into the shop's entranceway, just out of sight. He was no fan of the media. They were, in his opinion, a bunch of sensationalists who profited from other people's misfortune. He shivered in the northwest wind and turned up his jacket collar. A wave of frigid air seemed to bounce off the stone walls of the adjacent church, hitting him squarely in the neck. The marked news-mobile had disappeared behind buildings on the opposite side of the street. He knew he'd have to deal with the reporters. It was part of the job. Robichaud reluctantly moved out of the shadows and began crossing Rue Principale.

Ty, Greg and Jerry were ushered into the house by a disgruntled Richard Gaétan. Ty introduced himself and asked whether there was a telephone he could use. The constable gestured at the kitchen. "Wall phone. In there," he replied.

Ty waved at Greg, who shouldered his camera and began rolling film. Gaétan wasn't pleased. "The officer in charge isn't here," he shouted. "You'll need his permission."

Greg reluctantly hit the off button and looked inquiringly at Ty. "Best to shoot Bell and Howell, anyway. We'll do a wrap when Robichaud is here."

Ty retreated into the kitchen and Greg turned to Jerry Poirier. "The silent camera's still in the trunk. Want to get it?" He tossed Poirier the car-keys.

Ty spotted the wall phone in the kitchen and picked up the receiver, praying for a dial-tone. It was four minutes to six. The telephone was functioning and he dialed the recording line in the CKCF Television newsroom. Jason Moore answered.

"Make it brief," he told Ty. "We'll run a slide of you and a super, reading voice of Ty Davis."

"Anytime you're ready," Ty replied.

"Tapes rolling."

Ty counted down from three to one and began his report.

"At approximately one o'clock this afternoon, two young girls were on their way back to school, after lunch at home. According to one of the girls, a green station wagon pulled over to the curb near the corner of Crémazie and St. Laurent Boulevard in Montreal's northeast-end. She told police that the driver leaped out and forced her friend into the vehicle.

I'm in Saint-Sauveur, where an antique shop owner on Rue Principale saw a girl being carried out of a similar station wagon. Montreal and Quebec Provincial Police were dispatched to the scene, an old house just off the main street.

No girl has been found, here. But two bodies, those of a man and a woman, have been discovered inside. Both were shot to death in what police describe as a possible murder-suicide. I'll have more information on the late news tonight. This is Ty Davis, in Saint-Sauveur, for Flash News."

There was a loud clicking noise on the line. Moore came back on. "You went 52 seconds, Ty. That's just too long to hold a static shot of the slide on the air. So, look, I'll use your first fifteen or twenty seconds as a written lead for Art Bradley and pick-up your report from where you mention your location."

Ty grinned at the phone. "No problem, Jason. I guess we have to leave something for Bradley to talk about. I'll grab Robichaud for a clip and start shooting a wrap for the late show." He hung up and began walking toward the living room.

[3]

SERGE BLOUIN WAS SURE his overall senses had been sharpened. He sniffed at the cold air and surveyed the cityscape and the river below. He was certain the ritual had worked. He could smell meat cooking, probably from as far away as a restaurant along Dorchester Boulevard. There were voices which seemed to flow on the wind and, from his vantage point in the high super-structure of the Jacques Cartier Bridge, Blouin became certain of two things. He could see more clearly than ever before and ... he could fly.

The sun was low in the sky as he prepared himself. His ascent had not gone unnoticed. There was already a traffic-jam on the bridge. Two police officers were attempting to climb after him and rush-hour commuters watched in suspense, concerned about a potential suicide and at the same time angry that their trip home had been delayed.

Blouin felt a tingling sensation in the muscles along his arms. He wondered what the people below would think when he simply sailed over the St. Lawrence River and disappeared into the evening sunset. That was his last thought, before he leapt from the bridge and plummeted to the pavement below.

Ty emerged from the farmhouse kitchen at the same time Detective-Sergeant Robichaud walked through the front door. Robichaud's face was scarlet. Constable Gaétan was standing next to Greg, who had removed the sound-camera, harness and battery-pack from his shoulder and was gripping the hand-held Bell and Howell. Gaétan approached his superior.

"I told them not to film anything without your permission."

Robichaud's complexion now resembled that of a Florida sun-bather suffering from over exposure. "Goddamn right!" he exclaimed. "This is a crime scene. How'd you people get in here in the first place?"

Ty turned on his best, diplomatic smile. He stuck out his hand and stepped forward, meeting the detective eye to eye. "Ty Davis, Sir. *Flash News*. Your public relations officer, Peter Loughlin, contacted my office." He gestured at his colleagues. "This is Greg Peterson and Jerry Poirier. Constable Gaétan, here, made it very clear that you're calling the shots. We have not used our cameras and we will not do so without your approval. At least, not inside the house."

Robichaud appeared taken aback. "No. Well, good." He glowered at Gaétan and shook hands with Ty. "What, exactly, did Lieutenant Loughlin tell you?"

Ty noticed that some of the blood had drained out of the detective's cheeks. "Actually, he spoke to my assignment editor, Jason Moore. But essentially, it was enough to lead us to this location where we were hoping to be able to assist, in any way we can, in getting information out to the public on the missing girl. Constable Gaétan was kind enough to let me use the telephone so I could begin to do just that."

Gaétan relaxed his shoulders, apparently glad to be off the hook for letting the reporters come in. "I told them we haven't found the girl," he said.

Robichaud sighed. "Alright, alright. Precisely what do you want?"

"Again," Ty replied, "*with* your permission, we'd like to get some film of the, uh, crime scene. Couple shots of those bodies. And I'd like, very much, to ask you one or two questions, if that's not too much to expect."

Robichaud seemed to be thinking it over. "And the Lieutenant gave his approval?"

"He tipped us off. Loughlin knows the drill. I'm sure he knew we'd be asking you to fill us in on the investigation. Usually, when there's a missing kid involved, he gives us all the necessary information. We don't go to air with it unless next of kin are properly notified."

"They *have* been." Robichaud added.

"But this," Ty waved at the bodies. "This is a new wrinkle. Look, detective, we don't want to interfere with your investigation. I think you'd be doing a public service to bring the story up to date. If we can, I'd like to have Greg follow you around for a while with his camera. We'll show you and constable Gaétan searching for the girl and so on. This would not be on *Flash News* until 11:30 tonight and, in the meantime, we can all hope for a happy ending. I'm sure the family would be glad to see that the police are doing everything they can."

The conversation was suddenly interrupted by the sound of footsteps coming up from the basement. QPP Sergeant Roger Tremblay emerged in a corridor leading to the bedrooms. He was obviously agitated. "I think you'd better see this," he told Robichaud.

Ty pointed to the sound-camera and signaled Greg to start rolling. He didn't wait for Robichaud to give the go-ahead. The detective was distracted by the urgency in Tremblay's voice. The QPP officer turned back and disappeared through the door to the basement. He was followed closely by Robichaud, Gaétan, Ty, Greg and Poirier. Greg turned on the battery-pack and, as they headed down the stairs, the camera was recording everything.

Jason Moore was already ninety minutes past the end of his shift when Peter Loughlin called in again. The newsroom had quieted down. Wire-copy on the Crémazie street abduction had identified the missing girl as eleven-year-old Jacqueline Morissette.

Loughlin sounded excited. "I'm sending a courier with a photograph," he told Moore. "And, we've just had another incident downtown. Not related, but I thought you'd want to hear about it."

"Uh-huh?"

"Huge traffic jam on the Jacques Cartier Bridge. South-bound lanes. A jumper."

"We don't cover suicides," Jason replied. "Encourages other wack-jobs."

"Right," Loughlin agreed. "This guy is already history anyway. Took a dive before we got to him. Thing is, rush hour traffic is backed-up all over the bridge approaches and I figured you guys might get something on the air. Warn commuters to take alternative routes to the south shore."

"We can do that. Bradley's on the air 'til seven. I'll get a paragraph down to him. But that's not going to help anyone who's stuck in traffic and not watching television. I'll also notify the "rolling-home" host on CKCF Radio. He'll get something out to people already on the road."

"Thanks, Jason. Any feedback from Saint-Sauveur?"

"Just a brief report from Ty Davis, off the top of our newscast. What are *you* hearing?"

"Robichaud talked with the shop-owner up there, the witness who saw someone carrying a struggling girl into that house. No sign of the kid, however. They're still searching the place."

Moore swiveled his chair around to face his typewriter. "We had that already. How come we didn't know about this abduction earlier?"

Loughlin went on the defensive. "An alert went out on the radio, Jason. Maybe you missed it. We were dealing with the girl's hysterical, eleven-year-old friend. We had to determine whether this actually happened the way the kid was describing it, get the information out to be on the lookout for the damned station wagon and interview the mother of the victim. We didn't get everything straightened out until, well, until I called you. The QPP was involved. Hell, it was just a little busy around here. Give me a break, eh buddy? Not a lot of time for me to start *personally* notifying the media, but you were first on my list."

"Okay, Peter. I didn't hear a lot of chatter about it on the police radio, either. And I guess I *did* miss the first alert. Look, I'm heading home after this. You have my number. The night-side lineup editor is Maggie Price. She'll likely be in touch with you as the evening unfolds."

"Well, I won't be here," Loughlin said. "I'm on the way out too. But, Maggie can call dispatch for updates. I'll alert them to expect it. Dispatch will probably ask her to talk to the officer in charge, but at least he'll know what she's calling about."

"Good," Jason smiled. "Have a couple of Molson's for me, on the way home."

"I plan to. It's been a helluvah of a day."

4

A FIELDSTONE FOUNDATION encompassed the farmhouse basement. Sergeant Tremblay led the way through an open area where the furnace and a washer-dryer were located. A partition separated the unfinished portion from a business office and family room. Vertical knotty-pine planks gave the walls a rustic appearance.

"Over here," Tremblay pointed. He walked toward floor-to-ceiling bookshelves at one end of the room. "We're underneath the kitchen," he said, "and I could be wrong, but I think the kitchen and adjacent living room are longer than this space."

Detective-Sergeant Robichaud wrinkled his forehead. "I'm not sure I understand," he said.

"I think this is some sort of false wall. This basement is at least ten feet shorter than the house upstairs."

Ty caught Greg's attention, to make sure the cameraman was capturing this exchange on film. Greg nodded in the affirmative.

"So," Robichaud replied, "let's pace it off. From the wall to the left of the stairs we came down, through that door and over to these shelves."

"Let me do that," Ty said, thinking it would make good visuals for his report. Clyde Bertram referred to it as "*reporter involvement*." Ty didn't give Robichaud an opportunity to object. He winked at Greg and disappeared through the door leading to the unfinished basement. Greg followed, camera rolling. Ty began pacing off the distance.

"Fifty-seven feet," he finally declared, standing next to Sergeant Tremblay at the bookshelves. "Now, we better measure things off upstairs, don't you think?"

Ten minutes later, sitting in chairs in the living room, Robichaud and the others were trying to make sense of an eleven-foot discrepancy between the downstairs and upstairs dimensions. End to end, the house was sixty-eight feet long.

While a decision was being made in Saint-Sauveur to find a way through the false wall, Werner Hochstrasser was making his way up Bruderholz Hill in Basel, Switzerland. It was a few minutes before midnight local time. He had agreed to meet Linus Blosch, a Swiss government tourism official.

Hochstrasser had been asleep when the call came in. Blosch had been insistent. "I have access to the *Wasserturm*, Sir. No one will be in the water tower, with the exception of security. I'll meet you at the reception doors. We can talk on the observation deck, if that's alright with you. I don't think it's wise to have this conversation on the telephone."

Ten minutes later, the two men stood high in the tower, over-looking the lighted city below. Hochstrasser, a slim man over six feet tall, walked with a slight limp and used a cane since a recent surgery. He wasn't pleased with the midnight summons or the need to mount the steep stairs. Elevators to the observation deck had been shut down for the day. Blosch, shorter and stockier, took little notice. He stood at a broad window, staring at the night gloom that hung over a distant view of the Black Forest in neighboring Germany.

Hochstrasser leaned on his cane. "Whatever gets me out of a comfortable bed at this hour better be important," he grunted.

Blosch turned away from the window. "The Council believes it is. We're preparing a full report and will await your directions." His face reflected the apparent seriousness of the situation. "We have a problem," he told Hochstrasser, "and the police are involved."

Greg watched, with the others, as Robichaud, Gaétan and Tremblay began removing books from the basement shelves. He aimed his camera in their direction but, after taking a few shots of the ongoing operation, kept it switched off. The Montreal detective had decided against using a chainsaw to gain access to whatever lay on the other side of the false wall. "Has to be some sort of locking mechanism. A concealed door."

Books began piling up on the floor. Ty held a microphone, ready to capture wild-sound when and if there was any new discovery. Jerry Poirier kept silent. Ty had noticed earlier that the junior reporter was unusually pale. He had seemed particularly upset when Greg had shot footage of the discarded blue and red cloaks in the living room.

"Here's something," Tremblay declared. He had removed enough books to reveal a structural pattern in the shelves. "See, here? There's a double thickness in the vertical boards, separating one section from another. All the rest are single planks only."

Greg turned the camera on. Robichaud nodded, in agreement with Tremblay. "Okay, let's get all of the books off, from this board," he waved a finger in an up and down motion, "over to the basement wall over here."

Books tumbled to the floor. Gradually, it became apparent that the entire section of shelving was isolated from the rest, seemingly as a separate unit.

"And this may be what we're looking for!" Robichaud exclaimed.

A metal button, about chest-high, was recessed in one of the alcoves. Ty caught Greg's eye to make sure the film was rolling. Tremblay pressed the button and there was a whirring sound from behind the bookcase. On the side where the QPP sergeant had discovered the double-thickness, the shelves moved outwards. Robichaud applied pressure on the opposite end and a four-foot wide doorway began revolving on a hidden track.

Elizabeth Davis was drinking tea. She still fantasized about drinking something much stronger in moments of stress, but Dr. Wayne Hall had been adamant. "Once an alcoholic," he'd warned, "always an alcoholic."

The Unity College professor in Newton Lower Falls, Massachusetts had nursed her through a severe post-partum depression three years earlier. Her habit of self-medicating had escalated and she had moved, with her children Catherine and Robin, to her parent's home in the small town. Her marriage was in jeopardy. Most days and nights, during her separation from Ty, were nothing but a blur until her father had introduced her to Dr. Hall.

"Some women," Hall told her, "experience actual psychosis. The so-called baby blues can sometimes produce this related disorder.

You're not there yet, Liz, but you've advanced past mere emotional letdown since Robin's birth and you are exacerbating the problem by drinking far too much alcohol."

Liz looked at the old clock on the mantel. It was after seven. Ty hadn't called since four o'clock and Catherine was sick. She realized there was no liquor in the house but, for the first time since her crisis in Newton Lower Falls, the craving seemed almost overwhelming.

Robichaud stepped first through the opening in the basement wall. Greg followed, leaving his camera on. The microphone was in a fixed position at the base of the camera. The detective seemed unaware that his every move was being recorded on film. "You and the others," he told Greg, "stay back, until we see what the hell this is all about."

Sergeant Tremblay pushed past Greg, in an apparent move to emphasize the QPP's presence. He seemed perturbed with Robichaud's air of authority. Jurisdictional issues in the case had yet to be established. Ty sensed the tension and used a palms-down gesture to signal Greg to wait. Montreal constable Gaétan and Jerry Poirier seemed to be in no hurry to find out what lay behind the bookcase.

Robichaud's first impression was loudly expressed. "Christ! There's a huge room back here."

"Gotta be at least ten feet to the wall," Greg shouted through the opening. "Then, as wide as the house is deep. Maybe thirty feet."

The detective flipped a switch and the room was bathed in a reddish light. "It is," he replied. "The rest of you can come in, now. Don't touch anything. Stay near the door."

Ty and Greg entered, followed closely by Constable Gaétan. Poirier lingered in the outer basement and then, reluctantly, stepped through. Ty's first impression was the pungent odor. "Incense," he said. "Smells like incense."

Greg switched on a Frezzi light, attached to his camera. The film kept rolling as the room brightened. "What are those?" He pointed at the floor.

A large circle had been drawn in what appeared to be white chalk.

Beyond the circle, there was a triangle. Words had been written in both. Meus, Dominus, Adjutor, Agla and Alpha Omega in the circle, accompanied by symbols that looked like Christian crosses. The words faced outwards from the drawing.

There was a circle within the triangle. The words Primematum, Anexhexeton and Tetragrammaton appeared on the outside of the diagram, written inwardly. In each corner of the triangle and outside of the contained circle were the letters MI, CH and EL. "Spells Michel," Greg said, aiming his camera at the floor.

"Beats me," Ty replied. "The whole thing looks, I don't know, like witchcraft or something."

Sergeant Tremblay was sorting through the contents of a roll-up desk at one end of the room. He began reading aloud from a loose-leaf folder he'd discovered. His hands were trembling.

"Oh Lord, we fly to thy power! Oh Lord confirm this work. That which is working in us becomes like dust driven before the wind. Let our true nature appear. Behold the Lion, who is the victor of the tribe of Judah, the Root of David. I will open the book and the seven seals thereof. Give us the power. Nothing shall harm us forever, by Eloy, Elohim, Elohe, Zabahot, Elion, Esarchie, Adonay, Jah, Tetragrammaton, Sady.

I'm a good Catholic boy," Tremblay said, trying to force a smile. "I don't recall hearing anything like this in Sunday school."

Robichaud walked toward another partition, several feet beyond the triangle. "Another door, here. That's all Greek to me," he told Tremblay. He swung open a wooden door and disappeared into a second, much smaller room. It, like the larger space, was essentially barren of furnishings. Ty didn't wait for permission. He, Greg and the camera followed closely behind.

There were two items in the anteroom; a refrigerator and a chest freezer. The detective went to the refrigerator and opened it, momentarily stunned by what he saw. Inside, on the refrigerator shelves, were four bottles containing a clear liquid. Floating in the liquid were what appeared to be a human brain, a kidney, a liver and a heart.

Greg filmed the contents. Ty stared in disbelief. Robichaud seemed to have been holding his breath. He exhaled sharply and began walking toward the freezer. The camera panned over to capture his movements as he stood, briefly, beside the appliance and then gingerly lifted the lid." "Good God!" Ty shouted. Inside the freezer, a plastic bag tied securely around the head, lay the naked body of a young girl.

5

By the time Mobile 7 pulled into the parking lot behind CKCF Television, it was pushing ten o'clock. Snow still covered the paved lot, but the Montreal temperature was at least ten degrees warmer than it had been in the Laurentians. The snow was rapidly turning into a soot-colored slush and the wind had subsided. Greg carried the equipment back to the photo department and, to Ty's surprise, Jerry Poirier decided to call it a day.

The David Spear lab had processed the film from Saint-Sauveur on a priority basis and Ty had two phone messages waiting for him. Maggie Price, the lineup editor was busily typing leads for the eleven-thirty newscast. "Liz called you," she said, turning briefly from her typewriter. "Sounded upset. Something about Catherine. And you had a call from Réal Gendron, the police reporter from *La Voix* newspaper. I left his phone number at your work station."

Ty pulled off his coat and hung it over the back of his chair. He was so tired his bones ached. "Thanks, Mag'. This thing up north is going to be headlines for days. I didn't see Gendron there, so I imagine he wants to play catch-up."

Maggie nodded. "Editing is waiting. You got some good stuff?"

"About as good as it gets, from a news point of view. As bad as it gets for the family of Jacqueline Morissette." Ty picked up his phone and began dialing home. It rang eight times, before he finally hung up. "Maggie, what exactly did Liz say about Catherine?"

"Just that she was not feeling well. Running a mild fever. I have to say, though, Liz sounded awful."

"What do you mean, awful?"

"Just down, I guess. She wanted me to try to reach you in Saint-Sauveur, so I rang your beeper. When you didn't get back to me, I assumed you were too busy."

"Did you call her back?"

"Sorry, Ty. I just didn't have the time."

Ty smiled, wearily, and headed into the film editing suite. He'd have to check with the police before going to air, to make sure the Morissette family had been properly informed of the tragic events in the Saint-Sauveur farmhouse.

Greg Peterson was thinking about Suzie and a cold beer, as he pulled Mobile 7 into a laneway next to his mother's duplex in Montreal's Park Extension district. He'd been a television cameraman long enough to have seen some pretty disturbing things, but the image of the young girl in the freezer stuck with him. He wondered about the nature of evil. How was it possible that such unspeakable acts could be committed if evil did not exist as a force in nature? What dark under-current flowed just beneath the surface of the human psyche? Was civilized behaviour merely a veneer? Greg needed to hug Suzie. He needed to be hugged back. Maybe he needed more than just one beer.

"Allo my frien'." *La Voix* reporter Réal Gendron sounded upbeat and enthusiastic, on the telephone. Ty found it difficult to respond in kind.

"Réal, long time no speak."

Gendron chuckled. "You don't call," he replied. "Some fun up north, eh?"

Ty tucked the phone in the crook of his shoulder and began typing a lead for Art Bradley to read on the air. "Just putting the story to bed," he said. "What's with you? Normally you beat *my* ass to these crime scenes."

"Dental appointment," Gendron made a smacking noise with his mouth. "Too much junk food, I guess. By the time I got back to the paper, aroun' six, I figured it would be faster and easier to listen to you and talk to the cops on the phone."

Gendron was better connected to the Quebec Provincial Police than Ty ever would be. He had a wide readership. His reports on Montreal's underbelly earned him a loyal following, not only among the police hierarchy and local politicians, but by organized crime itself.

"You know about the girl?" Ty asked.

"Sad," Gendron replied. "Very sad. Got the information from Georges LaFlamme, the QPP's go-to guy on missing persons. Know'im?"

"Heard of him," Ty said. "Kid was in a freezer. What are you hearing about the two stiffs upstairs?"

"Here's the thing," Gendron seemed to be enjoying inside information. "You left Saint-Sauveur before Tremblay and Robichaud foun' the wallets."

"Had to get back, Réal. Show biz', y'know."

More chortling at the other end of the line. "The dead guy is a big-wig at La Corporation Énergie. His name is Francis Duguay, forty-three years old. The woman was only twenty-two. Marlene Brannigan. English."

"What kind of big-wig was this Duguay?"

"Big enough. Regional Manager at the corporation. Had a lot of government connections. Oversaw some pretty substantial contracts on Hydro development, that sort of thing. Looks like the woman was a Saint-Sauveur native. Nobody important."

Ty pulled the paper out of his typewriter and replaced it with another sheet. He began typing the information into a new lead for Bradley. "Anything else?" he asked.

"Whatever Duguay was into, it wasn't sex. Pathology will have to confirm it, but it doesn't appear the Morissette girl was sexually assaulted."

"What about all those symbols, or whatever they were, on the floor of the basement room?"

Gendron paused before responding. "Hard to tell, my frien'. Satanists, maybe? The human organs found in that refrigerator did not belong to the eleven year old. Her body was intact. So, there's another body somewhere. Probably an adult, judging from the size of the heart. LaFlamme is sending the troops, tomorrow. They plan to dig up the grounds aroun' that house. It's out of his hands anyway. Now it's a matter for the homicide boys. Montreal cops are probably out of it. The QPP will be running the show."

"Stay in touch," Ty said. "You're getting more information on the phone than I got through the entire evening."

"Not a problem. Just read *La Voix* tomorrow morning, eh? "All the news you need to know.""

"Very funny. Bye Réal." Ty hung up the phone and leaned back in his chair, reading the lead he'd written for the eleven-thirty newscast.

Susan Waldon greeted Greg at the top of the stairs. Marg Peterson was seated in the living room, sipping on a cup of tea. She had the television tuned to *Flash News*. "I don't like that Art Bradley," she said offhandedly. "Your friend, Ty, does a better job."

Greg grinned at the remark. "He's still the top rated anchorman in Montreal, Ma."

"Well, I'm sure he thinks too highly of himself. He's pompous."

Greg knew there was no arguing about it. Once his mother had made up her mind about something, that was the end of the conversation. On this issue, however, he didn't want to argue anyway. At a personal level, he felt the same way about the *Flash News* anchor.

Suzie had disappeared into the kitchen and Greg followed. When he caught up with her, she had already opened a bottle of Molson's. "Figured you could use this," she said.

Greg took the beer from her and set it down on the kitchen table. "This first," he replied, pulling her close and wrapping his arms around her. "You smell good."

"And you look exhausted."

"Want to see why?"

The *Flash News* theme resounded through the house. Marg Peterson was watching the news, a nightly habit before going to bed. Greg grabbed the beer off the table and he and Suzie walked into the living room. The farmhouse in Saint-Sauveur was full-screen on the old RCA Victor television set.

Ty signed out news Mobile 14. The day had etched itself in his face as he lifted the car keys off a hook on Jason Moore's pegboard. Maggie Price looked concerned. "Pretty rough, eh?" she patted his shoulder.

"Couldn't be rougher," he replied. "Eleven years old. That kid didn't have a chance.

What the hell is it all about, Mag?"

"Life sucks and then you die."

"Yeah, but Jacqueline Morissette should have had a lot of life left."

"No kidding! Sometimes I wonder, myself, what kind of world we live in. We just never know, do we?"

She and Ty walked out of Moore's office into the newsroom. Ty slipped his coat on and dropped the keys into his inner pocket. "Something about this one, though, Mag. Something more than just a murder. I can't help but think there was some kind of plan for this kid. There was a feeling in that basement room. It was almost tangible."

"What sort of feeling?

"The only word I can think of is … evil."

The NDG district was cloaked in the mid-March snow. It hung in the trees outside Ty's Oxford Avenue flat, weighing the branches down and sliding off in rapidly melting globs. Ty parked in the garage behind his home and gradually made his way up the stairs. He tried to be as quiet as possible, not wanting to wake anybody. It was approaching one in the morning. He placed the Mobile keys on the telephone table and hung his jacket in a closet off the hallway. His stomach gurgled and he realized he'd had nothing to eat since lunchtime.

"Daddy?" it was Catherine's voice.

Ty walked briskly into her room and sat on the edge of her bed. "How you feeling, Punkin'?" He held his hand on the seven year old's forehead. "Mom said you had a fever."

Catherine sat up and leaned on the backboard. "Better," she replied. "I was sick."

"To your stomach?"

"No-o-o. Just sick."

He put his arm around her and eased her back into a lying down position. "I'm sorry I wasn't here to help. But, I'm glad you're feeling a little better now." Her forehead was damp but reasonably cool. "I think the fever has broken. Just try to get some sleep. No school tomorrow, y'know."

34

"It's Saturday," Catherine said. "You're silly. We never go to school on Saturday."

She closed her eyes and, for a few moments, Ty rubbed her legs beneath the blankets. He couldn't help but think of another little girl, who would never see another Saturday again.

[6]

THE ROOM WAS DIMLY LIT. Overhead lighting was directed at the autopsy table, but a second lamp was aimed at a tray containing the contents of Serge Blouin's stomach. Dr. Laurent Pouliot stared at a sample through a microscope next to the tray. He checked again, not quite believing his eyes. Then he wrote something into a logbook on an adjacent table.

There had been no doubt as to the cause of death. Blouin had jumped from the Jacques Cartier bridge. His body had been sent to the forensics lab over the weekend. Pouliot conducted the mandatory autopsy Monday morning in his usual meticulous manner, finding what he expected to find. Broken bones. Severe trauma.

It was the nature of his last meal that confounded Pouliot. He took a deep breath and examined the slide one more time. It was undeniable. The substance found in Serge Blouin's stomach was digested human flesh.

Activities at Saint-Sauveur slowed to a stop when a team of provincial police officers found no evidence of another body in the grounds near the farmhouse. The heart, kidney, liver and brain would have to remain a mystery for the time being. Another thorough search of the house itself revealed no further clues.

The remains of young Jacqueline Morissette, together with the organs from the refrigerator and the bodies of Francis Duguay and Marlene Brannigan, were dispatched to Montreal. Circumstances of death seemed clear. *Why* they died was quite another matter.

The case was discussed by Sergeant Roger Tremblay, with his captain. The captain, in turn, bumped it up through the ranks to the level of Chief Inspector Adrien Cousineau, who sat at a large desk on the third floor of the QPP's Parthenais Street headquarters.

Sergeant Tremblay was summoned to Cousineau's office before noon on Monday and was seated in an upholstered leather chair opposite the desk.

"You've written a full report?" the Chief Inspector inquired.

"Yes sir."

"And what do you conclude?"

Tremblay shifted his weight nervously in the comfortable chair. "I'm not certain a conclusion can be reached without further investigation."

"Then review what you *do* know, Sergeant Tremblay."

"Yes Sir. It started with the abduction, in Montreal, of eleven-year-old Jacqueline Morissette. The lone occupant of a 1963 Chevrolet station wagon grabbed her off the street near Crémazie and St. Laurent."

Cousineau coughed into a balled fist. "Then it's a matter for Montreal municipal."

"It was, until the abduction led us to an apparent murder-suicide." Tremblay proceeded to recount the whole story.

The Chief Inspector listened intently and then held up one hand, to indicate he'd heard enough. "These bodies, upstairs in the farmhouse," he coughed again and swallowed some water from a glass on his desk, "what do the ballistics tell you about the gunshots?"

Tremblay seemed surprised by the question. "Ballistics?"

"Yes. How and by what weapon were these people shot?"

"It was a .45 automatic pistol, Sir. The woman was hit in the back of the head. The man, in his mouth."

"And you concluded murder-suicide?"

"The pistol was on the floor beside the man's body."

Cousineau stroked his chin. "If you were going to kill somebody, Sergeant Tremblay, would you shoot them execution style, in the back of the head?"

"I. Well, sir, I really don't know."

"I don't think you would. You would probably face the individual catching him, or *her* in this case, completely by surprise. Especially if you knew the person you were shooting. This woman, what was her name?"

"Marlene Brannigan. A resident of Saint-Sauveur."

"And you say they were naked?"

"As the day they were born, Sir."

"So there's no doubt he *knew* her. Why, then, would he force her to kneel down and then fire his weapon into the back of her head. It's simply too methodical. She would have seen it coming and tried to resist somehow."

"Yes Sir. I see."

Cousineau smiled. "No need to agree with me, Sergeant. You were the officer in the field. I'm just thinking out loud. Has there been a determination from ballistics about the man? Has it definitely been established he killed himself?"

"Not officially, Sir. Body's at the lab."

"Then your report is not complete, Sergeant. When you hear from the lab, finish it up. I want to see it. And, by the way, tell this Montreal detective that the Morissette homicide is still in the municipal jurisdiction. Sounds to me like we're going to need a cooperative effort to figure this one out." Chief Inspector Cousineau lit a cigarette, coughed once and inhaled deeply. Sergeant Tremblay was dismissed.

The Key of Solomon bookstore faced historic Place d'Armes in Old Montreal. Ty walked through the front doors of a structure that could have dated back to the city's earliest beginnings, when it was called Ville Marie. The façade was weather-worn and the walls were the work of masons long dead. He was immediately struck by the scent of burning incense and was momentarily transported to the secret room in Saint-Sauveur.

Walls of books confronted him. A glass-encased counter supported the store's cash register and lay to one side near the entrance. Ty assumed that books contained in the display case were particularly old and valuable. An elderly man stood behind the register, quietly thumbing through one of them.

He glanced up, adjusted his bi-focals and scowled, as though Ty were more of an intrusion than a customer. "Can I help you?" he asked, in a raspy voice.

Ty leaned on the counter. "Ty Davis," he said. "I'm doing some research."

The old man's face was now expressionless. "What sort of research?"

"I have to say I know very little about the subject of occultism. That seems to be the main focus of your bookstore, is it not?"

"Occultism is a broad area. What discipline are you hoping to explore?"

"Discipline?" Ty shrugged his shoulders. "I suppose I'm interested in something like, uh, witchcraft."

"Well," the store owner pointed, "over in that row we have numerous books on witchcraft, but you might spend hours trying to find whatever you need to know. Be more specific and perhaps I can steer you in the right direction."

"Words," Ty said.

"Words?"

"Let me try to explain. I work for a television station here in Montreal. I'm a reporter. I spent much of Friday in a certain farmhouse in Saint-Sauveur where the bodies of a kidnapped girl and her two abductors were found. On the floor of the room where the girl was discovered locked in a freezer were a circle and a triangle. They contained words I've never seen before. The killings might have something to do with some sort of ritual."

"Indeed." The store owner seemed to display a renewed interest. "These words. What were they?"

Ty reached into his pocket and withdrew a notepad. He opened it and read aloud. "In the circle were the words Meus, Dominus, Adjutor, Agla and Alpha Omega. There were also a number of crosses drawn there. There was another circle inside the triangle, along with the words Primematum, Anexhexeton and Tetragrammaton. Also, in each corner of the triangle were the letters MI, CH and EL."

"Kabalistic," the old man wheezed. These are so-called *names of power*. Meus, Dominus, Adjutor means *my Lord the protector*. Agla is unknown. Certainly you've heard the expression the Alpha and Omega of life?"

"I suppose so," Ty replied. "But what does it all mean?"

"To begin with, this isn't witchcraft per say. It's demonology. The circle and the triangle are used in a conjuration ritual."

"You mean, as in conjuring a demon?"

"That's precisely what I mean. The sorcerer, that is to say the conjuror, stands in the circle. Usually the words you just read to me are written outwardly from the circumference."

"They were. Why is that?"

"To prevent the magician from being possessed by whatever he calls into the triangle. The crosses you refer to were not Christian crosses. The four points of these crosses represent the elements, fire, earth, water and air."

"In the triangle," Ty marveled at the shopkeeper's knowledge, "the words were written inwardly."

"To *contain* the demon."

"Why would anyone do this kind of ritual?"

"The object of a conjuration is to invoke the name of the Archetype, God if you will, as the protector of the conjuror's soul. Then, to demand certain powers of the entity brought into the triangle, or to demand that the entity do his *bidding*."

"What kind of *bidding*?"

"Depends on the sorcerer's ambitions. It can range from an attack on an enemy to endowing the conjuror with inhuman powers."

"Like what?" Ty asked.

"Possibly like restoring his primordial conditions of youth, grace, strength, perfection. Even physical immortality."

"And people really believe this stuff?"

The old man's phlegmy voice dropped in tone. "I have studied much in my life, young man. I dismiss nothing as impossible."

[7]

WERNER HOCHSTRASSER was insistent. He crossed the *Mittlere Brüke*, Basel's central and oldest bridge, wondering how he could convince Frankl Anderegg. When he finally arrived at Sandoz Labs the chemist reacted with his usual scepticism "It's still being researched," he protested. "Much too early to say whether the drug would be useful. It could even be dangerous."

Hochstrasser stood his ground. "It has been synthesized, has it not?"

"Well, yes, but …"

"Then it will serve the purpose. I have so advised the council."

Frankl Anderegg, an admirer of the renowned Swiss chemist Albert Hofmann, had carried on a covert research program, long after Sandoz halted production of *lysergic acid diethylamide*, LSD, in 1965. He had done so largely in his own home. Often, however, he availed himself of state of the art facilities at the labs.

The company had marketed LSD, under the name Delysid, from 1947 until the mid-sixties. It had taken it off the market in the face of growing governmental concerns about its proliferation among the general public.

"This," Anderegg shook his head, "is premature, Werner. It is a powerful psychomimetic agent, not to be trifled with."

"Have you used it?"

"I have. Under the strictest conditions and the minimum possible dosages."

Hochstrasser appeared unimpressed with precautions. "And what was the result?"

"It was long lasting. The effects are not dissimilar to entheogen's psychedelic properties, but much more intense."

"What exactly is it?

41

"*Rivea corymbosa*, the seeds of the Mexican morning glory species. It is used by aboriginal groups in that country. They call it Ololiuqui."

"And you say it can be powdered and compressed into pill form?"

"It can. Or it can be produced as a liquid."

"Then do it. Say two-hundred pills. Maybe a quart of the liquid.

Hochstrasser retrieved his cane from the arm of his chair and limped out of the room.

Saint-Félix-de-Sébastien, a farming community near the Quebec-Vermont border, had supported Our Lady of Lourdes church for more than two centuries. Families who had lived off the area's old seigneurial lands for generations were traditionally supportive of their parish, but the congregation had dwindled. Church attendance fell off dramatically by the late fifties and early sixties, the dawning of Quebec's so-called Quiet Revolution.

Key members of the province's Francophone elite began questioning the role of the Roman Catholic church in general. Even the tax exempt status it enjoyed on vast property holdings was being challenged. Gradually, Our Lady of Lourdes fell into disrepair. The parish priest attempted to find alternative routes to financial liquidity, renting the building out to the town for a variety of recreational activities.

Contrary to his own convictions about gambling, the church hall became a meeting place for bingo nights. A local rock and roll band rehearsed in the hall, leaving all manner of electronic paraphernalia and musical instruments in the care of the parish. A farm-equipment company set up temporary offices. A hair-salon occupied two rooms in the rectory. In the end, however, Our Lady of Lourdes was not economically viable. The devout among the families of Saint Félix-de-Sébastien, migrated to a much larger, affluent parish in nearby Bedford and for a period of nearly two years the building stood empty.

In 1967 the church and its property were sold to private interests. Papers were appropriately signed and a distinguished silver-haired man who drove a Mercedes moved into the rectory. Laurent Picard cleared out the old pews, some of which were put up for auction along with other church memorabilia. Extensive renovations took place.

The building was under lock and key and rumors began to spread about the nature of Picard's enterprise. Lights shone in the various rooms,until the wee hours. Cars were often parked in the adjacent lot and the comings and goings were the subject of much speculation among the townspeople for the first few months after the sale. Eventually, however, what went on behind the stained glass windows of the old church lost appeal. It was, now, a private property.

Jérôme Poirier was apologetic, greeting Ty in the newsroom late Monday afternoon. "I did some soul searching over the weekend," he confessed. "After what we all went through, on Friday, I really wondered whether I'm cut out for this." He rocked back and forth, from one foot to the other. "And there's something I didn't tell you, up there in Saint-Sauveur."

"What's that?" Ty asked, not really caring one way or another.

"I. Well, it's difficult." His face reddened.

"Okay."

"My father," he added. "He has one of those cloaks."

Ty was immediately more interested. "You mean, like the cloaks in that farmhouse?"

"*Exactly* like that. His is blue."

"Well, what the hell!"

Poirier pursed his lips. "I've never seen him wear it. It's just that I found it, one day, when I borrowed one of his shirts. It was hanging in a bedroom closet of the family's chalet in Venise-en-Québec."

"The little town facing Missisquoi Bay." Ty was familiar with the area.

"We've had a vacation home, there, for years. I have no idea what to make of the cloak, or why my father would have it."

"Did you ask him about it?

"It was summer at the lake, two years ago. I didn't think much about it at the time. I admit it was odd, but I put it out of my mind. Water skiing and girls took precedence, I guess. I had just turned nineteen a couple of weeks earlier."

"What about your mother?"

"My mother died of colon cancer five years ago."

Ty winced. "I'm sorry."

"No, that's okay. Something I've had to deal with is all. She lived long enough to see my brother, Yvan graduated from the law faculty at McGill."

"Oh yeah? That's a blessing. Where's Yvan now?"

"Gone up the 401 to a brilliant career in Toronto. He's in finance at a Bay Street firm."

"And you live at home?"

"Just me and good old Dad, rattling around in twelve rooms."

"Where's that?"

"Outremont. My father isn't home all that often. He works most of the time and takes frequent trips to the country house."

"By himself?"

Poirier hesitated before answering. "Uh, well, sometimes he has, *you* know, female company?"

Ty could tell, from Poirier's expression that his father's private life troubled him.

Where's he work?"

"He's a vice-president at La Corporation Énergie."

Ty nearly choked on his own spit. Réal Gendron's words echoed in his brain. He'd said that Francis Duguay, who had abducted eleven year old Jacqueline Morissette, was a "big-wig" at the corporation, overseeing important government contracts on hydro development in Quebec. Somehow, the blue cloak in Venise-en-Québec was a clue to an ever growing mystery surrounding the farmhouse in Saint-Sauveur.

[8]

JASON MOORE WAS IN DEEP thought. He turned the volume down on the police radio and was mulling over details of the previous Friday. He intended to review the matter with Clyde Bertram, prior to the evening news, and he planned to involve Ty Davis. Jason prided himself on a good memory but decided to work out the chronology of events on paper. He rolled a fresh sheet into his typewriter.

Girl kidnapped.

Chevrolet station wagon spotted in the Laurentians.

Witness sees a young girl being carried into a farmhouse at Saint-Sauveur.

QPP and Montreal both involved in the investigation.

Officers on the scene discover two bodies upstairs and the girl's in a hidden room.

Strange markings on the floor of the room.

Ty believes they signify some sort of ritual.

Human organs found in refrigerator.

Weekend police search of Saint-Sauveur property comes up empty.

"That'll do," he told himself. Jason spotted Ty in the newsroom, talking with Jerry Poirier, and flagged him down. "Let's have a chat," he said to Ty, pointing at Bertram's office.

The news director was busy doing paper work. His office, as usual, harbored an enter at your own risk atmosphere. Cigar smoke hung heavy in the air. "Last minute touches to the budget," he said, holding up the ledger he was working on. "Fiscal year is ending."

Ty and Jason sat in the chairs opposite Bertram's desk. Jason handed over his list.

"Sorry to interrupt, Clyde, but this story isn't going away."

Bertram scanned the page and handed it back. "I agree. Whaddya know that's new?"

Moore glanced briefly at Ty. "I can't say we know a great deal

45

more about the investigation. It's ongoing, of course. But Ty, here, had a very interesting talk with a bookstore owner in Old Montreal."

Bertram leaned back in his chair. "I'm listening."

Ty wasn't sure how to begin. His conversation with the old man at the Key of Solomon was so outlandish, he felt almost foolish discussing it. "Clyde, you're not going to believe this, but …" He proceeded to outline the entire episode.

For a few moments, there was dead silence. Bertram re-lighted his cigar and leaned forward, placed his elbows on the desk and addressed Ty. "The *devil* is in the details," he grinned at his own joke.

"Well, Clyde, I didn't think you'd find the whole idea worth pursuing."

"Hell I don't! Look, the French language newspapers are on top of this thing now, and it's *our* story. We have nothing new, according to you, Jason, on the police investigation. This moves the story forward. Go with it, Ty. Use some of the footage from Friday and highlight all of the developments to date. So far as I know, nobody's picked up on the significance of those symbols. Good. Good. Jason, you've got your six o'clock lead. Ty, jacket and tie. You're on-set with Bradley for a live de-brief. And I don't want to see any grisly shots of that girl in the freezer. This is a family newscast." Bertram puffed out a fetid cloud of smoke and returned to his ledger.

The *Flash News* theme sounded. Art Bradley sat in the central chair behind the anchor desk and camera one focused on a close-up. "Tuesday, March 17th. This is *Flash News*, I'm Art Bradley." The booming voice resonated throughout the studio. An exterior shot of the farmhouse in Saint-Sauveur came up on screen and Bradley dropped his tone to a dramatic rumble. "A young girl's murder has police baffled. Was she the victim of a Satanic cult? We'll have a *Flash News* exclusive report."

In the control room, director Steven Collyer barked orders. "Take camera two."

Ty Davis was seen sitting to Bradley's right. The anchorman lowered his chin slightly, staring up at the camera in order to give prominence to his eyes, and turned to camera two. "It all started on

Friday, when eleven-year-old Jacqueline Morissette was abducted in Montreal's northeast end. *Flash News* senior reporter Ty Davis followed this grim story to a house in the Laurentian Mountains. Ty?"

Ty heard Collyer's voice in his earpiece, directing him to camera-three on a single shot. A script assistant began counting him down to the film, as he addressed the third camera. "Thanks, Art. *Grim* is an understatement. The child's body was discovered by police, stuffed into a freezer in the basement of the house. She'd been asphyxiated."

As the ten count ended, film rolled. It showed Ty, Detective Robichaud and Sergeant Tremblay standing beside the freezer. Ty continued to voice over. "A plastic bag had been tied around her head. Her death, however, is only a small part of this story."

The refrigerator was up on screen.

"In a refrigerator next to the freezer, police found four bottles."

A long shot of the bottles. Bertram had ordered Ty and Jason to refrain from sensationalism. No close-ups allowed.

"These bottles contained human organs. To be precise, a heart, liver, kidney and brain."

The film cut to bookshelves.

"All of this," Ty added, "in a hidden section of the farmhouse basement … behind this wall of books. And on the floor," He paused as a shot of the circle and triangle came up. "these strange drawings. I spoke to an expert in the field of occultism about this circle, this triangle and the bizarre words they contain. I was told they were likely part of a demonic conjuration ritual. How did the murder of an eleven-year-old girl fit into this? We can only guess."

The scene changed to show the stairs, leading up from the basement, followed by more general shots of the house, exterior and interior.

"We do know that upstairs, in this house, two bodies were found. They were both naked and, in the interest of good taste, we won't show them to you. However, police now believe that forty-three-year-old Francis Duguay was Morissette's abductor, that he was responsible for both *her* death and that of twenty-two year old Marlene Brannigan, and that after he shot Brannigan he took his own life."

Collyer shouted "Take camera two." Ty and Art Bradley were back on a two-shot.

"A weekend police search of the surrounding property turned up no evidence of any other bodies. The human organs, found in the refrigerator, remain unexplained. Art?"

Bradley thanked Ty and turned away to a single shot on camera one. The de-brief was over.

In a shadowy corner of Our Lady of Lourdes church rectory, Laurent Picard set his martini glass down. A television set, opposite his recliner chair, cast dancing light across the walls of a large room adjoining the church proper. Picard watched Art Bradley begin his next news item and switched off the television. The room was washed in darkness. Picard was making a mental note to get as much infor-mation as possible on *Flash News* reporter Ty Davis.

9

GREG PETERSON GREETED his girlfriend on Friday evening, March 20th, at Central Station.

Her train pulled in shortly after the supper hour and Greg was determined to treat her to an expensive meal. "Moishe's," he said. "Best steak in town."

Suzie handed her suitcase to him and gave him a hug. "Sounds delightful. Where's that?"

"Not far. Up on the Main ... Saint Lawrence Boulevard. Or would you prefer something else? We could eat Italian. Whatever you want."

She smiled. "Steak is fine with me." She leaned over and picked up an overnight bag.

Greg grasped the handle of the heavier piece of luggage with one hand. He held Suzie's with his other, as they crossed the smooth floor of the railway station and began walking toward the parking garage. So far, a weekend with Suzie seemed wide open. It wasn't likely he'd be called in on overtime because local stories were at a premium. The week had produced no new developments in the Morissette case.

Art Bradley, the self-styled internationalist, had won several arguments at the mid-afternoon production meeting. "North Vietnamese regulars are planning another attack into the south," he argued. "The Viet Cong are massing in the jungles around Saigon." Bradley, at his pontificating best, insisted on a history lesson for all those gathered at the boardroom table. "After the Tet Offensive in '68, the war wound down," he pounded the table for dramatic effect. "Then, in 1970, as the U.S. began the slow process of troop withdrawl, the North Vietnamese invaded Cambodia. Well, they appear to be at it again."

Clyde Bertram agreed that rumors were now rampant that Richard Nixon was gearing up for renewed bombing runs into Hanoi and Haiphong.

"Besides," Bradley gloated, "there's nothing happening, locally, except Moore's goddamn bicycle thefts."

About the same time Greg and Suzie were ordering steaks at Moishe's, the top story on the *Flash News* hour Friday evening at six was international. Ty, like everyone else, had endured the Bradley tirade, rolling his eyes at Jason throughout. He arrived home shortly after seven, switching off the two-way radio in Mobile 14 and parking along Oxford Avenue, in front of the flat he and Elizabeth rented.

Two days of sunshine had melted all of the snow along the street and sidewalk. A huge, icy pile of it still decorated the small front lawn where city snow-blowers chose to spread the winter's accumulation. Remnants of a snow fort he had built for Catherine and Robin had collapsed in the early spring weather.

The sun had set, but a street lamp cast a gentle, golden glow on the immediate area around his front stairs. Ty was proud of the home he provided for his family. Each brick structure, along the avenue, housed four units ... two upstairs and two on the ground floor. Inside, a foyer stood at the head of a long hallway. A huge living room off the hall featured a log-burning fireplace. Leaded glass windows fronted on Oxford.

A wooden archway, carved in the Victorian gingerbread style, led from the living room into a full-sized dining room. Three large bedrooms were further down the hall, then a bathroom and a kitchen complete with breakfast nook and walk-in pantry. There was even a maid's room off the kitchen, but of course there was no money for a maid. It made the perfect location for their washing machine.

As Ty walked up the front stairs, he remembered how empty the place had seemed when Liz had taken the children to her parents' home in Massachusetts. He worried, once again, that their marriage was on the verge of a meltdown. Liz had been silent on the subject of his preoccupation with work. He had expected an argument, when he'd returned from Saint-Sauveur on the previous Friday. Instead, she had been fast asleep.

Nothing further had been said. No quarrels had ensued. Ty was sure her silence was a precursor ... the *calm before the storm*.

* * *

Lineup editor Maggie Price was on the warpath. She intended to give Clyde Bertram an earful on Monday, about the constant harassment from lineup at the Toronto based National Television Network, of which CKCF TV was an affiliate. Rumors had circulated for months that NTN was poised to purchase CKCF from the private owner, Futura Films Corporation. To date, there had been no confirmation of a bid being made by the network. Head office executives, in both Toronto and Montreal, were holding their cards close to their collective chest.

Advocates of a takeover within CKCF argued that Futura Films had imposed far too many budget restrictions on the various departments. Maggie had to agree, at least with *that*. Much needed newsroom equipment had been promised but never materialized after Futura bought the station in the mid-sixties. Bertram's favourite line was "we can't even get new pencil-erasers out of those cheap bastards." Production had suffered greatly, at the local level, under the auspices of Futura Films.

Two children's shows, that had been staples since CKCF first went on the air, had been cancelled. A weekly *talk and call-in*, hosted by a popular weatherman, was expecting the axe to fall. Studio directors and script-assistants attached to the production department felt the proverbial Sword of Damocles hanging over their heads.

Maggie, on the other hand, had enjoyed free rein when it came to putting a newscast together. So far as she knew, no one in the news-op felt the heavy hand of editorial control from above. Purchase bid or not, NTN was already attempting to impose its influence on news content. Lineup Toronto had shown particular interest in the Morissette abduction and subsequent events. It seemed to Maggie that Toronto was always *hot to trot* when it came to negative news out of Quebec. Anything to do with what NTN saw as outrageous statements from the separatist movement in the province usually led the national news at eleven. Montreal's crime rate was of equal interest, and apropos of a perennial pissing match between the two cities. Negative made news.

Maggie accepted that determining its own lineup was the network's prerogative. Lately, however, she had come to expect nearly nightly calls from NTN requesting video feeds and reporter/anchor voice-overs and demanding that one or more of the network-generated reports be used by all affiliates.

Art Bradley and at least two of CKCF's reporters were only too pleased to cooperate. Bradley fancied himself, one day, at a national anchor desk. He kowtowed to the Toronto types whenever the opportunity arose for national exposure. Maggie, however, wound up doing all the work. It was time-consuming and was always at the expense of her main duty ... that of putting a local newscast to air at eleven-thirty. Bertram was going to have to bite somebody's head off. She wasn't going to put up with it anymore.

To anyone who suggested that an NTN takeover was desirable, Maggie had already prepared a response. "Be careful what you wish for."

10

THE MONKLAND TAVERN, just south-east of Ty's home, was a good meeting place for a quick beer and a brief meeting. There were the usual die-hard drinkers who showed up early in the morning for their first cold one. By the end of the day, Monday the twenty-third of March, some of them were incoherent, asleep, or had been shown the door. Usually, around four-thirty in the afternoon, the business-men began arriving. Most were intent on downing at least two beers before heading home to their families. A few of the jacket and tie set were still parked in their chairs when Ty Davis and *La Voix* police reporter Réal Gendron sat down at their table at five-forty-five. Gendron had called Ty earlier that afternoon. He had something of interest to show him.

"What are you drinking?" Ty asked. "And what are you doing this far into the West End?"

Gendron had a manila envelope on the table in front of him. "As to the first question," he grinned, "I'm a Labatt-50 man. As to *this*," he tapped his fingers on the envelope, "I drove out here into Anglo-land, because I thought it would interest you."

Ty laughed. "Well, much appreciated."

A waiter, wearing black cotton pants a white shirt and a black vest, stood next to their table. He held a note pad in one hand and a ballpoint pen in the other. "What 'kin I get fer you gents?"

They put in their orders and the waiter disappeared through a door next to the tavern kitchen. Gendron opened the envelope. "These are official photos," he said. "Even *I'm* not supposed to have them, but I have a good frien' in the police lab." He turned the two photographs around and slid them across the table to Ty. "Meet your Jacques Cartier Bridge suicide, Serge Blouin, or what's left of him after his swan dive."

Ty studied the shots. One of them was a full-length view of

Blouin's body, lying on an autopsy table. The skull, above the eyebrows, had been pulled back exposing his brain.

The chest had been opened in a T-shaped cut from one shoulder to the other and down the middle to the groin. "Nice," Ty said.

"Ever seen an autopsy?" Gendron asked.

"Never had the privilege."

"It tells the pathologist a lot about the individual. Not just how he or she died, but whether they had sex prior to death, whether they had an illness and, much more importantly in this case, what they ate for their last meal."

Ty looked on, inquisitively. "I get the feeling you're about to tell me."

"*C'est vrai*," Gendron replied. "*Monsieur* Blouin, here, was a cannibal. His stomach contained proof."

"Good lord! You mean, he ate … people?"

"*Exactement*. That's precisely what I mean. Anyway, that was the nature of his *last* meal."

The waiter returned with their beers. Ty's was a Molson. He took a long pull on the bottle, ignoring the glass beside it. "Unbelievable. What about this second photo?"

"That's where this gets really interesting," Gendron took a swallow of his Labatt-50. "I had a lengthy conversation with the QPP Chief Inspector Cousineau about the Saint-Sauveur incident."

The second photograph was that of Blouin in a face-down position. The *La Voix* reporter stared at Ty. "See anything you recognize?"

Ty felt the hairs rise on the back of his neck. On Blouin's right buttock was a healed scar, what was left of an old puncture wound. It was the same shape that had appeared on the bodies of Marlene Brannigan and Francis Duguay in the Saint-Sauveur house.

Maggie Price came in early. She knew that Clyde Bertram would be in his office, working against an April deadline for submission of his newsroom budget. She decided to risk her good health and wade through Bertram's cigar smoke, knocking and then entering the news director's office. "Hate to interrupt, Boss, but I got a beef."

Bertram recognized the disapproving expression on Maggie's face and put the cigar into an ashtray on his desk. "No problem,

Maggie. You're my excuse to take a break from all of *this*." He indicated the ledger and a mass of papers in front of him.

Maggie sat opposite the desk. "It's this, Clyde. The goddamn network is driving me crazy."

"How so?"

"To begin with, Art Bradley is a *vedette* ... a star, or so he thinks. And he's not helping. NTN's lineup editor is constantly asking for stories. I don't mean they just want a video-feed of our six o'clock pieces, they want me to rework the whole damn thing. That means going to the original script, rewriting everything and getting a reporter, or Bradley, to voice what amounts to a brand new story with an NTN signoff. Bradley's gung-ho, of course, because it means national exposure. One or two of the reporters, if they're assigned to the night shift, are equally enthusiastic."

Bertram responded with his usual "I'm listening."

"Well, Clyde, all of this takes me away from my obligations to *Flash News*. I mean, it's time-consuming and frustrating as hell. On at least three occasions, Toronto hasn't been satisfied with my rewrite. They've asked me to do it again, cut it down, add a sentence here or a sentence there. Then I have to deal with the techs to get the whole thing to T-O and get Bradley, or whomever, into a studio to do the voicing. By the time it's all done, I've wasted an hour or more."

Bertram grinned. "They don't own us yet. Leave it with me, Maggie. I'll talk with the NTN news director. If they can't use the six o'clock piece, intact, then they can shove it as far as I'm concerned. Worst case scenario is they use the six o'clock report, cut the *Flash News* signoff and you get Bradley to voice a special one for NTN. No more rewrites. The techs can handle the video feed. *You* work for *me*, not Toronto."

Maggie stood up and turned to the office door. "That's the way I see it."

"And I agree," Bertram smiled again and picked up the smoldering cigar.

11

DR. DENIS DESJARDINS ENJOYED the good life. His family background of old money, higher education and sound genetics served him well in the Laurentian community of Sainte-Agathe-des-Monts. The Centre Hospitalier Laurentien, the local hospital, valued his affiliation and his enormous, post-and-beam style home on the shore of Lac des Sables was envied by all who entered.

On the evening of Wednesday, March 25th, a waxing moon was partially concealed behind storm clouds moving in from the west. The beachfront, beyond a massive deck at the rear of the house, was mostly in darkness and it was beginning to snow. Inside, Dr. Desjardins sat at the head of a long, wooden table facing the living room. Occasionally the clouds parted and the moon slid into a patch of open sky. A silvery light played over the vaulted ceiling.

Desjardins was concerned. He had read the newspapers and he had seen the television news reports. His craving for a spiritual understanding of his privileged lifestyle had gone unsatisfied by long-standing attendance at the Catholic church of Sainte-Agathe. In fact, it had driven him to question the very existence of God. At fifty-three years of age, he'd needed a greater understanding of creation. Books had accumulated in his study. He'd reached out to numerous scholars. Nothing had satisfied his need to find some proof that invisible, cosmic forces were actually a reality, that there was a reason for his life, that death was not the end of everything. Nothing had satisfied. Nothing, that is, until he'd met Francis Duguay.

Desjardins picked at his dinner. His wife and two children were visiting relatives in Montreal and he was deep in thought. There was an unobstructed view, from his position at the table, through sliding doors on the outer wall of the living room. The doors were surrounded by huge glass panels fronting onto the deck and the beach beyond.

* * *

Ueli Berlinger picked his way along a snowmobile track across the frozen Lac des Sables. A deep-throated rumble was at his feet, as winter waves flowed beneath the surface of the ice. Berlinger was dressed in white and carried a heavy bag. The bag contained his livelihood. It was a C3A1 sniper rifle manufactured in 1960 by Parker Hale in the United Kingdom. It was a bolt-action rifle. No external magazine, 7.62 x 51 mm ammo, although he usually needed only one cartridge to do the job. A telescopic lens, to the 40 power, provided him with a bright, clear view of the target.

Berlinger hunched down every time the moon dropped out of the clouds, but that was unnecessary. His white clothing and the chalk he had used around his eyes, forehead and mouth served as adequate camouflage against the snow. He moved toward the house, his feet making a crunching noise as he made his way to the lake side of a concrete boat dock. The dock was probably a hundred feet long. A sweeping expanse of beach ran up to a staircase and outdoor deck. Lights shone inside the building.

He had two choices. He could simply climb the stairs and try to conceal himself on the deck, or he could position himself on a lifeguard tower at the end of the concrete wharf. The wooden structure, which rose at least ten feet above the dock, would put him on an even level with the house and the deck. It might even be above floor level, offering a downward trajectory. He opted for the latter.

Berlinger slowly walked to the beach, staying in the shadows, then abruptly turned around, stepped up on to the dock and jogged its length to the lifeguard stand. Luck was with him. The moon stayed behind the clouds. He mounted a short staircase at the base of the tower, lifted his bag to the platform and pulled himself up. He'd been right. The platform was at least two feet higher than the floor of the house.

Assembling the rifle took only minutes. He used a bipod to give the long barreled C3A1 additional stability. There were special crosshairs on the telescopic lens to aid with judgement of distance and accurate shot placement. Berlinger laid down on his stomach and looked through the lens. His target came into view, seated at a table about thirty feet from the windows. He estimated the total distance, muzzle to target, to be 86 metres … an easy hit. Actual target: a three centimeter or 1.2 inch portion of the victim's brain stem. Berlinger wanted a quick kill.

Moments later, Dr. Denis Desjardins reeled backward. His chair fell over. His body hit the floor and his life's blood spilled out of a hole in his neck. Desjardins would never have to worry about the existence of God again.

Visibility on the Eastern Townships Autoroute was minimal. Jerry Poirier kept the windshield wipers going and tried to stay at least half a dozen car lengths behind his father's Caddy. A sense of guilt accompanied him, all the way from the parking garage at La Corporation Énergie, where he'd waited since five-thirty. "After all," he told himself, "my mother's dead. Dad has every right to get on with his life."

Jean-Jacques Poirier called his son, at CKCF TV, late in the afternoon. Jerry was in the editing suite with Ty and the message had been short and sweet. "Heading to the chalet in Venise-en-Québec. See you tomorrow."

Jerry strained to see through the windshield. Heavy snow had swept down from the Laurentians and flat terrain through the Montérégie region wasn't helping. A stiff wind lifted white curtains across the highway from open fields to the right and left. His '68 VW bug usually held the road well, but temperatures had dropped just enough to cover the surface in an icy glaze. Trucks roared past, seemingly unaware of the wall of snow they kicked up in front of vehicles in the slow lane.

As he drove, Jerry reviewed his days with Ty Davis and Greg Peterson. Journalism courses at Ryerson Institute felt like an ancient memory. The challenges of becoming a *Flash News* reporter were daunting, to say the least. He leaned forward in the car seat, now barely able to make out the tail-lights of his father's car. Jerry felt certain of one thing. He had to know why a blue cloak, exactly like those found in Saint-Sauveur, hung in a closet in Venise-en-Québec.

* * *

"Far fetched!" Clyde Bertram exclaimed. "How do you make a credible connection between Marlene Brannigan, Francis Duguay and this ... this nut job on the Jacques Cartier Bridge?" Ty stood beside the news director in the open newsroom. Bertram was tearing copy off the CP wire. "It's too much of a stretch."

Ty was adamant. "Same puncture wound," he replied. "Same place on the right buttock." He held up the photograph Réal Gendron had given him. "And this was no ordinary nut job, Clyde. This guy had been eating human flesh."

"That's confirmed?"

"Direct from the police lab where the autopsy took place."

"Who *is* this Serge Blouin, anyway? I mean, what's his background?"

Ty slipped the photograph back into its manila envelope. "I made a few phone calls, Clyde. I think we have more to go on than just the puncture wound."

"I'm listening."

"He lives in Sainte-Agathe-des-Monts. He's a personnel manager at the Centre Hospitalier Laurentien."

"So?"

"So, think about it. Brannigan is from Saint-Sauveur. Duguay rented that farmhouse. Blouin lived just a few miles away. They all had similar scars on the right buttock and Blouin had a belly-full of God knows what. They could have known each other." Bertram appeared unimpressed. "The operative words, Ty, are *could have* known each other. We need more than that to go with a story."

"What about the cannibalism?"

"What about it?"

Ty shrugged. "We're still missing a body, Clyde. Someone belonged to the brain and other parts found in that refrigerator. Serge Blouin apparently preferred that sort of thing to a T-bone steak."

12

It was a fast turn in the wrong direction. His father had been a hundred feet ahead of him when the Caddy took a sharp left off Route 7 onto a farming road. To the best of Jerry's recollection he was unfamiliar with it. Traffic had thinned out since St.-Jean-sur-Richelieu. At Iberville, he'd slowed down and dropped back. Only two vehicles separated his Volkswagon from his father's car.

Now, well past the Richelieu River, even the snowfall was beginning to let up and Jerry was gripped by a worry he'd be spotted. Jean-Jacques Poirier was alone on the farming road, a route that would take him *away* from the lake and the family cottage at Venise-en-Québec. It was flat country and a straight run, stretching into the snowy distance. Jerry stopped at the intersection with Route 7. He decided to wait until his father's tail-lights were swallowed up by what was left of the blizzard.

An eighteen-wheeler thundered past and the driver laid on the horn. Jerry had stopped *his* car in the middle of the lane. He instinctively closed his eyes as a veritable wave of snow hit the windshield. When he opened them, he looked to his left. There was no sign of the Cadillac. Gradually, he swung on to the farming road, proceeding at a slow pace and determined to find out where his father was headed.

A workhorse stared at him from a fenced-in corral. Jerry noticed he was wearing a woolen coat, but the horse didn't appear overly enthusiastic about his freedom. The coat was covered in snow and its owner's eyes seemed to ask "what the hell am I doing here?" Jerry assumed the farmer was still in the milk-house and would return the horse to its stable when chores were done.

The Volkswagon crept along. Jean-Jacques' Cadillac was long gone into the night and Jerry still had no idea where the road was taking him. There were no curves, no intersections and no helpful signs indicating a juncture or a town ahead. Farms slipped by. Jerry momentarily lost his bearings and nearly clipped a roadside mailbox. It was difficult to tell where the pavement ended and the soft-shoulder began.

He wanted to believe that the blue-cloak, at the family chalet, was just a coincidence. Perhaps it was merely a carry-over from some Halloween masquerade party his parents had attended. It might have hung in that closet for years before he'd discovered it in the summer of his nineteenth birthday. Something told him, however, that the truth was much darker. He couldn't dismiss as mere coincidence that the dead man in Saint-Sauveur worked for the same corporation where his father was a vice-president.

Polo's Restaurant and Bar, otherwise referred to by CKCF personnel as "The Hole," was a city block away from the television station. It was a home away from home for *Flash News*; an extension of the work-day, away from interruptions and management oversight. Ty, Greg and Jason Moore sat in a corner. Nick, the barkeep, had refilled their pitcher of beer and the three men were in hushed conversation.

Moore poured some beer into his glass and addressed Ty. "Bertram is right," he asserted. We can't jump the gun on these things. A step at a time. Let's review what we know and go from there."

Ty felt impatient. "Jason, for Chrissakes, Réal Gendron isn't waiting. *La Voix* already ran a piece on the cannibalism. I mean, that's a story in itself don't you think?"

"Not if we waste it and miss the bigger story."

"Whaddya mean?"

Moore swallowed some beer. "Look at all the loose ends. We can't tie them all together, yet. We've got a murdered eleven-year-old, two dead kidnappers, some human organs in a refrigerator and a jumper on the Jacques Cartier bridge. This Blouin character has, shall we say, a rather exotic diet. How's it all connect? Plausibly, I mean. That's what Bertram wants to know and I think he's right. I think we have some work to do."

"To begin with," Ty replied, "They all live within a few miles of each other. Brannigan, Duguay and Blouin. And they all had the same healed scar on their right buttocks. Like I told Clyde, there's still a missing body. Those human organs had an owner. And, like *you* say, Jason, Blouin was a cannibal."

Moore screwed up his face. "Still circumstantial. I live a few miles away from Pierre Elliott Trudeau, but I don't know him, personally. Maybe he's got a scar on his left knee, just like the one I have from a cartilage operation. Doesn't mean he's a buddy of mine. The police are still looking for the body those organs were harvested from, so we can only speculate that someone was planning to *eat* the goddam things. Then, Blouin jumps off a bridge and the only way we can connect him to Saint-Sauveur is that he lived and worked in the region. Where do you see a story in this?"

Greg had been listening to the two-way conversation, passively, his eyes moving back and forth between Ty and Moore. "Maybe the answer lies on the floor of that secret room. Maybe all of these people were members of the same, I dunno, *cult* or something."

Moore smiled. "Maybe so, Greg. But we can't prove anything unless we do some more digging."

The sign read "Bienvenue à Saint-Felix-de-Sébastien. Reduce Speed." Jerry Poirier figured he'd driven about eight miles since turning off Route 7. It appeared he was on the outskirts of a small farming town that he knew he'd never seen before. The snowstorm had mostly dried up. A few flakes continued to hit the windshield of his VW bug, but he realized that most of it was being lifted off the ground by a gusty wind. There was still no sign of his father's Cadillac.

Jerry eased back on the accelerator as widely-spaced farms were left behind and he began passing a series of small homes along the village's main street. He realized he hadn't eaten since lunch time as a small *casse-croûte* on his right made him think of a cheese-burger and fries. It was already eight o'clock but supper would have to wait.

No one was on the sidewalk. It didn't really make any difference. He couldn't just approach a complete stranger and ask whether they knew Jean-Jacques Poirier. Jerry passed a gas station, a bank and another small restaurant, all in darkness. There was a farmers' co-op where the lights were still on and, directly opposite, a huge stone church. Text on a smooth-faced granite slab to one side of a driveway revealed

Our Lady of Lourdes church to be a historic site. But that was not the reason Jerry slammed on his brakes. At least twelve cars were parked in a lot next to the church and one of them appeared to be his father's 1972 Cadillac.

He decided not to pull into the parking lot, drove past the driveway and pulled into a space about a hundred yards up the street. What business would his father have with a church? He had no idea. Since his mother's death in 1967 Jerry had stopped attending church in Outremont. He didn't believe his father had *ever* accompanied his wife, his brother or him. Jean-Jacques, for all intents and purposes, was a non-believer.

Jerry walked back along the sidewalk and crossed into the church driveway. He couldn't figure out why so many cars would be lined up in the parking lot on a Wednesday night. Just to make sure he wasn't mistaken about the Cadillac, he wandered over to check it out. There was no mistake. His father's overcoat lay across the back seat and, in a subdued light showing through stained-glass windows in the church, he could make out a familiar burn mark in the driver's side upholstery. His father was a relentless consumer of Belvedere cigarettes.

Gradually, he approached wooden double doors at the side of the building. His mind was racing. Jerry realized he'd been following the Caddy because he suspected his own father of being involved, somehow, with a brutal crime. He hadn't been able to simply confront him about the blue cloak. In fact, now, he would find it impossible to explain why he'd followed him all the way out of Montreal. It came as a great relief that the church entrance was locked. As he turned away, frustrated and riddled with guilt, Jerry paused. Emanating from behind the huge doors was a chorus of voices. It was not a hymn. It sounded more … like chanting.

13

MARCH, IN ACCORDANCE with an Almanac reference, had come in like a lion. It appeared to be "going out like a lamb." Thursday, the 26th, was bathed in a warm spring sunshine. Jason was about to make the day even brighter for Ty, Greg and Jerry. Shortly after nine in the morning, he tapped on the glass partition surrounding his tiny office and made a *come here* gesture. Ty, who was scanning the French newspapers for any updates on the Morissette murder and related events, was seated at his typewriter. He picked up his coffee cup and walked into the assignment-editor's sanctum.

Moore, as usual, had the police radio blaring. "Hold on, Ty." He turned the volume down and smiled. "Remember we all agreed, last night, there was more work to be done on the Saint-Sauveur thing?"

Ty nodded. "I still think we ought to run a story on Blouin's cannibalism, but yeah of course I remember."

"Well, here's the deal. I had a tête-à-tête with Bertram this morning and he's agreed to free you up to follow the whole story. No assignments from me, today or tomorrow. Go with your own ideas and see what you can come up with."

"Cool."

Moore chuckled. "Mind you, I'd like you to run 'em by me just the same."

"No problem. I'll tell you, right now. I assume you're going to give me a camera?"

"Greg Peterson," Moore replied, "and Jerry Poirier will be tagging along, wherever you go. Maybe, give Jerry an opportunity to do a couple of standups. See how he is on-camera. Not for air. We'll screen the stuff and see whether he's ready."

"Gotcha. Anyway, I don't believe we'll get anywhere with this story until we go back to where it all started. It's a nice day. You and Clyde have given me the green light, so Greg, Jerry and I will spend the day basking in Laurentian Mountains sunlight."

"The farmhouse?" Moore asked.

"Not specifically. But Detective-Sergeant Robichaud interviewed a witness *near* the house. I never got to her. That's where I intend to start."

Moore reached over and turned up the volume on his police radio. He gave Ty a thumbs-up and said "Good luck. Let's stay in radio contact, eh?"

La Petite Perle, an antique shop on Rue Principale in Saint-Sauveur, was as quaint as its name. A blue and white canvas awning had been unfurled and hung over the front door. A welcome mat, obviously hand made, invited customers across a threshold into an earlier century. Ty stepped around a butter churn. A Boston rocker that might well have suited Whistler's Mother sat on a wide-plank floor that was literally covered with all manner of antiques. In fact, it was difficult to see very much of the floor.

Ty had asked Greg and Jerry to wait in Mobile 7, until he had a chance to speak to the proprietor. He wasn't expecting to be greeted by two enthusiastic dogs. They came bounding out from behind a partition at the back of the shop, followed closely by a middle-aged woman. She was carrying a third dog in her arms. "Those," she pointed at the two animals who were now excitedly sniffing at Ty's legs, "are my meet-and-greet specialists. They manage to beat me out of the office every time a customer comes in."

Both dogs at Ty's feet were brown-colored and approximately the same size. Both, it seemed, were pleased to have company. The shop owner continued with the introduction.

"That's Max," she indicated. "He's so happy to see you, he's likely to pee himself. And the other one is Mike. They're what's known as Nova Scotia tolling duck retrievers, tollers for short." She proceeded to pat the small, black dog she was holding. "This one is Pearl. We don't know a great deal about the parentage. My shop is named after her and she considers herself superior to all of this customer relations stuff." Pearl's large, black eyes stared blankly at Ty. There was virtually no expression of interest. She had much more important things to do. Places to go and lie down ... and food dishes to see.

Ty scratched Max behind the ear. Mike circled him, demanding equal time and equal attention. Pearl, it seemed, had become bored with the encounter and had dropped off to sleep. "My name is Ty Davis," he told the shop-owner. "I'm a reporter with CKCF Television in Montreal."

"Yvette," the woman replied. "I'd shake your hand, Mr. Davis, but Pearl would wake up and object. I take it you're not interested in antiques?"

Ty shook his head. "I like antiques. I just can't afford them. Actually, Yvette, I'm here because …"

"Because you want to know more about what happened across the street."

Ty grinned. "I hope you don't mind. I know the police have already talked with you."

"Not at all. Terrible thing, that."

"Absolutely the worst. Well, look, first of all I was here and in that house on the day they found the little girl and the two bodies upstairs. What I'd like to find out from you is whether you might have seen any activity across the street, in the days or weeks leading up to the event."

Yvette stroked Pearl, bent over and put the little black dog down on a cushion by the rocking chair. "She's old, now," she said, referring to Pearl. "Sleeps most of the time. I think I've seen *you* on television."

Ty nodded. "So, you're familiar with *Flash News*?"

"It's how I practice my English," Yvette smiled. "I have no objections to telling you what I know."

"Would you mind telling a camera?"

"You mean, on television?"

"Well, yes, it would be on *Flash News* eventually. Just a short interview. I'm doing an investigative report that would involve a number of elements in the story. I can let you know when it would be on the air."

"What fun," Yvette rubbed her hands together. "I'm sorry. I know this is a serious matter, but I've never been on television before."

"There's a first time for everything, they say. If you don't mind, then, I'll ask my colleagues to come into the shop. We can set up right here."

"Do you think Max and Mike could be on TV too? I don't think we'll be able to keep them from jumping up and down. I suppose I could lock the dogs in the office."

Ty shrugged his shoulders. "No need for that. If they're in the shot, they're in the shot. No problem."

Yvette's face showed her excitement at the prospect. Ty turned toward the front door.

"I'll be right back," he told her.

Ty waved at the car and Greg climbed out of the driver's seat. "Good to go?" he asked.

"All set, Greg. Bring the tripod, unless you think the harness is better. Actually, bring 'em both in. You're the expert. You choose, once you see the layout."

Jerry Poirier stepped out of the back seat. Greg popped the trunk and handed him the heavy, wooden tripod.

Inside *La Petite Perle* Yvette was brushing her hair, using a framed mirror that was probably stylish in Queen Victoria's time. "I must say, Mr. Davis, I look a mess."

"You look just fine, and there's absolutely no reason to feel nervous. We'll just have a conversation. Forget about the camera. Just talk to me.

She pulled her hair into a bun and inserted a mother-of-pearl comb into it, holding it neatly in place at the back of her head. Greg set up a light-stand and said "anytime you're ready." The camera was mounted on the tripod.

"You want us to sit?" Ty asked.

"Nah. Standing would be better. The background will show up more. Lots of atmosphere in this place."

Ty stepped into frame, his back to the lens. "You can stand right here, in front of me," he motioned to Yvette. "Just look at me. No need to look at the camera."

Greg adjusted for a single shot of the shop owner, shooting over Ty's left shoulder. "Rolling," he said.

Ty cleared his throat. He held the microphone midway between himself and Yvette, in order to balance the audio. "Give us your full name please, Yvette."

"Now?" she asked, once more checking her hair comb which had slipped out of place.

"Yes. I just want this for a reference. It's not part of the interview."

Her cheeks reddened and, despite Ty's directions, she addressed the camera. "Yvette Comtois, sole owner of *La Petite Perle* here in Saint-Sauveur." She shook her head, making sure that the ponytail hadn't come loose. Max and Mike darted in and out of frame. Pearl sighed, briefly opening one eye, and promptly went back to sleep.

Ty thanked Yvette for the ID and carried on. "Now, I understand that on Friday the thirteenth of this month, you were shoveling snow outside your shop, here, and that you spotted something disturbing. Could you describe *what* you saw."

Ty knew he wouldn't find her answer to be useful. He was aware of what she'd seen on that day, but wanted to take her mind off her appearance and simply get her talking. And she *did* talk, recalling the old model Chevrolet station wagon's arrival, the struggling girl being carried into the farmhouse and her subsequent conversation with Detective-Sergeant Alain Robichaud.

Ty let her finish and then *really* began the interview. "Had you ever seen the man and woman before the incident on the thirteenth?"

"Oh, yes. Yes, I knew Marlene Brannigan. She lives, or I should say *lived*, right here in Saint-Sauveur. As for *him*, well he moved here about a year and a half ago. Rented over there. I saw him around from time to time. Kept pretty much to himself."

Ty realized that Yvette Comtois had her ear to the ground when it came to small town gossip.

"Do you know *where* he lived, before moving here?"

"Oh, yes. His name was Francis Duguay, you know."

"So I understand."

"Word around town is he came from somewhere around Saint-Luc, a few miles south of Montreal."

"Do you have any idea, from what you heard around town, *why* Mr. Duguay decided to pack up his things and move all the way up here?"

"Somebody chasin' him, I guess. No, I really don't know that. But he was a strange one, that's for sure."

"What makes you say that?"

"Just the way he was so secretive 'n all. Always looking over his shoulder. Like he was being watched. And, when he talked with people, there was a *look* about him."

"A look?"

"Yes. I saw it in his face one day, right out there on Rue Principale. Almost," she hesitated, "animal-like."

14

THE CENTRE HOSPITALIER LAURENTIEN tried, several times on Thursday, to reach Dr. Denis Desjardins by phone. There was no reply at his home on Lac des Sables. Desjardins had been due for a patient consult shortly after the noon hour. The patient had arrived, waited an hour and given up.

At roughly three o'clock, Desjardins' wife, Carole, and the couple's two children left Carole's sister's home in Montreal and headed north. There was very little traffic on the Laurentian Autoroute and they took their time on the return trip. They had no idea what awaited them at the huge house by the lake. At five o'clock, after a brief stop for a mid-afternoon snack and restroom visit in Laval, the trio pulled into the couple's driveway in Sainte-Agathe-des-Monts. It was after five-thirty when Carole managed to collect her shattered nerves and call the Quebec Provincial Police, to report her husband's murder.

Ty spent some time walking up and down Rue Principale in Saint-Sauveur. He hadn't really learned anything new from Yvette Comtois, except her impression that Francis Duguay wasn't quite right, that there was something unsettling about him.

"Of course," she had said, "I was right. Look at what he did to that poor little girl."

Greg and Jerry tagged along, as Ty spoke to passersby and merchants along the main street. No one was helpful. Mobile 7 was back on the road, heading to CKCF TV, when Jerry decided to reveal the details of his previous night's adventure into the Montérégie.

He stammered, slightly, as he began. "I, uh, I d-don't know whether this means anything. But, well, you know about the cloak I saw in the family chalet, Ty?"

"Yeah. And, Jerry, I haven't mentioned it to anyone else. Do you want to discuss this now?"

"For a couple of reasons. Yes."

"Okay. He glanced over at Greg. "*You* should know that, two years ago, Jerry saw a blue cloak ... similar to the red and blue ones in Saint-Sauveur, hanging in a closet at their cottage in Venise-en-Québec. It might have no bearing on the Morissette case and I haven't pursued it as an angle in the overall story."

"Jeez!" Greg exclaimed.

Jerry continued. "But, there's more *to* it. My father is a vice-president at La Corporation Énergie."

Greg, who was driving the car, turned his head to face Jerry in the back seat. "Correct me, if I'm wrong, but isn't that where this ... Duguay worked?"

Ty interjected. "It is. But that's as far as it goes. Could be coincidental. Both the cloak *and* the corporation. Besides, we're talking about Jerry's dad here."

"That's what I had thought," Poirier said, "until last night." He recounted his entire experience, from the corporation to the church in Saint-Félix-de-Sébastien.

For a few moments there was silence in Mobile 7. Then Ty spoke up. "It's interesting, Jerry. But what does it really tell us?"

"There was something going on in that church. I'm sure it wasn't, you know, a usual church meeting. The doors were locked. Whoever was *in* there didn't want to be seen ... including my father. There was some sort of weird singing too."

"How was it weird?"

Jerry thought it over. "Maybe Gregorian? But different. Not pleasant. A lot of discord and minor notes. For lack of a better word, it didn't sound ... Christian."

The Bank for International Settlements is contained in an imposing building in Basel, Switzerland, it's architecture reminiscent of an era colored by two world wars. Werner Hochstrasser stood in an alcove off a gigantic, pillared hall highlighted by marble floors and crystal chandeliers. It was shortly after nine o'clock on Friday morning.

Security in the building is ranked a number one priority. No agent of the Swiss government is entitled to enter the *BIS* without permission.

The bank controls police power over the premises and enjoys immunity from criminal and administrative jurisdictions. There is a distinctive, foreboding presence that hangs in the very air of the place, likely carried through the decades from its founding in 1930 by Hjalmar Schact who later became Adolf Hitler's Minister of Finance.

Hochstrasser was never bothered by the atmosphere. He was intent on one thing … a transfer of funds to Ueli Berlinger in Ottawa, Canada. It was accompanied by a simple note to Berlinger. The note mentioned no names but advised the recipient that a list would be provided … that the job in the Laurentian Mountains of Quebec was not yet done. Further transfers would be necessary.

La Voix carried a front page headline on Friday the 27th. It read "Professional Hit in Laurentians." Ty sat at his typewriter, trying to decide what possible relevance the story might have to his own investigations. He made a mental note to give Réal Gendron a call.

The La Voix piece reported that a Dr. Denis Desjardins had been shot to death at his home on Lac des Sables in Sainte-Agathe-des-Monts. Ty froze in his chair. Suddenly, he realized that contacting Réal Gendron would not be necessary. Dr. Desjardins was affiliated with the Centre Hospitalier Laurentien, the same hospital where the Jacques Cartier bridge jumper, Serge Blouin, had been employed in the human resources department.

He pushed his chair back, grabbed the newspaper and headed for Jason Moore's office. The assignment editor was engrossed in his day-file. "Morning, Ty, how's it feel to be self-assigning for another day?"

"Actually, Jason, I think I might be on to something. And, it doesn't appear that my good friend Réal Gendron has connected the dots yet."

"You talking about the Sainte-Agathe murder?"

"You know about it, then."

"Yeah. I read it this morning. What *dots* are we connecting here?"

Ty sat down beside Moore's desk and placed the La Voix story in front of him. "Look closer at the story, Jason. The good doctor was affiliated with the same damned hospital where Serge Blouin was a personnel manager."

"The guy who dove off the bridge?"

"Exactly."

Moore seemed to be considering the information. "Interesting. Very interesting. Mind you, I'm not sure we can make anything of it. Could be another coincidence."

Ty appeared frustrated. "Yeah, but I'm willing to bet they knew each other. I mean, Desjardins had to have had dealings with the hospital's personnel department."

"What if he had?"

"Then they *knew* each other."

"And you think that Blouin's suicide is somehow connected?"

"I don't *know* it. I just *feel* it."

Moore straightened some papers on his desk and grinned. "See this day-file? It's pretty much empty today. I can't afford to spring you from regular assignments on Monday, but, if you think there's something in this *La Voix* thing to pursue, go right ahead. You've got all day today. Greg and Poirier are at your disposal."

"Thanks, Jason. I think we're dancing around the edges of a very, very big story." He stood up and walked slowly back to his typewriter, lost in thought.

Elizabeth Davis couldn't seem to slow down her mind. She'd managed to get Catherine and Robin off to school, bathed, breakfasted and dressed, but she felt agitated. She had snapped at Catherine, when the seven-year-old objected to the dress she'd chosen for her to wear. Ideas occurred to her like rapid-fire rounds from a machine gun, so disorganized she couldn't discern their meaning. She found herself talking much faster than usual, changing subjects and obviously confusing the children as they tried to understand and cooperate.

Liz realized she had not been sleeping well. In fact, for at least three nights, she hadn't seemed to need much sleep at all. Unknown to Ty, she had gotten out of bed and paced up and down the hall in their Oxford Avenue flat ... wanting to, and yet unable to focus on anything.

Liz was distantly aware that her behavior, this morning, had frightened and confused Catherine and Robin. She was also aware that she and Ty hadn't had sex for over a month. "Hell," she thought, "we haven't even had a decent conversation."

15

STUNNING SCENERY BORDERS the Laurentian Autoroute north from Saint-Sauveur into Sainte-Agathe-des-Monts. A transformation, from wintry weather of the previous week to bright sunshine and temperatures in the thirties, accompanied Ty, Greg and Jerry. It boosted their spirits, despite the grim nature of their trip into the mountains. As Mobile 7 passed Saint-Sauveur, Jerry jokingly asked whether they could just take the day off, find a good restaurant and report back to Moore that they needed to book into an expensive hotel. They'd been on the road for two hours.

Rue Saint-Vincent, in Sainte-Agathe, was less than a mile off the autoroute. Greg drove into a visitors' parking lot adjacent to the Centre Hospitalier Laurentien, where Ty had learned the body of Dr. Denis Desjardins was being temporarily held in the hospital morgue. It would be turned over later in the day to provincial authorities. An autopsy would follow. Police would still be at the family house on Lac des Sables, collecting evidence and interviewing family members and closest neighbors.

"Your choice," Ty told Greg and Jerry. "Stay put and enjoy the sunshine until I sniff around a bit, or come in. We may or may not get any cooperation from the hospital. This whole thing might have nothing to do with what happened in Saint-Sauveur."

Greg opened the driver's side door. A flock of crows suddenly exploded into the air, from trees surrounding the parking lot. "Feels like spring," he said offhandedly.

Poirier climbed out of the back seat. "It *is* spring," he said, "at least, officially." He stretched his arms and legs and inhaled the fresh air. "I, for one, would like to go with you, Ty."

"Okay. Greg, you might as well bring the silent camera with us. Just in case we're given permission to use it."

"What about sound?"

"Who knows?" Ty replied. "Let's see, first, whether anybody is willing to talk to us."

The trio made its way toward an emergency entrance off the parking lot. Greg paused at sliding doors that opened automatically and they walked over to a reception area, set behind a wall of glass. A perky young woman greeted them.

Ty stepped up to the window. "We're from CKCF Television in Montreal," he told her. "Could you tell me how to get to the office of the hospital's Medical Director?"

She smiled and pointed. "Elevator , there. *Deuxième étage,* second floor."

Ty thanked her and headed for the elevator bank. He pushed the 'up' button and when the doors opened, a nurse and an orderly dressed in a green uniform pushed a bed out into the corridor. An IV tower, attached to one corner of the bed, fed clear liquid into the veins of a patient who appeared to be asleep. A bag of orange colored urine hung just below the blankets. "*Je m'excuse,*" the orderly maneuvered into the open hallway. Greg held the elevator doors open until the bed was clear. "*Merci monsieur.*"

The second floor office of the Medical Director was divided into two areas. A secretary sat in an ante-room off the main section. A door to the director's office was closed and a brass plaque on the door bore the name "Dr. Thérèse Lanctôt." Ty introduced himself to the secretary and asked to see the doctor.

"*Un autre journaliste?*" she inquired.

Ty nodded. "Have you been getting a lot of calls from journalists?"

The secretary switched to a fluent English. "All morning," she replied. "There's one of your colleagues with Dr. Lanctôt right now."

"Well, perhaps the director would see us at the same time." Ty smiled widely. "We have an expression in English. Kill two birds with one stone?"

She shrugged. "Haven't heard that one. But I'll check." The secretary pressed an intercom button beside her telephone. "Dr. Lanctôt. I have another journalist here in the office. He wonders whether ... you'd wish to kill two birds with one stone?" A mischievious look passed over her face.

For a moment, there was no reply from the director's end. "*Quoi?* Two birds?"

The secretary grinned, showing a dimple in each cheek. "He says it's an English expression. Sorry for the joke. He'd like to come in, while you're with *Monsieur* Gendron."

"Wait a minute," Ty suddenly leaned over the desk. "Did you say Gendron? Is it Réal Gendron from *La Voix*?

"It is."

"He's a friend of mine. I'd really appreciate it, with Dr. Lanctôt's permission of course, if …"

Suddenly, the director's door swung open. Gendron waved at Ty. "Allo, my frien.'"

"Beat me up here this time." Ty said.

"All the news you need to know, eh?"

"Yeah, yeah. Blah blah." Ty and the others walked through the open doorway.

Dr. Lanctôt was standing behind her desk. She appeared a little perturbed at the idea of an impromptu news conference that wasn't *her* idea in the first place. "You are, *Monsieur* …?" she held out her hand. Her brow was furrowed.

Ty shook the hand. "Davis. Ty Davis. These are my colleagues, Greg Peterson and Jérôme Poirier. Thank you for seeing us, Dr. Lanctôt."

Gendron's eyes still conveyed an impish expression. "I was just telling the doctor, here, that it would be very helpful if I could see the body of Dr. Denis Desjardins."

Lanctôt sat down. "No pictures," she declared. I can let you talk with our morgue attendant. But no photos."

Gendron raised his hands in a gesture of resignation. "*Pas de problème*. No problem," he replied.

Ty wasn't ready to give in, just yet. "Dr. Lanctôt, Réal works for a newspaper, as you know. I am a television reporter. We both deal in pictures. What if we talk with this morgue attendant, and agree to take just a few shots of the hospital exterior and some very general pictures of the morgue itself. We understand that you'll be turning the body over to the coroner's office and that it will be object of a criminal investigation. We give you our word. No photos, or film, of Dr. Desjardins' body."

Lanctôt pursed her lips. "I can't stop you from shooting outside," she said. "I *can* stop you from using cameras *inside* the morgue. Dr. Desjardins was highly regarded in this community. I'm sure his family has enough to deal with, without seeing it plastered all over the media."

Gendron interjected. "We understand your concerns, Dr. Lanctôt." He winked at Ty. "And we sympathize with the family. However, this story has already been, as you say, plastered all over the media. We're simply trying to do our job."

The director didn't seem persuaded. Ty jumped in. "What if we put you in touch with Chief Inspector Adrien Cousineau of the provincial police? If he agrees to let us into the morgue with our cameras, would you permit us to take a few shots? And we promise, it would be nothing gruesome. Nothing to upset the Desjardins family."

"You would just photograph the room? Not the body?"

Ty shook his head affirmatively. "Not the body. You have my word."

"Then call the Chief Inspector. Here's my direct line." Lanctôt wrote a telephone number down on a sheet of paper and handed it to Ty. "I'll talk with this, Cousineau, but I'll also call Dr. Desjardins' wife. If Carole objects, I'm sorry, that will be as far as it goes. Agreed?"

"*Certainement.*" Gendron nodded. "*Merci*, Dr. Lanctôt." He asked to use a telephone. The director pushed her own to the front of the desk and Gendron began dialing the number for QPP Chief Inspector Cousineau. He knew it by heart.

Jason Moore was worried about a communiqué dispatched to the media. Quebec's Common Front of workers, established the year before on behalf of 250,000 public and semi-public employees, was talking strike. Moore sensed an explosion in the labor movement's attempts to bargain with the Quebec government.

It was Friday. The communiqué stated that all attempts at negotiations had failed, in the face of a government refusal to deal with the Common Front and Quebec's insistence on bargaining *only* with individual unions. A strike would embroil three union *centrales*, including the Quebec Federation of Labor, the Confederation of National Trade Unions and the Quebec Teachers Corporation. Government offices, schools and hospitals would be targeted in what could become a de facto labor revolution in the province.

Moore carried the dispatch into Clyde Bertram's office. The news director was on the telephone. He raised a hand, to indicate the call would be over in a moment. "Gotta go, Dear."

Jason realized Bertram was talking to his wife. "I can come back," he said, still standing beside the desk. Bertram simply hung up. "Sit," he told Moore. "You have *urgent* all over your face. What's goin' on?"

Moore sat down, as instructed, and held up the communiqué. "This looks ominous," he waved the dispatch over his head. "Looks like the Quebec Common Front is at it again, and it doesn't seem like just a twenty-four-hour warning strike in the works."

"What are they saying?"

"That negotiations have gone to hell in a hand basket. First ... the warning strike, as early as tomorrow. Who knows, a general walkout could be the next step."

"What would that involve?"

Moore was aware that Bertram was expecting him to fill in the blanks. "Big trouble," he replied. "Hospitals, schools, government offices ... you name it."

"What about essential services?"

"Unions would provide up to a third of regular staff. Senior staff and medical practitioners would stay on the job."

Bertram leaned back in his chair. "So, the machine would keep on working."

"That's not the point," Moore disagreed. "We're talking about sixty-one hospitals, clinics and health centers across Quebec. Some of these outfits have agreed with the unions' definition of essential services. Some haven't, and *they* would consider any walkout as illegal. Christ, the government itself appears ready to reject *any* strike notice or essential services procedure. Not to mention the fact that a general walkout could, literally, *shut down* the government."

"What do the unions want? What're the demands?"

"Guarantees," Moore said. "Things that don't even exist in the private sector. They want a guaranteed minimum wage, across the board, and they want guaranteed job security. Under that last demand, once hired, the government would have one sonofabitch of a time trying to get rid of a worker. In other words, job protection would be ensured."

Bertram smacked his lips. "Any timeline on this?"

"Like I say. We could see the first round as early as this weekend."

"Get on it, Jason. Pull Ty back from the Laurentians. I want him reassigned."

16

QPP Chief Inspector Cousineau had no objections. He agreed that photographs of Dr. Desjardins' body could be disturbing to the family, but did not feel that general shots of the morgue at Centre Hospitalier Laurentien would compromise the police investigation. He told Dr. Thérèse Lanctôt that the ultimate decision, as Medical Director, was entirely hers. She hemmed and hawed but reluctantly gave her permission.

Ty, Greg, Jerry and Réal found themselves in a basement hallway, facing double doors marked Pathology — Employees Only. Gendron pushed his way through, as though visiting a morgue were a routine occurrence. The others, including Ty, wrinkled their noses in reaction to an immediate assault of chemical odors.

The pathology department was divided into two sections. The hallway led, first, into a laboratory filled with the usual paraphernalia. Two men in lab coats were laboring over microscopes and test tubes. One of them glanced up, as the four entered. "You the reporters?" he asked.

Ty responded with another question. "Dr. Lanctôt telephoned we were coming?"

"In there," the lab technician indicated the second room, sealed off by what appeared to be heavy steel doors."

"Looks like a bank vault," Ty tried to sound humorous. The technician didn't seem amused. "You want to talk with Donald.

"As in duck?" Ty asked, still trying to provoke a smile. He didn't succeed.

"Donald Quesnel. He's expecting you." The tech went back to his test tubes.

Gendron was grinning as he pulled back on the heavy doors. "You should stick with your day job, Ty. Comedy's not your forté."

"I thought it was funny," Ty said, as Donald *Duck* Quesnel stood up from behind a battered old desk. The morgue was softly lit and at least fifteen degrees cooler than the lab. One wall displayed a series of six closed cabinets, framed in stainless steel. There was an autopsy table in the center of the room and, apart from the desk and chair, there was no other furniture.

Gendron shook Quesnel's hand. "I believe Dr. Lanctôt explained, *Monsieur* Quesnel, that we intend to take some pictures of the morgue. We'd also like to see the body of Dr. Desjardins."

"And," Ty interjected, "if you don't mind, perhaps a few questions for you?"

"The director explained," Quesnel replied. "No photographs of the body, *n'est ce pas?*"

"Right. No shots of the body."

Gendron was already taking stills of the morgue itself. Flash bulbs illuminated the darkened room in staccato bursts of light. Greg followed suit, using the Bell and Howell silent camera.

"When was Desjardins' body brought into the morgue?" Ty asked Quesnel.

"Late Thursday night. Actually, early this morning."

"Has it been determined how long he'd been dead?"

"*Sais pas*. I don't know. His wife found him yesterday afternoon."

"Shot, is that right?"

"He has a wound through the neck," Quesnel nodded.

"So, he could have been lying on the floor at his home for some time before his wife discovered the body."

"Again, *Monsieur*, it's a matter for the police to determine. There will be an autopsy, but not here."

"I understand that, Mr. Quesnel. Just trying to get a timeline on all of this. Let me ask you another question. What sort of a man was he? Was he, as far as you know, a good doctor?"

"Everybody liked him. He operated a private clinic, right here in Saint-Agathe, but he was here at the hospital every day. The patients always looked forward to his rounds. He treated them well."

"What do you mean about treating them well?"

Quesnel shrugged. "Just seemed to be very kind. How do you say in English? A good bedtime manner?"

"Bed *side*," Ty smiled. "Can you give me an example of this *kind manner*?"

"Well, very recently, there was a terrible accident on the autoroute. A Saint-Agathe man was killed when he hit some black ice near exit 58. Dr. Desjardins knew the family. He had the ambulance bring the man to his own clinic, rather than the hospital, then took it upon himself to notify the family."

"Is that normal procedure? I mean, to have the body at his clinic?"

"No. But he felt it would be easier … less traumatic I suppose, for the family."

"What happened then?"

"The doctor advised the victim's wife that, if she chose cremation for her husband, he would make all of the arrangements. He told her it would not be wise to see her husband in the condition he was in."

"And she did that? She chose *not* to see the body? Wouldn't she have to make a formal identification?"

"Dr. Desjardins spared her that. This man was well known in town. There was no doubt as to his identity."

"So he was cremated."

"*Oui Monsieur.*"

"Locally?"

"The crematorium is on the outskirts of Sainte-Agathe. The Ouellette Funeral Home."

"Hm-m-m. A brief question about another Sainte-Agathe man," Ty said. " Did you know the hospital's personnel manager, Serge Blouin?"

"*Oui.*"

"To your knowledge, did Dr. Desjardins have contact with Blouin for any reason?"

Quesnel seemed taken aback by the question. "Why do you ask? Blouin committed suicide you know."

"Yes, I know. I just wondered whether … I'm just trying to get some background on Dr. Desjardins. You know, people he knew. People he hung out with?"

A pause. Quesnel cleared his throat. "I don't see the relevance."

Ty smiled. "Perhaps not, Mr. Quesnel, but that's what we reporters do. We ask questions."

"Well, I don't understand the significance. Blouin is dead. Dr. Desjardins is dead. If they were friends, so what?"

"So they *did* know each other?"

Quesnel's face reddened. He realized he'd already answered the question. "I saw them, *de temps en temps*, eating lunch together. In the hospital cafeteria."

Greg suddenly announced that he had enough footage of the morgue. Gendron had stopped shooting stills and was jotting something down on a notepad. Ty assumed he hadn't drawn his own conclusions about the Jacques Cartier bridge suicide and its possible connection to the Desjardins murder. He fired an approving glance at Ty and addressed the morgue attendant. "Can we see the body, now?" He put his camera down on Quesnel's desk, to indicate there would be no further photography. Quesnel, in turn, walked over to the wall of stainless steel and pulled open a drawer marked with the letter "D." The six cabinets were labeled "A" through "F." A slab, supporting the remains of Dr. Denis Desjardins, slid out into the room. The body was wrapped in a blood-stained sheet.

"Can we see it?" Gendron asked. Quesnel drew back the sheet from Desjardins' face.

"*All* of it?" Gendron requested.

Quesnel obliged. As the rest of the body was revealed, it was abundantly clear what had killed the doctor. The bullet had made a gaping hole, now surrounded by coagulated black blood, in Desjardins' throat near his Adam's apple. But that wasn't what caught their attention. On the body's right buttock, appearing like a vaccination mark gone wrong, was a healed scar. There could be no doubt that Dr. Desjardins, Serge Blouin, Marlene Brannigan and Francis Duguay shared a common secret that had gone with them to the grave.

17

IT WAS INTENDED TO BE a peaceful demonstration. On Saturday morning, March 28th, rank and file members of the CNTU, QFL and QTC marched, along Ste. Catherine Street waving placards and blocking traffic. A mass rally was scheduled for noon in front of the Hydro Quebec head office on Dorchester Boulevard, where Premier Robert Bourassa kept a Montreal office. The twenty-four-hour warning strike marked the first time public servants had taken to the streets since a three week strike in the civil service in 1966.

Something happened as the marchers reached the downtown intersection of Peel and Ste. Catherine. A motorist, intent on turning south on Peel and fed up with delays, hit the accelerator when a group of picketers stood directly in front of his car. One of the strikers was knocked off his feet by the impact. Another threw out his arms in a Superman-style effort to stop the car, and suffered two broken arms. A third man landed on the hood of the vehicle and was knocked unconscious.

"Hey! Fuck you, eh." A big man, carrying a sign that read *On veut le respect,* leaped off a sidewalk and grabbed at the driver's door handle. The door swung open, as the car slowed down, and the motorist was dragged out on to the pavement. His car kept going, running up on to the sidewalk and crashing through the plate glass windows of a tobacco store on the corner.

A pedestrian, seeing the violence begin to unfold, rushed into the Dominion Square building and dialed the police emergency number. It was unnecessary. A police contingent was already in place and reinforcements were already on their way. Sirens could be heard wailing in the distance. By this time the angry motorist had been surrounded. He was wrestled to the ground by the big man who had rushed his car. Picketers dropped their signs and piled on.

On the previous evening, Ty Davis had thought it was a case of insult to injury. His beeper had gone off while he, Greg and Jerry were returning to the television station. They'd exited the autoroute and Ty had made a payphone call to Jason Moore. Now, not only was he being temporarily pulled off the Morissette murder, he was being told to take Mobile 14 home and remain on twenty-four-hour call. Labor trouble was brewing. He might have to work the weekend.

There was an iceberg atmosphere at home. Catherine and Robin had been put to bed early. Liz had not prepared any supper. She'd glared at him when he told her he might have to report into the station Saturday morning. And it was then that he realized there was something different about the living room in their Oxford Avenue flat.

"What the hell, Liz?" She was sitting on a couch he'd never seen before. His favorite easy-chair, in front of their TV set, had also been replaced. "Where'd this stuff come from?"

There was no response from Liz. Only her utterly cold stare. Ty tried again. "Where's my chair, Liz? What happened to the couch?"

"Like it?" She ran her hand across the rounded arm of the couch. "It's new. I got a deal."

Beads of perspiration burst out on his forehead. "I can *see* it's new, Liz. *Why*? Where'd the old stuff go?"

"They took it."

"Chrissakes, *who* took it?"

Liz smiled defiantly. "The Sally Ann."

"You *gave* my chair to the Salvation Army?"

"Yep."

"Liz, this isn't making any sense. Why would you do a thing like that?"

"I felt like shopping. The kids and I."

Ty tossed his overcoat on to the new chair and flopped down on top of it. "Where'd all of this *come* from. He made a sweeping motion with his arms. "How much did it cost?"

"I told you. I got a deal."

"Yeah, but how much? What sort of deal? And how'd you pay for it?"

"That's the deal. Nothing down. A hundred a month. We'll own it in just eighteen months."

"Jesus, Liz. We can barely make ends meet now. What were you thinking?"

She'd lapsed, again, into silence, now staring straight ahead and ignoring any further questions. Liz Davis, it seems, had gone on a shopping spree.

The fuse was lit. The explosion wasn't far away. Three Montreal Police squad cars and two ambulances were at the intersection of Peel and Ste. Catherine on Saturday morning, when Ty walked into the area from two blocks west. Crowds of curiosity seekers milled among the union demonstrators and a tow truck was winching a car backwards, out of the display window of a tobacco shop. Greg Peterson was filming the action. He handed Ty a microphone.

"Here's what's happening. Motorist gets pissed off and runs into three guys. He's hauled out of his vehicle while his car is still moving. They beat the shit out of him and the vehicle jumps the curb and crashes. Of the three guys who got hit by the car, two have been sent to the hospital. Cops say one appeared to have fractured both wrists. The other had head trauma. Hit his head on the hood of the car when he tried to duck out of the way. The motorist also got shipped to hospital. In a cruiser. He's prob'ly gonna be breathing through his mouth for a month. Broken nose. Shattered teeth."

"Holy shit! Where'd you get the info'?"

Greg pointed at a heavy-set man in a flannel shirt. "I got here as the first ambulance was leaving. "*That's* the guy who yanked the motorist out of his car."

"Here." Ty gave the mic' back to Greg. "Might's well just keep shooting wild sound. Maybe I'll snag the big guy for an interview and see where things go from there."

Glass fragments and pieces of the tobacco shop's outer wall tumbled on to the sidewalk as the tow truck gradually eased the car out of the display window. Some of the demonstrators began cheering. East-bound traffic on Ste. Catherine Street was now backed up as far west as Mountain and some motorists were heading south on one-way streets toward Dorchester Boulevard. Ty noticed that the crowd had increased in size and was getting larger all the time.

College students, who had heard earlier in the week that there might be a Common Front protest, had planned a sympathy march of their own. They filed in from the north. Another group, apparently made up of radical elements in the Quebec separatist movement, moved in from the east. Some of them carried baseball bats.

"Hey!" Ty flagged down the burly man in the flannel shirt. "Ty Davis. *Flash News*."

The man shrugged, all but ignoring him. He said "*Ici on parle français*," and promptly turned his back on the possibility of an interview. Ty was about to go after him when there was a piercing scream from someone near the Dominion Square building. Greg swung his camera around. Ty grabbed the microphone again and they both pushed their way through the crowd and across Peel Street.

Police officers were already kneeling beside a woman who was lying on her back. One side of her coat had been ripped across the shoulder and she was bleeding profusely. A hockey stick, apparently thrown like a spear, lay beside her. The business end of the stick had been sawed off and razor blades protruded along its entire length.

"Good God!" Ty exclaimed. "She could have been killed."

"*Solidarité!*" the demonstrators began shouting in unison. "*Solidarité! Solidarité!*"

Just east of Peel, near Metcalfe Street, several of the demonstrators began rocking a police squad car back and forth. "*Solidarité!*" they shouted. "*Abat* Bourasssa ... down with Bourassa." The rocking motion failed to overturn the squad car as half a dozen police officers, swinging night-sticks, rushed the perpetrators. The officers were badly outnumbered. Two of them were attacked and struck down by their own batons. The others retreated.

Further to the west, a gang of thugs not related to the union demonstrators, began smashing shop windows along Ste. Catherine. Fights broke out spontaneously, and a French-language radio station's news car was set on fire. Someone had tossed a Molotov cocktail. Ty and Greg weren't sure which way to turn. "Keep rolling!" Ty yelled. "Follow me!" He began moving toward the firebombed car, voicing a report as they maneuvered through the melee.

"*I'm on Ste. Catherine Street,*" he began. "*Near Peel. The so-called*

Crossroads of Canada, Peel and Ste. Catherine this morning have become a battleground. Rank-and-file members of three unions, making up what's come to be known as the Common Front labor movement, began a march early today at Guy and Dorchester. Despite traffic tie-ups, it was an entirely peaceful gathering as they moved north to Ste. Catherine. The plan ... to protest the state of collective bargaining with the government of Robert Bourassa. Unknown to the union members, others were planning something quite different. Violence erupted when a motorist, heading east on Ste. Catherine Street, drove his car into a group of the marchers, injuring two men. He was pulled out of the driver's seat and severely beaten. His vehicle, gearshift still in 'drive', rolled up on to the sidewalk and through the display window of a tobacco store. No one injured in the shop. By this time groups of college students and, apparently, radical separatist elements had infiltrated the union demonstration. The march was fast becoming a mob.

Demonstrators tried to overturn a police squad car and failed. Two police officers were slightly injured when they were beaten, literally, with their own night-sticks.

Shortly after that, a woman was struck by a hockey stick riddled with razor blades. I've just left her, bleeding on a sidewalk, near the Dominion Square building. Emergency personnel are with her, as I try to get through this growing crowd to a car that's on fire to my west."

Sirens interrupted Ty's report. From his position he could see that someone with a fire-extinguisher was spraying the car and he paused, momentarily.

"I don't know if this microphone is picking that up. But it sounds like police reinforcements ... possibly the riot squad itself ... are approaching the scene."

Ty was suddenly shoved hard by someone wearing a black jacket, bearing the insignia "*Québec pour les Québécois.*" The attacker backed off when Greg aimed the camera at him.

"As you can see, this is no peaceful demonstration. The mood is definitely ugly and getting uglier by the minute."

Ty motioned to Greg to pan the camera in a 180-degree sweep. The two of them were still a block or more away from the burning car, when half-a-dozen police motorcycles burst on to Ste. Catherine street from Peel. They formed a crescent, driving on a steady course directly through the crowd. Screaming people dove for cover and the motorcycles were followed by at least fifty officers in full riot gear.

Ty found himself literally tugging Greg back toward the intersection, using his mic cord like a leash. He kept voicing his report.

"*It appears the car fire is being brought under control. The action is shifting, now, back to Peel and Ste. Catherine where the violence first broke out. Police motorcycles are being used in what appears to be an attempt to disperse the crowd. Shops are being looted and vandalized as I speak. But riot control is underway. Officers ... dozens of them carrying protective shields are wading into the midst of the demonstration.*"

There was a sharp popping sound, followed by smoke.

"*Tear gas!*" Ty exclaimed. "*The police are firing tear gas canisters into the crowd. People are running in all directions. And here come the paddy wagons.*"

Four heavy vehicles moved up Peel Street and stopped just south of Ste. Catherine. Ty watched, as several muscular young men tried to break through the police cordon. The shields were used to push them back. Scores of demonstrators and spectators, coughing and hacking from the tear gas, began heading north on Peel, trying to get away from the eye-stinging cloud. A woman and a young child had collapsed in the middle of the street, and the woman ... arms around the young boy ... was rocking him back and forth in her arms.

"*The police are definitely taking charge here,*" Ty continued, "*But at what cost? What had been intended as a peaceful message from civil service workers to government negotiators has left what may be a permanent scar on the process of collective bargaining in this province. The Common Front wanted public support. This is not the kind of support they were after. This is Ty Davis reporting from Peel and Ste. Catherine ... the Crossroads of Canada ...for Flash News.*"

[18]

THE CHAOS ON STE. CATHERINE STREET made nationwide headlines. Ty's compelling report from the heart of the riot was CKCF's lead story at six and again at eleven-thirty. The National Television Network harassed Maggie Price until she gave in and reworked everything with an NTN signoff. Art Bradley voiced it. Portions of the Davis piece, along with accompanying visuals, were fed to ABC New York. Maggie spent a good portion of her Saturday evening fielding calls from radio and television outlets on both sides of the border.

French language newspapers, including *La Voix*, were sympathetic to the Common Front, stating that a peaceful demonstration had been hijacked by thugs and troublemakers. All of the papers, both French *and* English, recalled the history of the labor movement. They pointed out that public servants had been granted the right to strike in 1965 and that when the unions staged a three week walkout, a year later, the government had refused to accept their *essential services* procedures and encouraged hospital and schoolboard employers to do the same. On the heels of the Saturday riot, calls were already being made by union leaders, for a general strike throughout the public and para-public sectors. April 11th was being touted as a possible strike date.

At least forty arrests were made in relation to the weekend violence. Damage to retail stores, restaurants and motor vehicles along Ste. Catherine Street was estimated in the hundreds of thousands of dollars. Montreal area hospitals treated a variety of injuries, ranging from cuts and bruises to fractured limbs. The Mayor's office declared it was nothing short of a miracle that no one was killed.

Ty spent what was left of the weekend trying to make sense of Elizabeth's increasingly odd behavior. On Sunday morning, with spring sunshine as incentive, he suggested they take Catherine and Robin on a trip up Mount Royal. Liz had been unresponsive. Even the children's enthusiasm for the idea hadn't moved her out of a growing despon-dency.

Catherine hugged her mother, in an effort to lift her out of the depression. "It's okay, Mom," she rested her head in Liz's lap. "It smells like dog poop out there anyway."

Ty found himself wandering from room to room. He tried sitting in the new chair by the TV set, but couldn't bring himself to praise Liz for what she referred to as "a great deal." He missed his old chair and still hadn't figured out how their monthly budget would handle an additional hundred dollars. Then it occurred to him that, possibly, Liz's parents might be able to help.

Charles and Sarah Walkley had moved to Newton Lower Falls, Massachusetts shortly after Catherine's birth. Charles gave up teaching at Loyola College in Montreal in 1964 when Boston's Unity College underwent extensive staff changes. Several young lecturers failed to meet its standards. The college was searching for seasoned academics and was offering professorships to replace them. For Charles, then in his fifties, it was an opportunity to increase his salary and please his wife at the same time. Sarah, who had been born in Massachusetts, had often spoken of selling their home and moving to the United States. Both of them liked the Boston area.

Ty waited until mid-afternoon, Sunday, when Liz decided to take a nap. Catherine and Robin were playing quietly together in Robin's room, as he lifted the telephone off the small table in the hallway and carried it as far as the cord would allow into the dining room. He tried to keep a sense of urgency out of his voice when Charles picked-up at the other end. "Hey, Charles," he said, sounding as up-beat as possible, "it's Ty calling."

They talked trivialities for the first few minutes, touching on the change in weather, their health in general and the possibility of getting together over the summer. The tone changed, slightly, when Charles referred to an item in *The Globe* about labor troubles in Quebec. Ty filled him in on the events of the previous day and eased into the subject of Liz's mood swings.

There were a few moments of silence on the line, as Charles

absorbed the information. "Have you consulted anyone, Ty?"

"Not yet. She's sleeping just now, Charles, but I wondered whether your colleague, Professor Hall, would be willing to, I don't know … talk with Liz."

Charles sighed, audibly. "Wayne isn't *at* Unity any longer. He retired about a year ago, after suffering several minor strokes. I actually haven't spoken to him for several months now. Perhaps it might be better if you found someone, locally."

Ty thought it over. "I suppose I could ask around. Nobody comes to mind, though. Do you think you might just call Professor Hall? I mean, he knows the background. He was a tremendous help to Liz when she needed it most."

"I'll do that, Ty. I can't guarantee anything, but Wayne is a good friend. I'm sure he'll agree, if he's well enough."

"Much appreciated, Charles. Give my love to Sarah."

"Will do. And kiss the grandkids for me. I'll let you know about Professor Hall."

The line went dead.

Twelve miles upstream of Basel, Switzerland, on a hill overlooking the Rhine River, Werner Hochstrasser stood in the shadow of the *Basler Münster* church. The day was bright, but a stiff breeze swept up from the river. Hochstrasser walked slowly, using his cane to mount stairs leading to the Gothic cathedral's porch. He paused, briefly, to stare into the distant foothills of the Black Forest and Jura Mountains.

Ulrich Sennhauser was late. They had first agreed to meet near the Tomb of Desiderius Erasmus, in the bowels of the ancient building, but had ultimately ruled that out because of heavy tourist traffic. Sennhauser, a renowned archeologist, had wanted to attract as little attention as possible to excavations behind the cathedral.

Hochstrasser glanced at his watch. Statuary on the huge structure depicted prophets and kings, roses and angels. He wondered whether even the biblical Abraham could have sensed the true nature of mankind … the seemingly infinite number of biological processes he studied in his own lab at the University of Basel.

Hochstrasser's leg hurt. He was searching for something to

sit down on when Sennhauser came up the stairs. "Sorry for the delay," he said. "I had to leave my team with strict instructions."

"Have you prepared the *bidding*?"

"According to your specifications, yes. No one is aware of the temple but myself and other members of the Council. The dig is officially out of bounds to anyone else."

"How do you explain this to … your team?"

"I have made it clear that this is a highly sensitive project, with extraordinary significance to the history of Cathedral Hill. The site is truly spectacular and I have hand-picked the few colleagues who have seen the tunnel."

"Are they members of the Order?"

"They are all Elders."

Hochstrasser smiled in approval. "The initiate is a young woman from the Biozentrum. Anderegg has synthesized the drug. We should be ready for the ceremony within a week. Precisely three days after the full moon."

Sennhauser nodded. "I don't know how long I can keep my discovery from going public. It is part of a Celtic settlement, pre-dating the Romans. We're talking about a temple that actually survived some 2,500 years." His eyes shone with excitement. "The earthquake of 1356 wiped out the strongest, Roman fortifications. This structure was, somehow, buried intact."

"I can see you are caught up in it, Ulrich. Remember, a secret is only a secret … as long as it is kept."

Sunday morning seemed as good a time as any. Jerry Poirier decided to head south to the family cottage on Lake Champlain. His father had complained of a mild hangover and intended to spend a quiet day in their Outremont home. Jerry told him he wanted to see whether the ice had gone out on Missisquoi Bay. Shortly after breakfast, he drove down Route 7. The sun was at his back. Flocks of geese sailed overhead and his spirits would have been high if his mission had not been so serious. Jerry planned to see whether the blue cloak still hung in his father's closet at Venise-en-Québec.

He'd tried to convince himself, since following the Cadillac to

Our Lady of Lourdes church, that the cloak had no significance … no bearing on the disturbing events in Saint-Sauveur. He had been unsuccessful. In fact, Jerry couldn't put it out of his mind. By itself, he might have dismissed the cloak as a coincidence. He wasn't even sure, these two years later, that it was a duplicate of those found in the Laurentians. What ate away at him, however, was the fact that his father and the Morissette kidnapper, Francis Duguay, were colleagues at La Corporation Énergie. This was accompanied by the fact that Jean-Jacques Poirier was an atheist. There was the additional mystery of the old church in Saint-Félix-de-Sebastien. Jerry turned off the highway just short of Pike River, and drove his VW bug down a curving farm road toward the bay.

What was left of the heavy snowfall just four days ago was rapidly disappearing from surrounding fields. Flocks of crows wheeled into a southwest wind, landing in the rutted mud where corn would soon sprout. Despite himself, Jerry began to feel better. Thoughts of summers past, when his mother was alive, cheered him as the lake came into view and he began following the bayside road. There was open water along the shoreline, but a gray blanket of ice still covered Missisquoi Bay.

Fishing shanties had been pulled onto the beach near the Château Blanc, where Jerry had kissed a girl for the first time in the summer of his thirteenth year. He passed the dance hall, continued heading north for about a mile and turned right into a paved driveway. The chalet, with its picture windows aimed at the lake, stared back at him.

He fished in his coat pocket for the house keys, found them, and climbed out of the car. Cold air off the frozen water made him shiver as he walked up a stone pathway toward the small porch in front of the house. Jerry's hands began to shake as he inserted a key into the lock and swung open the outer door. The main entrance was off the porch. He unlocked it and stepped into the living room. It seemed even colder inside, almost as though winter had found a place to hide.

If his father had actually visited the chalet, as frequently as he'd told Jerry, there was no evidence of it. Curtains were pulled tight over all the windows. Sheets were draped over upholstered furniture …

his mother's long established custom to prevent colors from fading in sunlight. Jerry inhaled the familiar scent of the place, a combination of old wood and kerosene. An oil-fed space heater stood against one wall in the living room. There was an open fireplace between two of the picture windows, but it contained no ashes. "Another indication," Jerry thought, "that no one's been here since last summer."

He experienced a growing trepidation as he walked through the room and down the hallway toward the bedrooms. The door to *his* bedroom was open. Both his brother's and that of his parents were closed. Jerry took a moment to glance into his bedroom and memories flooded in. He hadn't spent more than a couple of weekends here since going off to the Ryerson Institute in Toronto. Then, throughout the previous summer, he'd pounded the pavement looking for a job. So much of his life had changed. The *room* ... had not.

Now that he was here, Jerry was reluctant to enter his parents' bedroom. He wasn't sure he really wanted to know anything more about his father's private life. But, as he wrestled with the idea of simply leaving he found he couldn't turn back. The door swung open and he moved inexorably closer to the closet. Was that his mother's perfume, hanging in the air? He realized it couldn't be. She had been dead for five years. Slowly, now fearful of what he'd find, Jerry opened the closet.

There was the usual array of summer clothing inside. A bathrobe. Shoes, slippers and several hats on an overhead shelf. Suddenly Jerry was gripped by an intense feeling of dread. Cold perspiration ran down the center of his back. Hanging between a rain coat and an L.L. Bean jacket were not one, but two cloaks. One blue. The other, red. Two words were inscribed along the necklines ... *Münzplatz, Zurich.*

19

HIGH WINDS TORE ACROSS Montreal island on Monday the 30th of March. Quebec Provincial Police Chief Inspector Adrien Cousineau sat in his corner office of the QPP headquarters, looking out on to Parthenais Street. He idly watched a city bus avoid a trash can that had blown out of a nearby alleyway. Cousineau debated with himself whether or not to call someone to make sure the garbage pail didn't cause an accident. He was interrupted by a knock on his door.

A police constable, who served Cousineau as a secretary, opened it and stepped inside. "*M'excuse*," he stood at attention, appearing almost military like. "Three gentlemen to see you."

Cousineau pushed his chair back from the huge desk. "Réal Gendron?" he asked. "I'm expecting *him*. Who're the other guys?"

"A Mr. Ty Davis. Works for a television station. English. And a colleague, Jerry Poirier."

The Chief Inspector scowled. "Alright. Show them in."

Gendron entered first, followed by a hesitant Davis who immediately walked over to Cousineau's desk and extended his hand. "Ty Davis, Chief Inspector Cousineau. Réal and I are old friends. I hope you don't mind I tagged along."

Cousineau *did* mind, although he didn't say so. He stood up, shook Ty's hand and sat down again. "Réal," he nodded, "Nice to see you. I presume you want to know what we have, in the case of Jacqueline Morissette?"

"As we discussed, Chief Inspector, when I called you this morning. My friend, Ty here, was with your Sergeant Roger Tremblay and Montreal Detective-Sergeant Alain Robichaud when the girl's body was found in Saint-Sauveur. I thought you might be interested in hearing some of *his* observations in the case. We've worked together many times in the past."

Cousineau appeared surprised. "What sort of observations?"

Réal sat himself down in one of the leather-upholstered chairs surrounding the desk. Jerry remained standing when Ty sat down. Ty smiled at Cousineau. "For one thing, Chief Inspector … "

"Let's dismiss the formalities. My name is Adrien."

"Alright, Adrien. For one thing, the two people who were found dead in that house … Marlene Brannigan and Francis Duguay both had peculiar marks on their right hips or buttocks."

"*C'est vrai.* What did you make of that *monsieur*?"

"Nothing, at the time. But are you aware, Sir, of the man who committed suicide off the Jacques Cartier bridge on that same day?"

Cousineau glanced down at an open folder. "I believe the name is Serge Blouin. The autopsy revealed some fascinating things about him, if I recall."

Ty nodded enthusiastically. "He was a cannibal!"

"Precisely. But what you seem to be indicating, *Monsieur* Davis, is that this is connected to the Morissette murder?"

"Blouin worked at the Centre Hospitalier Laurentien in Sainte-Agathe … the same hospital with which the victim of this latest murder, that of Dr. Denis Desjardins, was affiliated."

"And so?"

"Well, my colleagues and I were able to see Desjardins' body in the hospital morgue. He had the same mark on *his* hip."

"Let me understand this," the Chief Inspector clasped his hands in front of his chest. "So, Brannigan, Duguay, Desjardins and Blouin all had the same …" he seemed to search for a word.

"Scar," Ty replied. "By extension, if Brannigan and Duguay killed eleven-year-old Jacqueline Morissette, possibly the doctor and Serge Blouin were in on it somehow."

Cousineau wrote something down on the folder. He grinned at Gendron. "Your friend *did* have some observations."

Gendron grinned. "He usually has. But on to the reason we're here, actually. Has there been any progress in your investigation of the girl's murder?"

"Not so much. We *are* sure, however, that Brannigan and Duguay were killed by a professional."

Gendron straightened his back in the chair. "You mean, Duguay *didn't* shoot the woman? It *wasn't* murder-suicide?"

The Chief Inspector held up the folder. "This is Sergeant Tremblay's revised report. I spoke with him shortly after he returned from Saint-Sauveur and I asked him to check with our ballistics people. Apparently, the angle of the .45 slug that killed Duguay was downward. If he stuck the pistol into his own mouth, the bullet would have been on an upward trajectory. It would have … well, it would have blown his brains out. Instead, it pierced the lower jaw and exited his back, just above the spinal column. We concluded that someone *else* shoved that pistol into his mouth and pulled the trigger."

"What about Marlene Brannigan?"

"She was shot, as you know, in the back of the head. So it seems Duguay went down first. She was forced into a kneeling position and shot, execution style. The revolver was wiped clean. Duguay's fingerprints were the only prints we found on the murder weapon. The killer wanted us to believe it was murder-suicide. We don't believe it was."

Ty couldn't remain silent any longer. "Then, Dr. Desjardins and both Brannigan and Duguay were all victims of a professional hitman?"

"So it would seem, Monsieur Davis. So it would seem."

"What about the gun? Was it registered?"

Cousineau shook his head. "No serial number. Filed off. Could've been Duguay's. Could be the killer brought it in, used it and dropped it."

"Will you be checking on those, uh, scars?"

"We will. Thank you for that."

"No problem. One more thing, Chief Inspector. Donald Quesnel, the morgue attendant at Centre Hospitalier Laurentien?"

"Yes?"

He confirmed for me that the Jacques Cartier Bridge jumper, Serge Blouin, and Dr. Desjardins were not only colleagues—they were also … friends."

It seemed like an out of body experience, although Liz Davis had no true idea of what an out of body experience was supposed to feel like. She made sure that Catherine and Robin ate a good breakfast, dressed them and walked them both to Terrebonne Avenue to meet their school bus. She was certain she'd engaged in conversation with the children, but had no memory of it. Walking back to the flat, the freshness of spring air, sunshine and birdsong failed to make an impression. Now, sitting alone in her kitchen, she tried to remember what Ty had said he had to do this morning. Something about a police interiew. She couldn't be sure.

Dust filaments, highlighted by a shaft of light through the kitchen window, seemed to possess a hidden meaning. They swirled in a column that ended at her feet, as though beckoning somehow. Liz thought of Alice's rabbit hole, before she left reality behind and dropped into Wonderland. She wasn't sure how the bottle of pills came to be in her hand, or why she'd emptied its contents on to the kitchen table.

"This one makes you taller," she thought, "and this one makes you smaller."

She popped one into her mouth, totally unaware of its chemistry. Then she swallowed another ... and another.

20

CLYDE BERTRAM WAS FUMING. He stormed into Jason Moore's office, shortly after ten on Monday morning, demanding to know why Ty Davis was still self-assigning. "Goddamn it, Jason, this isn't the time to release our senior reporter on a whim!"

Moore was ready for him. "Hardly a whim, Clyde. "He's with Réal Gendron and Gendron got us in to see the point man, at the QPP, on the Morissette murder investigation. You're the one who suggested this is *our* story, and we shouldn't let the French papers take it away from us."

"That may be true," Bertram shot back, "but that was before this Common Front thing carved us a new asshole on the weekend."

"We're not losing track of that either."

Bertram wasn't convinced. "So tell me this … what's your game plan for tonight's show? What's Davis going to be providing in the way of a report? Have we got something substantial on the kid's murder, or are we just whistling in the wind?"

Moore grinned. "Let's see what Ty has to say when he gets back. I'll trot him into your office and we'll kick it around."

"Sometimes," Bertram raised an eyebrow, trying to appear fierce, "I'd like to kick the seat of your pants. Don't play boss with me, Jason. I make the decisions around here. Remember that."

"Look, Clyde, no disrespect intended. If Ty has nothing new on Morissette, we aren't going to drop the ball on the Common Front. Nobody's forgotten what happened on the weekend, much less the strike *last year* at La Presse. I've pulled stock footage of some of the stuff that went down last October."

"Like what?"

"So far, and I thought Art Bradley could voice over some of this, I have film of the five-month-long lockout at the newspaper, a clip of Mayor Drapeau on his and Bourassa's anti-protest bylaw and the huge confrontation between 15,000 demonstrators and police. That whole episode is what really gave new life to the Common Front, in the first place."

"Don't forget that demonstrator who was killed."

"The student activist?"

"Yeah, the girl was central to labor's reaction. Clubbed to death by police."

"I've got that. Even the left-wing publication that declared it was a "police baton wielded by the state and felt by the entire working class of Quebec."

"Alright, alright. History is one thing. What's happening *today* is the issue. I want to see you and Ty, as soon as he gets back."

Bertram stalked out of Jason's office.

Ueli Berlinger's daily life could be measured in city blocks. His gym, favorite theatre and apartment were all on Bank Street in Ottawa. Just around the corner, on Slater Street, was his storage locker containing everything he needed for his professional obligations to the Order of the Sword.

Berlinger had a routine. He kept his body trim by attending the gym three days a week. At forty-seven, Berlinger had the physique of a man in his late teens or early twenties. He enjoyed foreign films at the Bytowne Cinema and, on this Monday morning, he'd eaten a hearty breakfast and had already watched an award winning-movie entitled *Le Charme discret de la bourgeoisie.* Now, as he stood in the storage locker on Slater Street, he was taking inventory … perhaps the most important part of his routine. He was constantly restocking, preparing for any eventuality.

His C3A1 sniper rifle sat in its container, on one shelf. There would soon be a need to order a new supply of 7.62 X 51 mm ammunition, although there was plenty of that for the immediate future. There were telescopic lenses, two or three bipods to give the rifle additional stability for long range kills and, in a separate part of the locker … explosives. On occasion, when the Order required it, Berlinger's explosive of choice was a combination of nitro-benzene and tetranitromethane. The toxic substances were in closed containers and at least ten feet away from any possible sources of ignition. He'd installed an air conditioner in the locker, keeping the temperature steadily at only two degrees Celsius.

Explosions could be carefully measured in their intensity. The deadly combination was easily detonated by a tip-to-tip electrical charge, allowing him to decide on an appropriate distance from the target and to set an accurate propagation diameter or extent of damage. He used a high-speed oscillograph to record the voltage on his discharger at the very moment of detonation.

Berlinger's list was up to date. He felt satisfied and began to think of lunch. Obesity was one of his greatest fears and he was always conscious of weight gain. His father, Hasjürgen, had been a very large man, indulging in copious quantities of food and alcoholic beverages.

Born in 1905, Hasjürgen had been caught up in the early days of Nazi Germany, joining the National Socialist German Workers Party in his late twenties. In 1940 with the creation of the Waffen SS, he had become part of Adolf Hitler's personal bodyguard, a force of nearly seven-hundred carefully selected troops. Hasjürgen rose quickly from Obersturmführer or first-lieutenant to SS Standartenführer ... full Colonel.

Ueli's mother, Anja (Delfs) Berlinger was of Swiss-German descent. Her sympathies for the violent acts of the Reich were often the subject of family discussions. Anja was proud of her husband's accomplishments and had no tolerance for anyone who would not acknowledge the superiority of the German race. She had been beautiful in her time, and a boon to Hasjürgen at party functions.

Ueli inhaled deeply as he raised the door to his storage locker. There was something exhilarating about the smell of the place. Death was in every corner. He was the Reaper.

Mobile 7 pulled into the parking lot behind CKCF Television. On the trip back from Parthenais Street, Jerry Poirier had described the red and blue cloaks he'd found in his father's closet at Venise-en-Québec. Ty and Greg listened intently.

"Let's keep it under wraps, for the present," Ty advised. "They may have nothing to do with Saint-Sauveur, Jerry. And who the hell knows what the label *Münzplatz, Zurich* means?"

"Maybe not," Jerry replied. "But we should find out, don't you think?"

Greg began unloading equipment from the car. "How? I mean, short of going to the police."

"Chrissakes, Greg!" Ty exclaimed. "That's the last thing we want to do. At least, for now."

They walked through the guard's entrance off the parking lot. Greg planned to change cameras, complaining about a focus problem with the one he'd taken out of Mobile 7. "See you guys later."

Jerry went upstairs with Ty to the news department and the two of them were immediately summoned to Jason Moore's office.

"Bertram's on the warpath," he told them. "Wants you and me front and center."

Ty was well aware he'd been given a great deal of latitude in pursuing the Morissette story. He'd been expecting this. "I'm prepared," he said.

Moore appeared apologetic. "It's going to have to be solid. Bertram wants you back on the Common Front developments."

Poirier seated himself in Ty's work-station and pawed over some wire copy. Ty and Jason headed for Bertram's office. The News Director was puffing away on a House of Lords cigar. Moore rubbed his eyes and left the office door open. A river of smoke flowed out into the newsroom proper. "You called, Boss?"

"I did. Look, Ty, I know this kid's murder is your current passion, but there's been nothing new and you haven't been generating any updated reports on the matter. Where do we stand?"

Ty sat down, ignoring the cigar smoke. "Clyde, I just got back from QPP headquarters and I can definitely tie up a bunch of loose ends now."

"I'm listening."

"Well, you said it was a stretch to try to credibly connect Marlene Brannigan, Francis Duguay and the Jacques Cartier bridge jumper Serge Blouin. I can *do* that now."

"Okay."

Chief Inspector Cousineau confirmed several things. First of all … Blouin's cannibalism is a matter of police record. Blouin's body and those of Brannigan and Duguay all had the same unusual, puncture wound on their hips. The QPP is looking into that, as we speak. But here's the real mind-blower. This latest killing … this Dr. Denis Desjardins of Sainte-Agathe?"

"Yeah?"

"His body had the same mark. We saw it in the morgue at the Centre Hospitalier Laurentien. And that's not all. Our suicide guy, Blouin, was a personnel manager at the hospital, and the morgue attendant positively established that he was a friend of Dr. Desjardins."

Bertram's interest was piqued. "This is *starting* to sound like a *Flash News* report," he grinned. His cigar had gone out, but he kept the butt in the corner of his mouth.

"It gets better," Ty said. "Cousineau told us that ballistics prove the Duguay-Brannigan thing was not murder-suicide, after all. They were both killed. No fingerprints but Duguay's on the .45 automatic, but the cops are convinced it was a professional hit."

"So, how does all of this connect to the Morissette girl?"

Ty realized he was making headway in the argument that he needed to stay on the case. "If Brannigan and Duguay were taken out by a hit man … maybe it was the same guy who murdered Dr. Desjardins. Let's face it. They all lived and worked a few miles away from each other. They all had the same marks on their buttocks. We know there was something pretty strange going on, in that Saint-Sauveur house. I think we're looking at some sort of cult connection. The Morissette girl was going to be part of a ritual. And somebody didn't want *any* of this to go public. Somebody, or some group had to have wanted these people dead."

Bertram glanced at Moore. "Let's pull stock footage on the kid in the freezer. Use some of your interview with that antiques dealer, Ty, and the stuff you got at the Saint-Agathe hospital. Work all of the angles, but leave the cannibalism *out*."

Ty was taken aback. "Why? It's part of the story."

"Because it's not clear whether Blouin's dietary habits have anything to do with it. It'll confuse the issue. I think the story, here, is the hit man. The deaths of Desjardins, Brannigan and Duguay all have that in common. Mention Blouin and Desjardins' friendship and these ... these puncture wounds, as a sidelight. We really don't know what *they* mean."

"Not yet," Ty emphasized. "But they're germane to the overall story."

Bertram nodded. "Agreed. And Jason, let's go with Art Bradley on the Common Front issue."

"Like we discussed?"

"Like we discussed."

The meeting was over. Jason returned to his office and Ty told Jerry Poirier to get the hell out of his chair. Moments later, his phone rang. Switchboard had just had a call from the Montreal Police. Elizabeth Davis had been taken, by ambulance, to the Reddy Memorial Hospital.

21

DESPERATION ACCOMPANIED Ty, as he maneuvered through traffic on Park Avenue. The message from the police had been unclear. He had no idea what to expect of Liz's condition or whether Catherine and Robin were still in school or had come home for the lunch hour, as was their custom. When the switchboard operator had relayed the information to him, she hadn't asked any questions of the police. His subsequent efforts to reach someone at the Reddy Memorial, who *knew* what had happened, were unsuccessful.

"Go. Get outta here," Clyde Bertram told him. "The story will wait. Family first."

Ty couldn't help wondering, as he turned Mobile 14 on to Sherbrooke and headed west toward Atwater, whether his family would endure. Liz and he had broken up once before. He had thought, prior to her stay in Massachusetts three years ago, that their marriage was on shaky ground. What now? Had there been some kind of accident or was it something to do with Liz's strange behavior lately ... possibly a breakdown.

He hit the horn as a cab driver shot down Atwater hill and cruised through a yellow light heading south. He experienced a momentary urge to chase him down and cut him off. Ultimately he made a careful turn on to Atwater, arriving a few minutes later at the intersection with Tupper. There was a parking lot just beyond the Reddy. Ty realized he'd been hyper-ventilating and he felt dizzy and nauseous, walking toward the hospital's front entrance.

A middle-aged woman sat a reception desk in the lobby. Her smile was less than sincere. "Can I help you?" she asked, showing a discolored front tooth. Ty was reminded of a bureaucrat, working a customer's window at the Motor Vehicles Bureau.

"My wife, Elizabeth Davis, was brought here by ambulance. Can you tell me what room she's in?"

The receptionist mulled it over. "Was it trauma? If so, she would be in emergency."

Ty was losing patience. "I don't know. I don't know. The … the police called my work. Could you just check your admissions records?"

"The *police*," the receptionist parroted. "Well, in that case, your wife has probably not been assigned to a room."

"I honestly don't know." Ty rocked back and forth, from one foot to the other. "That's why I'm asking *you*."

She began looking through some paperwork. "What did you say the name was?"

"Davis. Elizabeth Davis."

Another minute passed. Ty was on the verge of losing it, when she finally tapped the sheet of paper with a forefinger. "Davis," she said, displaying little enthusiasm for her discovery. "Here it is. Elizabeth Davis. Your wife is in the psych-ward."

"You mean psychiatry?"

The receptionist remained stone-faced. "Second floor," she said, pointing to a door marked *Stairs*. "Or, you can use the elevator, just over there."

Ty took two and three stairs at a time, pushed through double-doors on the second floor and emerged at what appeared to be some sort of nurses' station. There were three uniformed nurses behind a circular counter. A tall white-haired man in a lab coat was engaged in conversation with two Montreal police officers. Ty interrupted. "Excuse me. My name is Ty Davis. I believe my wife, Elizabeth, was brought here?"

The man in the lab coat swung around and put his hand out. "I'm Barry Nelson," he said, "*Dr.* Barry Nelson. Your wife is doing well, Mr. Davis. We pumped her stomach and …"

"Pumped her stomach! W-what do you mean? Where are my children?"

Nelson placed one hand on Ty's shoulder. "Calm down, Mr. Davis. I can see this is all rather shocking to you, but I assure you, your wife and children are fine."

"Well, what happened?"

One of the police officers introduced himself. "*Monsieur* Davis. I can answer that. I'm Constable Yves Fortin. Your two children went home on their school lunch break. When your wife failed to meet them on the corner of your street …"

"Oxford and Terrebonne. Liz always waits for them there."

"*Oui*. This time, she did not. The kids walked to your home. When they rang the doorbell, no one answered. The little girl …"

"Catherine. She's seven."

"*Oui*, Catherine. She got your neighbor," Fortin looked at his clipboard, "a *Madame* Geraldine Mount. She telephoned us. We contacted your landlord, who came and opened your front door."

"What about my kids? You didn't let them go upstairs to our flat!"

"No *monsieur*. They stayed with your neighbor while we investigated. Elizabeth, your wife, was unconscious on the floor of the kitchen in your duplex."

"God! Oh God!"

Dr. Nelson, again, rested his hand on Ty's shoulder. "Calm, Mr. Davis. Elizabeth is okay. She's in no danger. Your neighbor is looking after the children."

Ty realized he was crying. He wiped at his eyes. "What? Why was she unconscious? What did she do?"

"There was a bottle of 10 milligram valium on the kitchen table. It appears she had swallowed quite a few of them."

"Jesus! She tried to kill herself?"

"I don't think so. As I told you, we got to her in time. The valium is no longer a threat. I've had an initial conversation with Elizabeth and I don't believe this was a classic suicide attempt. Let me ask you, Mr. Davis. Was your wife going through a depression? Was she symptomatic, I mean?"

Ty felt himself trembling all over his body. "She suffered through post-partum depression after our son, Robin, was born. She began drinking heavily. But all of that happened three years ago."

"Was she treated at the time?"

"A Professor Wayne Hall. My wife left me for a while. Stayed with her parents in Massachusetts. Dr. Hall is a psychologist who works, rather *worked*, with Liz's father at Unity College in Newton

Lower Falls outside Boston. Liz was under his care for several weeks. She stopped drinking. Seemed perfectly, uh, normal when she and the children finally came home."

"What about lately. Has she displayed any signs of depression?"

Ty leaned on the nurses' counter. He was sure he was going to be sick. "I'm sorry, Dr. Nelson. I … I really need to see Liz."

He smiled. The expression in his eyes seemed reassuring. "She's sleeping right now. If you could indulge me just a little longer, Mr. Davis, I think it would be very helpful in getting to the bottom of your wife's actions today. I promise. You'll see her shortly."

"Okay. I understand. Sorry. Yes … Liz has been acting *very* strange."

"How so?"

"Well, short-tempered, for one. Forgetful. Confused and sad. She barely speaks to me, and I know she hasn't been sleeping well. There've been several nights I've woken up and heard her walking up and down in the hall outside our bedroom. She has mood swings."

Nelson nodded. "How long has this been going on?"

"Three weeks, maybe. A month."

"Anything else unusual about her behavior?"

Ty suddenly remembered his chair. "The furniture." he said. "I came home from work a couple days ago and found our couch and my favorite chair had been replaced. Liz gave the stuff away to the Salvation Army and bought new ones. We didn't *need* new ones, and she didn't seem to understand we can't afford them."

"Uh-huh. That checks."

"Checks with what?"

"Let me tell you what I think is happening, Mr. Davis. Feelings of self-reproach. Loss of interest and vitality. These things are often displayed by someone who suffers from what we call chronic depression. The symptoms can last for years, and manic swings of mood can manifest themselves in periods of elation. When the individual is *down*, to use the street expression, they can exhibit appetite changes … not eat or eat too much. They complain of aches and pains, cramps … digestive problems. But when they're *up*, they seem almost normal. They manage to disguise their problem, at least to the untrained eye. But they also tend to speak more rapidly than usual. They are just overboard with their apparent happiness. An impulsive shopping trip, like the one you describe, is part and parcel."

"Yeah, but part and parcel of *what*?"

"It's called *dysthymia*. Chronic depression. Often, and you say Elizabeth was diagnosed three years ago, a recurrence can result in a focus on past failures. There is a lot of self-blame involved ... although this varies from person to person. Look, Mr. Davis, I've only had one opportunity to talk with Elizabeth. But I don't believe she was even *aware* of taking those pills. It's too early to say for sure, but I believe she may have experienced a psychotic break. That would explain her confusion ... forgetting that your children were coming home from school and that she needed to meet them on the corner. She would have become disoriented. She might have suffered actual hallucinations."

Ty tried to absorb the information. "So, why don't you believe she tried to commit suicide?"

Another reassuring smile. "Look at it this way, Mr. Davis. Delusional behavior ... hallucinations are scary. The person experiencing this sort of thing is often aware there is something terribly wrong. Paranoia sets in. An attempt to do self-harm can be the result, but it's not a well thought out plan, if you can understand. When I spoke to her, Elizabeth had no memory of taking that valium. She *did* tell me that she's been worried she was losing her mind. She's been feeling detached and anxious. The shopping was just an attempt to put up a bold front."

"So, what now?"

"The police are obliged to file a report. For the time being this has to be treated as an attempted suicide."

"What does that mean?"

"Unless I am entirely satisfied, through subsequent conversations with Elizabeth, that it was *not* ... the law requires a psychiatric evaluation over a seventy-two hour period."

"You mean, she can't come home?"

"If I can simply talk with her ... *observe* her, let's say overnight, and I conclude she is not a danger to herself, then she can be discharged. However, even in that eventuality, she's going to need family support. Family understanding."

"What about treatment? What do we do about the depression?"

Dr. Nelson smiled again. "Physical environment is a very important part of patient rehabilitation. Being at home is important. So is your attitude and, for that matter, the way your children react to her."

"How do you mean?"

"They know their mother was taken away in an ambulance. They're too young …"

"Five and seven."

"That's right. Too young to understand about emotional or mental problems. Just let them know their mother was feeling ill, that she's been looked after in the hospital and that she's getting well."

"But *will* she get well?"

"I'm jumping ahead of myself, here, Mr. Davis. But I think we have to rule out any physical causes. Hypothyroidism, for example. Once we determine *that*, we might try a mood stabilizing drug like lithium."

Ty glanced at his watch. "I've got to get to the kids, Dr. Nelson. Could I see Liz now?"

"Follow me." Nelson turned to the two police constables. "Do you fellas have what you need?"

Constable Fortin handed the doctor a card. "This is the number of my superior officer," he said. "We have what we need."

Ty thanked them for their quick action at his home and for saving Liz's life. Fortin shrugged his shoulders. "It's what we do, *monsieur* Davis. *Merci bien*."

Nelson led Ty toward a set of doors off the nurses' station. They required a coded pass card … before admitting anyone into the locked-down psych ward.

22

WALKING WAS DIFFICULT, but Werner Hochstrasser knew it was therapeutic. Using his cane as little as possible, he cut through the *Münsterplatz* on his way back from a late supper of *roesti*, olive bread and a caffé-latté. The shredded, fried potato sat heavy in his stomach, as he made his way along a paved walkway in the main square and passed Basel's city hall.

His leg throbbed. Hochstresser intended to be back in his office at the university by eight-thirty. There were some pills in his desk drawer that would relieve the pain, and he expected the late hour would mean he'd have no intrusions. He had to contact Laurent Picard in Saint-Félix-de-Sébastien and he wanted absolute privacy. It would be mid-afternoon in Quebec. During previous conversations with the Order's Canadian Regional Commander, they'd established an appropriate time frame for such contact.

All records of the Order, historical, financial and organizational, were locked in a wall safe in Hochstrasser's office. He was Supreme Leader of the Council, which oversaw all aspects of the organization, worldwide. The records had been handed down from one Supreme Leader to another, since the Order's founding in the mid-1800s. They outlined a complex network of operations in several countries, each representing a single *lodge*. Each *lodge* was overseen by a Regional Commander who was served by three Elders. The Elders recruited new members among high achieving university students, who were promised honors and financial rewards by the Council. Twenty new members were selected each year from the various *lodges*. Elaborate initiation ceremonies involving secret rites, costumes and mind altering drugs would then be employed.

In return, the students were sworn to secrecy and promised to dedicate their lives and their careers to the goals of the Order. Vast sums of money were generated as the students went on to distinguish themselves in politics, the sciences and the corporate world. In some countries, shadow governments were established, exerting great influence on democratically elected regimes. The so-called "scientific method" was applied to literally all forms of human endeavor, a carefully crafted means of infiltration at the highest levels. The Order of the Sword was tilted toward the Power Elite, while offering a strict belief structure, void of religious orthodoxy but capable of filling any spiritual vacuum. Its roots were Swiss-German. Its reach was global.

When Hochstrasser entered his office at the University of Basel, he felt the weight of it all on his shoulders. Now, a splinter group of followers in Quebec ... a group that could be traced back to Laurent Picard's *lodge*, had exposed itself to a police investigation. It mimicked the Order's ritualistic practices, while introducing its own. And *that* was the problem. "Child abduction and cannibalism," he muttered to himself. "Fools! All of them fools!"

He sat down at his desk and began dialing the overseas operator. He would make sure Laurent Picard was in constant touch with Ueli Berlinger. There was no time to lose.

Charles and Sarah Walkley flew into Dorval Airport Monday night. As soon as Ty had a few minutes with Liz, he'd telephoned her parents in Newton Lower Falls. They'd both been insistent. Sarah would look after the children. Ty could make himself available to the Reddy Memorial and stay abreast of any developments, and he could go into CKCF if necessary.

It was pushing midnight by the time Ty had caught them up to date on everything. "I'll get up with Catherine and Robin," he told Sarah, "and get them off to school. You guys are going to need a good night's rest." Sarah reminded him that they were used to rising early. "Whatever," Ty replied. "I can't tell you how much I appreciate this. I'm not sure how I could have handled the situation by myself."

Later, lying alone in their bed, Ty hugged Liz's pillow. It smelled of her. Tears welled up forming a salty wetness against his cheek and, gradually, he fell into a troubled sleep filled with disturbing dreams. In one of them, Liz was *next* to him, although he was aware that she was in the hospital. She hovered several inches off the surface of the bed and her face was very pale. Ty tried to touch her, to pull her down. His hand came away sticky, as though her body was somehow dissolving. He reached out to touch her face, begging her to "Come back! Come *back*, Liz!"

Suddenly, there were flames all around her. Her body was naked and covered in what seemed to be surgical incisions. A viscous fluid ran out of each one and her mouth was moving as the fire spread up her legs.

"What? What, Liz? I can't hear you!" He kneeled on the mattress, leaning in to hear more clearly.

"They *burned* the evidence," she wheezed. "*Burn-n-ned*!"

Ty sat bolt upright. He swung his legs off the bed and sat staring into the darkness. Then, for no reason he could imagine, he thought of the morgue attendant, Donald (Duck) Quesnel, at the Centre Hospitalier Laurentien. The dream played at the edges of consciousness, but a definite picture began forming in his mind. Somehow, in the dream-state, Liz had been the instrument his brain had used to unravel a mystery his conscious mind hadn't sorted out. And the morgue attendant had provided the information. Ty had known the answer all along.

"*A Sainte-Agathe man was killed*," Quesnel had said, "*when his car hit some black ice on the autoroute. Dr. Desjardins knew the family. He had the ambulance bring the man to his own clinic, rather than the hospital, because he thought it would be less traumatic for his wife. Desjardins told her it would not be wise to see her husband in the condition he was in. She made no formal identification, because the victim was well known in the community and there was no doubt as to his identity.*"

"Desjardins arranged for the cremation!" Ty remembered. But he already *knew* that. The dream was trying to offer another possibility, namely that cremation had concealed the truth. Desjardins had wanted to isolate the body for the purpose of surgically removing internal organs. That was the meaning of the incisions on Liz's torso and her unsettling words "*They burned the evidence.*" And that was why police couldn't find a source for their grisly discovery in the refrigerator in Saint-Sauveur.

Ty slowly stood up, now fully awake, and walked into the living room. He realized it was one more element in a story that seemed to possess the properties of smoke. You could see it, but you couldn't quite grasp it. If this were true, how could one prove that a highly regarded doctor had illegally harvested a heart, kidney, liver and brain ... from a dead man? How did one accuse a man who was already dead himself?

The living room was full of shadows. The only light came from outside. Ty looked through his front windows, expecting to see a truck or car passing. There was neither, but hanging low in the sky above buildings on the other side of the street, a cold moon spread its ghostly light on the pavement.

Tensions were building. Jason Moore was on the telephone, early Tuesday, with Quebec Federation of Labor President Louis Laberge. It appeared a Common Front general strike was looming. LaBerge was adamant. He told Moore that Quebec workers were facing one of the toughest government bargaining positions in history. Public service employees' salaries were far behind those in the private sector. Working conditions were, in LaBerge's words, "intolerable."

The unions were demanding an eight percent raise across the board, a weekly guaranteed minimum wage of one hundred dollars, a say in working conditions and equal pay for equal work regardless of region, sector or sex. The Bourassa government was offering zero-point-four percent and no deal on a guaranteed minimum wage. Essential services had yet to be defined. Newspaper reports were talking about "revolutionary syndicalism."

Moore was under pressure. Ty said he would try to report in later in the day, but he couldn't count on it. The French language *La Voix* newspaper had headlined a story on developments in the Morissette murder case, under a Réal Gendron byline. Moore was down to two reporter-camera teams and one of them wouldn't be available to him until after the lunch hour. Sports had commandeered one of them for an important news conference, called by Montreal Canadiens management. Moore decided to take his problems to Clyde Bertram.

"What did Gendron have to say?" Bertram wanted to know. "Haven't glanced at the French papers this morning."

Moore had carried a copy into Bertram's office. He held it up for Bertram to read the front page headline. "Basically, Clyde, it's what Ty's been talking about. Connecting the dots. I'm afraid we've been scooped."

"Well shit. What's the word on Davis? I know his wife is in hospital, but this is *his* story."

Moore nodded. "He might be in sometime this afternoon. We ought to go with what we have, even if it repeats a lot of the *La Voix* stuff."

Bertram appeared frustrated. "Has he mentioned what time he might get in? If not, we'll have to hand it over to another reporter."

"Initially, he said he might *drop* in. I don't know whether he meant to actually work on a six o'clock report."

"Alright. Play it this way. If Ty has the time, let him do a standup in the parking lot. Some neutral background. Trees … whatever. You get the librarian to pull stocks on Saint-Sauveur, that hospital in Sainte-Agathe, possibly use a clip from the morgue guy and even a brief comment from the QPP Chief Inspector. So, if Ty reports in at all, tell him to make it quick and dirty in the parking lot. We'll do the rest and he can get the hell outta here."

Moore grinned. "If I know Ty, he'll be pissed off about chasing Gendron's story."

"Fuck it," Clyde replied. "If *he* can't do it, get someone else on the thing."

"It could be a busy day." Moore paused. "This Common Front business is really heating up." He began briefing the news director on his conversation with Louis Laberge.

23

"I'm not like these people, am I? You don't think I'm crazy, do you?"

Ty sat on the edge of Liz's bed at the Reddy Memorial. Her private room was anything but private. The door was wide open and other patients in the psych ward drifted in and out. Ty held his wife's hand. "No. No, of course not," he replied. Dr. Nelson thinks you'll be out of here before you know it."

A wizened old woman with scraggly hair peered in from the corridor. She was engaged in what appeared to be a two-way conversation, but she was quite alone. Her eyes were constantly blinking. She muttered into thin air, paused as if awaiting an answer and nodded to acknowledge an imagined response. Then, quite unexpectedly, she gazed at Liz, smiled broadly, pirouetted on the ball of her right foot and propelled herself away from the doorway.

The old woman was quickly replaced by a young man in pyjamas. He was in a crouched position and his tongue darted in and out of his mouth. He spotted Liz and Ty, uttered a comment that sounded something like "blech-buh" and proceeded to hop away.

Ty was incredulous. "Is this what it's been like?" he asked Liz.

"All last evening. When they handed out the meds, after supper, things calmed down."

He shook his head. "Well, now that I've seen it first-hand, I can say without reservation, Liz, you are *definitely not* like these people."

"How long do you think I'll have to stay?"

Ty patted her hand. "It has to be a certain length of time, according to the law. Dr. Nelson said he planned to run some tests."

Liz suddenly pulled her hand away from his. "Law? What law?"

"Liz, I *know* you didn't try to harm yourself." He waved his arm at the door. "They don't know you like I do, but Liz, you *did* swallow that valium."

"I … I don't. I mean, I don't remember doing that."

"What *do* you remember?"

She hesitated, appearing on the verge of tears. "It's all so vague. Like a dream, y'know?"

"I *don't* know, Liz. That's why I'm asking."

"Alice in Wonderland," she said.

"What?"

"Alice in Wonderland. I remember *seeing* the pills. I don't know how they got there, but I … " she began to sob. "Oh God, Ty, m-maybe I *am* crazy."

"You're *not*. Dr. Nelson is pretty sure you had some sort of psychosis. Some kind of break from reality. But what about this Alice in Wonderland stuff?"

She wiped her eyes with a Kleenex tissue. "I remember there was sunlight coming in our kitchen window. Somehow, that made me think of Alice's rabbit hole .. I mean, in the story. Then I saw the valium on the table. One side makes you smaller. The other side makes you taller. I had no idea it was valium. I've no real memory of swallowing anything."

Ty felt a rush of concern. "Okay. Alice's pills were a mushroom, right?"

"Yeah. A mushroom. I decided that if I could get bigger, taller, stronger … that would make me better. I wouldn't be afraid anymore."

He leaned over and hugged her. "I promise," he said. "You have nothing to be afraid of. I love you. The kids love you. We'll get through this … together."

Liz grabbed his arm suddenly. "The kids! Oh my God, the kids!"

"It's alright, Liz. The kids are fine. Mrs. Mount looked after them when they came home from school yesterday. Last night, your parents flew in from Boston. Sarah and Charles are at the house and they plan to stay as long as we need them.

She flopped back on to her pillows. "What's happening to me, Ty? What kind of a terrible mother have I become?"

Ty handed her more Kleenex tissues and began to realize that Dr. Barry Nelson's observations were right on the money. Justified or not, his wife was being overwhelmed by self-doubt and a deep sense of failure. *Why* this was so was beyond his understanding.

Maggie Price reported in for her three to midnight shift about a half-hour early. It was a habit. She took the extra time to pour herself a coffee, look over wire-copy and the daily newspapers and get a handle on the six o'clock lineup. Maggie liked to head into the three o'clock production meeting relaxed and informed. Sometimes her best decisions were made in that first thirty minutes of the day. Often, the late news for which she was responsible *took shape* as a result of those decisions.

Clyde Bertram had a lot of respect for Maggie. He never worried about her priorities and felt he could always count on her to stay abreast of developing stories. He flagged her down as she passed his office and waved her in. The air stank of cigar. "So, Mag," he said, "ready for another day at the mines?"

She set her coffee down on his desk. "Have you heard from Ty? What's happening with Elizabeth?"

"I think she's doing okay. Moore says Ty was heading into the hospital this morning. He might come in briefly. Gendron scooped his story on the Morissette kid."

"You mean the possibility that all those people were involved in some sort of cult?"

"That and more. It seems … and Ty *knew* this … that Duguay and Brannigan were not a murder-suicide. The cops think they might have been murdered by the same guy who shot that doctor up in Sainte-Agathe."

"Desjardins?"

"Yeah, him. Gendron nailed all of that down in his piece, but left out the fact that every one of them, including this Blouin who jumped off the Jacques Cartier bridge, had some sort of puncture wound on their bodies. Apparently, all in the same place around the lower part of the hip."

"Why'd Gendron leave *that* out?"

"Probably for the same reason I initially advised Ty to do the same. Because we have no way of really knowing what these scars mean, or whether they mean anything at all."

"You change your mine about that?"

Bertram leaned back in his chair. "What do *you* think?"

"I'd *go* with it. Especially if it's more evidence that these people were connected. Even if we don't understand exactly what the connection *is*. The scars, or whatever they are, can't just be coincidence."

He grinned. "That's my take on it. Glad to see you agree."

As Maggie retrieved her coffee from Bertram's desk and stood up to leave, Ty walked through the door. He quickly filled them in on Liz's status and proceeded to outline his theory about the human organs, found in Saint-Sauveur. "If I'm right," he insisted, "Dr. Desjardins handed a body over to the crematorium to be disposed of. Christ, the wife of this poor bastard didn't even get a chance to see the remains. Desjardins told her the guy was too busted up."

"That's not even legal," Maggie said.

"No formal identification," Ty agreed, "that's right, Mag. Now here's the rest of my theory. The man who operates the crematorium, which by the way is part of his funeral home in Saint-Agathe, would have had questions if the body was covered in surgical incisions and not just banged up in the accident."

"So, he was *in* on it!" Maggie exclaimed.

"*Had* to be." Ty had his eye on Bertram, to see his reactions. The news-director didn't appear to be jumping out of his skin.

"We can't use it," he said. "It's only speculation. The funeral home operator would sue our asses."

Ty appeared disappointed. "What if I can *prove* it?"

"How?"

"What if forensics picked up fingerprints on those bottles ... the ones that contained the human organs? What if I go to interview the funeral home guy and I can pilfer something he's handled. It's just possible forensics would get a match."

Bertram considered the idea. "First things first, Ty. That's all very intriguing, but I think ... if you don't need to get right back to Elizabeth ... I'll get you to do a standup on, as you put it, connecting the dots that we are *certain* about. If the Common Front thing doesn't blow up in our faces first ... I'll send you, Greg and Jerry up north later in the week. How's that?"

Ty glanced at Maggie and back at Bertram. "You're the boss."

"And," said Bertram, "You're a news reporter ... not a cop. Let's see where this takes us before I let you play detective."

"What about the cannibalism?"

"You *know* my opinion about that."

"Did Gendron mention it though? I haven't read this morning's piece."

"Not a word. Despite their first reference to Serge Blouin's suicide and the subsequent autopsy report, *La Voix* hasn't brought it up again. I think we need to do the same. Even if Blouin can be tied to Brannigan, Duguay and Desjardins ... we don't know what the cannibalism means. It would just be a sensational bit of information going nowhere."

Bertram reached for his package of cigars, signaling an end to the conversation. Ty and Maggie headed out of the office. Ty, reluctantly, would fashion his evening report around the Réal Gendron story, adding only what he knew about the mysterious puncture wounds.

24

A GIBBOUS MOON, NOT QUITE FULL but well past half its illumination, cast a kaleidoscopic glow through the stained glass windows of Our Lady of Lourdes church. The telephone communication from Werner Hochstrasser had been disturbing. "It can all be traced back to you," he'd warned. Laurent Picard's hard soled boots echoed through the old building. The absence of church pews combined with surrounding fieldstone walls transformed the former place of worship into an acoustic chamber.

Hochstrasser had been careful not to make specific references to names and places. Instead, he spoke of news headlines and police inquiries which could be interpreted as simple interest. "Have you recently talked with our good friend in Ottawa?" he'd asked.

Picard was aware he was referring to Ueli Berlinger. "I have indeed. He's a hard worker."

"Work is never done, it seems."

"That's the truth. I've been meaning to catch up with him. He's been quite a success, I understand."

"He's good at what he does. There are always new challenges in that field."

Picard clicked his tongue. "I might have some thoughts on that."

"See that he gets them."

The line had gone dead. Picard paced up and down for a few moments. There was certainly more to discover about the breakaway sect in the Laurentians and he was sure Berlinger would fulfill any new contract that might come his way. The only comment from Hochstrasser that had not been couched in ambiguity was the warning ... "it can all be traced back to you."

Catherine woke up screaming at three o'clock Wednesday morning. Ty leapt out of bed encountering Sarah Walkley in the hallway outside the seven-year-old's bedroom. Both rushed to her bedside. Catherine was sitting upright. Her blankets had been tossed on the floor and her eyes were filled with night terrors. "Daddy, Daddy, Mommy's dead!" She began to sob.

"It was just a dream, punkin'. Just a bad dream. Mommy is fine. She's going to be coming home very soon."

Liz's mother stood by the bed, as Ty scooped the little girl up in his arms and squeezed her into his chest. Sarah looked as though she might burst into tears herself. "You remember what I told you this morning, Cathy?"

"Y-you said Mommy was just sick."

"That's right dear. And she's getting better. Your father is right, it was just a terrible dream you were having. We're all right here with you and you know what else?"

"What?"

"When you and Robin get up this morning, I'm going to make you pancakes and maple syrup for breakfast."

Ty placed Catherine back on her bed and picked up her blankets. "And you'll go back to sleep and the next thing you know it will be a bright, sunny day."

Sarah fluffed her pillow. Gradually, Catherine's eyes closed and she slipped away into another dream. In this one, her mother was riding a horse and the horse was wailing like an ambulance siren.

Dr. Barry Nelson was reading patients' charts when Ty arrived, around ten, at the psychiatric ward in the Reddy Memorial. He was leaning on the circular desk at the nurses' station, but straightened up and waved as soon as he spotted Ty. "She had a good night, Mr. Davis. We've put her through a battery of tests. Thyroid is normal so we can rule that out, but there *was* something."

Ty felt a twinge of concern. "You mean ... something physical? Not mental?"

Nelson nodded. "Why don't you come and sit down in my office. We can go over what we've learned so far."

Ty followed him into a large room. One wall displayed a series of diplomas, indicating Nelson's academic credentials. On another, a huge mural showed a scene that seemed almost unearthly. Nelson smiled. "*That*," he said, "is a work in progress. Patients do it as part of their therapy. It's always changing. Sometimes scary images or landscapes. Sometimes, well, just what you see ... a kind of mixture of Dante's "Inferno" and Van Gogh's "Starry Night." He sat down behind a huge, dark wood desk and invited Ty to be seated on a comfortable couch next to it.

Ty showed polite interest in the mural, but wanted to hear about Liz. "You said there was something about my wife that could have caused her ... her trouble?"

"Among other things, Mr. Davis, we did a lumbar puncture. A spinal tap. Liz said you were at work, so she consented to the procedure. An analysis of the spinal fluid indicated elevations of serum creatine phosphokinase or CPK activity."

"What does that mean in English?"

"Elizabeth, I believe, is suffering from unipolar or major depressive disorder. She is *not*, in my opinion, generally psychotic. Sometimes, albeit rarely in non-psychotic people, these elevations have been detected. We really don't know why, however we *do* know what seems to help in such cases."

"That's encouraging."

"Yes. Well, in Liz's case I think her break with reality, on the day she took those pills, may be related. Somehow, for that brief period of time, I think she slipped into a bipolar episode ... a condition that would have made her more susceptible to hallucinations."

Ty tried to comprehend the information. "You said there is a treatment for this?"

"And it's not too complicated. In a recent broad scope trial, with patients who had experienced CPK, it was found that a regimen of isometric exercise brought serum CPK levels back down into the normal range.'"

"What about the depression?"

Nelson handed Ty a brochure. "This outlines our usual approach to people who have major depressive disorder. Now, *understand*, Mr. Davis, in psychiatry there are no absolute guarantees. But, I think Liz is quite treatable with lithium carbonate. That, combined with exercise, some counseling and at least one session that would involve you and your children here at the Reddy, and I'm pretty sure your wife will return to her old self."

"And, if she doesn't?"

"Then there are other things we can do. Some of my colleagues believe lithium, as an antimanic, should be combined with other antidepressants. We can explore *that*, if Liz is not responding to the lithium alone."

Ty didn't feel reassured. "Is there a time frame? I mean, how long before we know?"

"Give it a month to a month and a half. It takes a while for the drug to get into the system."

"But what would have triggered all of this?"

Nelson smiled again. "I realize this has been quite a fright, Mr. Davis. Let me say *this*. Elizabeth is an otherwise healthy young woman. I've spoken with her, at length, and she's very bright. In general, women are especially vulnerable to this type of unipolar depression after giving birth. There are hormonal—actual physical changes in the body that can touch it off. Some types of depression can run in families, but Liz tells me her parents have never experienced anything like this and there are no siblings.

"Not alive," Ty replied.

"Meaning?"

"She had a younger brother. David was five or six when he was killed in an accident."

"Any history there?"

"None. He was just a normal kid, from all I've heard. Liz was five years older."

Nelson wrinkled his brow. "Well, events ... particularly traumatic events in a person's life can act as the trigger. An accident like that, or stress in a marriage for example. You mentioned you and your wife were separated at the time of her postpartum depression."

"Yes."

"I don't think we're dealing with anything we can't *fix* in Elizabeth's case. I'll advise you as we go along, of course."

"Can I see her now?"

"Absolutely. She's expecting you."

Ty thanked Nelson and headed for Liz's room. The mural on Dr. Nelson's wall wasn't helping to relieve his anxiety.

25

A RECEPTIONIST AT THE FRENCH LANGUAGE radio station CQAM
stared, wide-eyed, at six men who had stepped off the elevator and
pushed through double glass-doors into the lobby. Three of them
were carrying baseball bats. Five were wearing T-shirts that called
attention to bulging muscles. Just one was dressed in an Oxford shirt
and dress pants, while the apparent leader of the group was shaven
bald and had a lightning bolt tattooed on his neck. He stood directly
in front of her.

"Who's yer boss?" he demanded to know.

The receptionist felt her stomach do a *loop the loop.* "I, well, that
is … who did you wish to see?"

The big man towered over her desk. "Are you *deef*? I asked who's
the boss around here." He placed two fists on top of her typewriter.
"And I want to see him *now.* Got it?"

Her hands were shaking as she picked up a phone and dialed the
program manager's extension. "*Monsieur* Asselin," she told the
tattooed man as she waited for a reply. "*Maurice* Asselin. I'm calling
him now. Just give me a second."

The phone rang four times before Asselin picked up. The
receptionist tried to keep the fear out of her voice. "*Monsieur* Asselin.
There are several men here. They want to talk to you."

The program manager, a small man with a wispy moustache
and a Napoleon complex, delivered a curt reply. "What men? And
what do they want to talk to me about?"

"I really don't know. I think you'd better come out here. They're …
insistent."

"Alright. Alright. Tell them to wait." He slammed the receiver down.

Her face, now quite pale, turned upwards to address the intruder.
"He says he's coming. It may be a few minutes."

"Fuck this!" the bald man exclaimed. He turned to his compatriots.
"Two of you stay here and keep on eye on this bitch. He gestured at

the better dressed man. "Benoit … you and the other two with me."
He headed toward a door into the radio station proper.

On-air studios were on one side of a long corridor. A door,
marked Master Control, was on the left side. "You!" he pointed at
one of the men who looked as though he'd be at home in a wrestling
ring, "into Master Control. Tell them I have a message for Premier
Bourassa and Monsieur Jean Drapeau. Tell them I intend to go on
the air. And *you*," he indicated the last man, "head down the hall to
the front office. Find this … Asselin. Make it clear to everyone you
see that if they try to call the police we'll start bustin' things up …
starting with their heads."

At that moment, the program manager entered the corridor.
Maurice Asselin, who stuffed risers into his shoes to give him
additional height, thrust out his chest and confronted them. "Who
the hell do you think you are?" He used one hand, like a traffic cop,
in an effort to stop the thug with the baseball bat.

Lightning Bolt stalked down the hallway and grabbed Asselin
by the lapels of his three-piece suit. "Listen, you goddam prick, we're
borrowing your radio station for a little while. You can cooperate, or
you can go to the hospital. Your fucking choice."

Asselin was, literally, being lifted off his feet. "W-what do you
w-want?"

The huge man released his grip, lowering the program manager
down to the floor.

"It's simple. I want you to tell your employees there's some guys
in the station who will ruin their day if anyone calls the cops. Tell
them to do *nothing*! Understand?"

"Nothing. Do nothing. I … I'll tell them." Asselin looked as
though he might cry. "What, exactly are *you* going to do?"

Lightning bolt grinned. Asselin could smell beer on his breath.
"I'm going to deliver a message, or rather Benoit, here, is going to
deliver a message … on the air."

"A message?"

"Shut up and do as you're told. If you do *exactly* as I say, we'll be
outta here in no time. If you don't, or if any one of your employees
tries playin' hero, I'll fuck you up. My man here will follow you.
Nuthin' stupid. Remember?"

"Yes. Nothing stupid. Nothing stupid. I promise." Maurice Asselin was no longer thrusting out his chest as he disappeared into the offices beyond, prodded from behind by the man with the baseball bat.

In master control, the radio operator was cowering in a corner. He'd been playing a pre-recorded announcer track and spinning discs when Lightning Bolt's cohort stood behind him and ordered him to get ready for a live announcement. In the meantime, an old Claude Gauthier hit song entitled "Geneviève" was playing.

Lightning Bolt entered, followed by Benoit. He demanded a studio and a live microphone and the operator wasn't about to argue. "In there," he pointed through a plate glass window at an unoccupied room facing master control. "I, uh, I'll cue you. Know what I mean?"

"You point. He talks." He aimed his chin at the man in the Oxford shirt.

"Right. That's … right."

Benoit left master control and entered the studio. "Genevieve" came to an end and the operator cued the studio.

"Did you know," Benoit began, in a baritone voice, "that, at this very moment, there are hospital patients here in the city of Montreal who spent the night … sleeping in their own urine? This is a message for Quebec Premier Robert Bourassa and Montreal Mayor Jean Drapeau. We … the working people of the province … are not going to take this any longer. In more than sixty hospitals, management personnel aren't listening to the unions. Working conditions are unspeakable. Understaffing and inadequate pay have meant that the patients pay the price, in spite of labor's good faith at the bargaining table.

"In schools and universities, teachers' demands aren't being met. Class sizes are too large. Compensation is too small. The voice of the working class is not being heard. We are not represented by this government. We are at the beck and call of Bay Street, Saint James Street and Wall Street. This government has failed. I urge the unions of the Quebec Common Front to instruct their rank and file to *resist*, in a province-wide work-to-rule and in a general strike if necessary. Let civil disobedience be the order of the day. Messrs Bourassa and Drapeau … you *will not stop us. Solidarité. Vive le Québec.*"

* * *

Jason Moore got the call from Montreal Police lieutenant Peter Loughlin shortly after ten. A half-dozen squad cars had surrounded the radio station. CQAM's program manager, Maurice Asselin, had been standing at the street entrance off Papineau Avenue.

Loughlin was brief and to the point. "This guy thought he was Captain Marvel or some comic book super hero," he chuckled. "Told us he'd chased the bad guys out of the station."

"Not before they got their little manifesto out on the airwaves," Moore replied. "Any sign of these ... bad guys?"

"None. They must have had vehicles parked in the area. We're doing a sweep of the neighborhood, but it appears they're long gone, either into the city or over the bridge to the south shore. So, all we have are descriptions of the perps, from Asselin and a few of the radio station's personnel."

"What about names? Any of the witnesses hear a name?"

"Just one. Benoit was the guy who went on the air. But we think it was probably made up. They wouldn't have used a *real* name, I wouldn't think. But we're checking that."

Moore made a note on his steno pad. "Can we get audio of the actual manifesto, or whatever you want to call it, this Benoit read on air?"

Loughlin cleared his throat. "Excuse me. Got a bit of a cold. Yeah, CQAM keeps a 24-hour air-check. They're dubbing off a copy for our people to analyze. I think I can send one your way. Leave it with me. I'll get back to you on that."

"Sounds good, Peter. Talk to you then." Moore hung up and began dialing the number for CQAM radio. He would ask Maurice Asselin for permission to send a reporter-camera team to the station. If Loughlin's description of the program manager was accurate, he was pretty sure Asselin would be quite happy to strut like a rooster on the six o'clock *Flash News*.

26

TY PARKED MOBILE 14 in the parking lot behind the television station. On his way to work from the Reddy Memorial hospital he had mentally prepared an argument to convince Clyde Bertram his hunch about the Ouellette Funeral Home had merit. He *wasn't* prepared for the mayhem at CKCF. Moore was on the phone. Bertram had kept the overnight police reporter on overtime. Ty's ten-to-seven shift had been covered by another reporter in case Ty got tied up at the Reddy, and CKCF Radio's Keith Campbell was furiously pounding the keys on his Underwood. Phones were ringing. Moore's police radios were blaring and the teletype machines were churning out copy on the CQAM occupation.

CKCF Radio shared space with television, under the same corporate umbrella. Their studios were just down the corridor from the newsroom. *Flash News* reporters were often required to file radio reports on developing stories while covering for television. They held two microphones, one for radio and one for TV. Writers for television occupied one side of a long table in the newsroom. Writers for radio worked the other side. When he wasn't in his office Bertram often sat in a semi-circular slot at the head of the table, overseeing both news divisions. He believed in a hands-on management style. Writers were sometimes intimidated by his presence, calling him "Big Daddy" behind his back. Bertram had heard the nickname and he kind of liked it.

Campbell saw Ty walk in, balled his fists and waved his arms in the air. It was his way of silently pointing out that the proverbial had "hit the fan." Ty sat down on the TV side. "Busy day?" he asked Keith.

"I'll say. You haven't heard?"

Ty shook his head. "Heard what?"

"Drapeau's on his way to the station. Plans to respond to the CQAM thing."

"Sorry, Keith, I've been at the hospital with Liz. What CQAM thing?"

Campbell stopped typing and filled him in on the Papineau Avenue events that morning.

"Jeez! Shades of the October crisis."

The radio newsman nodded. "These guys weren't Common Front. They presented themselves that way, but the references to Bay Street, Saint James Street and Wall Street sort of gave them away. The *Vive le Québec* was a nice touch."

"Separatists, on the Common Front bandwagon?"

"Radical sovereigntists. Willing to shed blood if necessary and, *yeah*, using labor's confrontation with the government to further their own agenda."

Ty watched Bertram walk into Moore's glassed-in cubicle and stood up. It was 10:45 by the newsroom clock. "Thanks Keith. I'd better go see what they're planning. What time's the mayor supposed to get here?"

"About 11:30, according to his secretary. We're hoping to get a clip for our noon news."

Moore and Bertram were discussing the idea of bringing Art Bradley in for the Drapeau interview, when Ty walked through the door. Bertram glanced at his watch.

"I know you have family problems," he said, "But, if you're going to be an hour late for your shift, Ty, you've gotta let us know in advance."

Moore shrugged. "He's here, now. Let *him* do the bit with Drapeau. You'll get a much better interview with Ty than you would with Bradley. Bradley's got his nose up his ass when it comes to local news, anyway. We'd have to feed him the questions."

Bertram thought it over. "Bradley's our anchor. He won't like it."

"True. But he'll charge you an arm and a leg if you bring him in several hours early."

"Okay. I'm over budget as it is. Ty, you're the man. Can you handle it?"

Ty told him he was abreast of developments at the French language radio station, if that's what Drapeau wanted to talk about. "If he decides to make an announcement about Montreal's plans for the '76 Olympics, that's *all* he'll talk about."

Moore interjected. "No. We made it clear. This will be a response to what happened this morning. Apparently the Mayor's mad as hell that these guys got away with it. He'll be open to questions about the police response and the existence of fringe groups like the one that carried it out."

"Maybe we should remind him about Pierre Trudeau's *reason before passion* philosophy."

Bertram smiled. "When Drapeau's angry, passion makes a better news clip."

Ty seized on the opportunity to bring up his thoughts about the Sainte-Agathe crematorium. "Clyde, I'll do you proud with the Mayor. But I'm damned anxious to head up north again. I really don't think we should let things slide on the Morissette story."

The news director raised an eyebrow. "Bradley's going to be pissed he didn't get a crack at Drapeau. Tell you what, Ty. You handle the mayor. I'm bringing Maggie in, to prepare a piece for the six o'clock show on what happened at CQAM. That'll be lead story. I'll tell Bradley he's *cock of the walk* on the whole deal. We'll simply edit in Drapeau's answers to your questions and keep you out of it. That'll appeal to his ego and allow me to keep my promise."

"What promise?"

"To let you follow up on this theory you had about the funeral home operator and our dead Dr. Desjardins … cutting up bodies before incinerating them."

Ty smiled. "You're the boss."

"And, if you're going to try to play cop and lay hands on fingerprints of this guy, make bloody sure you do it without his knowledge. We've got enough lawsuits without looking for more of them."

"Consider it done." Ty snapped his heels together and saluted.

"Yeah, yeah. Get outta here. Wait for Drapeau at the front door. Greg's setting up for an off-set interview in the main studio."

* * *

A black 1972 Chrysler LeBaron pulled up in front of CKCF Television at 11:45 Wednesday morning. Mayor Jean Drapeau waited for his chauffeur to open the rear-seat door before stepping out on to the sidewalk. Two large men in dark-colored suits emerged, simultaneously, from the front and rear of the car ... quickly flanking Drapeau as he approached the TV station entrance. Ty was there to greet them.

The ensuing interview, in studio two, went smoothly with Drapeau reddening in the face only once when Ty asked him why police had found no trace of the men who had occupied CQAM Radio. The Mayor went on the defensive about response time, and the perennial efforts by provincial and municipal authorities to keep track of radical elements in the Quebec separatist movement. He acknowledged that building tensions between the Common Front and government negotiators had worsened relations between English Canadian and Québécois workers.

"This," he agreed, "had underlined the feeling among what he called *certain elements* in Quebec's Francophone majority that they were being denied a right to self-determination." Asked to define that term, he had emphasized his own federalist views, while skillfully avoiding the question.

When the interview was over, Ty and the Mayor shook hands amicably and Greg handed off the footage to another cameraman, who would take it to the David Spear Lab for processing. Drapeau's Chrysler LeBaron departed the station shortly after noon. Keith Campbell did *not* get his news clip in time for radio's major newscast at twelve.

"Get set," Ty told Greg. "We're going to Sainte-Agathe."

27

THE COMPLEXE FUNÉRAIRE OUELLETTE, on Rue St-Aubin in Sainte-Agathe-des-Monts, was housed in a Georgian style home. Ty couldn't help but think the distinctly British architectural design was somewhat out of place for the Laurentian Mountains of Quebec. It was essentially a two-story box. A paneled front door was located in the center, topped with rectangular multi-pane windows, five across. The entire structure was composed of red brick.

"Looks like a connecting building to the rear," Ty pointed out to Greg. "Probably the crematorium." There were chimneys on both sides of the home. Another protruded from the more contemporary section behind it.

"We'd better get the marked car out of the way." Ty added. "If this guy makes us out to be journalists, and I'm *right* about his involvement in harvesting those human organs, he won't talk to us at all. Park the mobile up the road, behind that hotel. From this moment on, I'm a potential client in search of information about cremation. If you and Jerry come in a few minutes later, back up my story. My father is terminally ill. I want to respect his wishes when he dies. Got it?"

Ty climbed out of Mobile 7. Greg rolled down the driver's side window before pulling away. "Are we just supposed to be friends? I mean, I'm no actor. What's my motivation?" His eyes had an impish expression.

Ty smiled. "Get the hell outta here, or I'll motivate your ass." Greg and Jerry drove off toward the hotel.

Inside the funeral home, there was no one to be seen. There were closets on both sides of the entranceway, presumably for those attending funeral services during the winter months and in need of hanging up heavy coats. No coats, or any other clothing, were in evidence. Ty walked into an open area where a sign indicated directions to the facility's various rooms. A chapel to the left. Viewing rooms to the right. Crematorium, past a central staircase that led to the second floor. Ty assumed there would be offices upstairs.

He hadn't quite reached the top, when he heard a female's voice. She was on the telephone and she sounded frantic. "In the embalming chamber!" she exclaimed. "Mr. Ouellette, that's right. Yes, I'm *sure* he's dead. It was horrible. He was lying on the table. Please, come quickly. I .. I'm very frightened." There was a pause. "No, *downstairs* in the embalming chamber. Mr. Ouellette was working down there this morning, preparing a body. Yes, I'll wait. No, there's no one else here."

Ty heard her hang up the telephone. He immediately backtracked down the stairs to the lobby. He realized he had only minutes to find the embalming room, before Greg and Jerry got back from the hotel, and he didn't want to be seen by the young woman until he'd had a chance to better understand what had happened. She'd obviously been talking to the police.

There were two viewing rooms on either side of a corridor, leading off to the left of the staircase. He walked to the end of the hallway, which turned again to the left. A washroom was located there, next to a door marked "Casket Room." He walked to the latter, trying to make as little noise as possible as he opened it and proceeded down another set of stairs.

Here was an office, probably used by Ouellette himself when he wasn't prepping bodies. In another room, Ty found himself surrounded by coffins of varying size, quality and color. Shelving contained an array of elaborately built urns, ready for the choosing by the bereaved. Some were decorated with flowers, or praying hands, or birds and butterflies. "Nice," he thought, "mask the grief with thoughts of eternal spring." He shuddered at the thought and began feeling claustrophobic in the closed space. That was when he spotted the heavy set of doors. There was a small, enamel plaque on the wall next to them. Inscribed on it were the words "Employees Only."

Ty took a deep breath and entered what the woman's voice had described as "the embalming chamber." There were two, stainless steel tables, tapered in the middle to allow bodily fluids to be drained away. And there were two bodies. The first was a female. She had most likely been the focus of Ouellette's attention. On the second table was that of a white-haired man, probably in his mid-fifties or early-sixties. He was fully clothed.

"Hello, *Monsieur* Ouellette," Ty said out loud. "You look decidedly ... dead."

Ty had only one objective in mind. He needed to follow through with his plan to get a fingerprint. Perspiration ran down his forehead into his eyes. He listened carefully, for any sound from the funeral home upstairs. There was none. Then he retrieved a steno-pad from his shirt pocket and hesitated, only momentarily, before reaching for the dead man's cold hand. Gradually he lifted the hand toward his own forehead, wiping the fingers across the sweaty surface and then pressing them firmly on to the paper. He gingerly replaced the pad in his shirt pocket.

Not satisfied with the effort, he desperately looked around the room for any object that might better retain the impression of the friction ridges on Ouellette's fingers. He spotted a metal cup. Ty grabbed it off a nearby countertop and repeated the procedure.

Ouellette's hand felt almost insect-like on his forehead. But the result of pressing the fingers on to the metal cup was successful. He could actually see the "loop and a whorl" patterns—not smudged, not distorted or overlapped. He realized he'd been holding his breath. Ty let out a lungful of air, returned Ouellette's arm to the position he'd found it in and got ready to leave. That was when he spotted something shiny, on the floor beneath the embalming table. He realized, instantaneously, that it had no business in this room. He was also aware he'd seen the object before. The mother-of-pearl hair comb, likely one-of-a kind, had belonged to Yvette Comtois, proud owner of La Petite Perle antique shop on Rue Principale in Saint-Sauveur.

28

ICE CREAM SEEMED LIKE a good idea. A mid-afternoon sun filtered through leafless tree branches along St-Aubin street, boosting temperatures into unseasonable highs. Greg and Jerry left Mobile 7 in the hotel lot. They'd begun walking the roughly half-mile back to the funeral home, when Greg spotted the malt shop. A boyish glee crept over his face. "What about some ice cream?" he asked.

Jerry, who was wearing a corduroy windbreaker, looked surprised. "You kidding? I'm freezing."

"Well, maybe they serve hot coffee. Me, I'm for two scoops of vanilla."

Jerry grinned. "Suit yourself. I guess I don't think about ice cream until some time in July." They turned into the small shop, ignoring the distant sound of sirens.

Ty slowly climbed the stairs from the casket room. He refrained from opening the door at the top, listening for any indication that the young woman he'd heard speaking on the telephone had descended to the first floor. There was no telltale sound. Taking every precaution to avoid unnecessary noise, Ty pushed open the door and stepped out into the corridor. His heart was racing so fast, he could feel a beating pulse in his temples. He held the small metal cup by its handle, making sure not to smudge the fingerprints he had stolen from … Ty realized at that moment he didn't even know Ouellette's first name.

He inched his way past the restroom and peered around the corner into the entrance area. No one was in sight. The rubber soles of his shoes squeaked unnervingly on the tiled floor, as he quickly made for the front door. "Yvette Comtois," he thought, "what possible connection?" He'd left the antique hair comb on the floor under the embalming table. Ty was aware he'd already broken several laws, ranging from illegal trespassing to interfering with a dead body.

Tampering with evidence in a possible capital crime had been out of the question.

He'd barely reached the sidewalk when two things happened. He heard the sirens and he spotted Greg and Jerry about two hundred yards up the street and walking in his direction. He whistled at them and urgently waved them back toward the hotel. Greg was munching on an ice cream cone. Jerry was carrying the Bell and Howell silent camera in one hand and what appeared to be a coffee in the other. As Ty left the sidewalk and followed them into the parking lot, two Quebec Provincial Police cruisers sailed past, sirens blasting, and headed toward the Complexe Funéraire Ouellette.

He was breathless and nearly hysterical, by the time he slid into the passenger seat of Mobile 7. Greg turned the key in the ignition. "What happened? You look like you're about to explode."

Ty's face was beet-red. He held the metal cup away from his body. "The guy's dead," he took a deep breath. "Ouellette's dead." Then he began to laugh. It wasn't because of anything funny. He couldn't help himself. "I fucking can't believe it. He was lying on a table in the ... ha ha ... embalming chamber. Dead as a fucking doornail."

"Jesus!" Greg said. Jerry, who was in the back seat sipping on his coffee, nearly choked on the hot liquid. "How?" he asked. "What's that cup you were holding?"

"Evidence," Ty replied. "At least I *think* it's evidence. I ... goddamn it ... I actually got fingerprints from the guy. I could be in a shit load of trouble."

Greg pulled out of the hotel lot and headed in the direction of the Laurentian Autoroute. "You mean they're on that cup?"

"Yeah. The cup. I pressed Ouellette's hand, or rather his fingers, on to the cup. Also on to a steno-pad I have in my pocket. And that's not all. Remember the woman we interviewed in Saint-Sauveur? The antique store? Remember she fixed her hair before you rolled film, Greg?"

"Uh-huh."

"Well, she used a mother-of-pearl comb to keep it in place. Remember that?"

"Sort of. I was busy setting up the camera."

"Okay. Get this. The comb was on the floor, underneath the embalming table Ouellette was lying on."

"Get outta here!"

"I'm not kidding. Look, I don't know what the hell to do now. I'd better radio in and talk to Jason." He plucked the microphone from the dashboard. When Moore came on, he recounted the entire incident.

"Did anybody see you?" Moore wanted to know.

"No one."

"Right. Good. Listen, I'm going to fill Clyde in. Why don't you guys get back to Montreal. Together we'll figure out how to handle the situation. 10-4?"

"10-4. Mobile 7 is 10-30, en-route.

"One more thing, Ty."

"Yeah?"

"The Reddy Memorial called. Liz will be discharged tomorrow."

Jason got the message loud and clear from Clyde Bertram. "Get in touch, immediately, with that QPP Chief Inspector Cousineau. Tell him precisely what went down and let him know that Davis is on his way to Parthenais Street with the evidence. Advise him that we're entirely aware Davis's actions crossed the line, but he firmly believed he was furthering the Morissette investigation and was only trying to help."

"What about the hair comb?"

Bertram shook his head. "Leave that out. That's an ace up Ty's sleeve. If Cousineau gets pissy about the fingerprints and if it turns out Ouellette was actually *murdered*, Ty might be able to hand them the killer on a platter. At the very least, this Comtois woman will be a person of interest. Cousineau may wind up *thanking* us in the end."

Moore stood up from one of the chairs next to Bertram's desk. "Hope you're right. Ty committed at least a couple of felonies up there."

"See what you can find out about the antique shop owner. Where she was born. Who her friends are. Anything at all about her background."

"I'll do my best, Clyde." He headed for his own office and, when

139

he'd sat himself down at the assignment desk, he reached for the two-way radio. Ty, Greg and Jerry reported they were just south of Saint-Sauveur, on the Autoroute. Moore told them to proceed to QPP headquarters in Montreal, then he picked up the telephone. The first thing he would do is inform the Chief Inspector of an incident on St-Aubin Street in Sainte-Agathe-des-Monts, before his own officers had even left the scene.

Max, Mike and Pearl came bounding out of the rear office, tongues out, eyes alight. The three dogs strenuously objected to anything that took their mistress out of their sight for any length of time. Pearl had a habit of sitting on cushions in the picture window, facing Rue Principale, waiting in anticipation of Yvette Comtois' return. Usually, her absence was brief. A walking trip to the grocery store or the dry cleaners generally took less than an hour. This time was different. Pearl had waited quite long enough, in her canine opinion. When she'd felt abandoned, she joined Max and Mike in the office and curled up in her basket. All three sprang to life when the bells, over the front door of *La Petite Perle*, announced an end to their seclusion.

Yvette greeted her pets with enthusiasm. Max and Mike made 360-degree tours of her feet. Pearl, who considered herself to be the center of the universe, required being picked up and cuddled. Nothing less would suffice. After the initial explosion of affection, Max and Mike indicated an urgent need to visit the backyard. Yvette deposited Pearl on the floor and accompanied the exuberant trio into a fenced in, albeit tiny, yard at the rear of her shop. Her long hair kept falling across her forehead and she pushed it back out of her eyes, as she waited for the dogs to do their business. Until that moment, she had not noticed that her mother-of-pearl comb … was missing.

Adrien Cousineau was incredulous. "You realize," he said, hands clasped across his expansive mid-section, "that you may have compromised the ability of my officers to do their job?"

Ty was seated in one of the leather upholstered chairs in the Chief Inspector's corner office at QPP headquarters. "I was very careful. I touched nothing, except Ouellette's hand and wrist."

"You might have *thought* you were being careful, *Monsieur* Davis.

But, you tell me you entered several rooms at the funeral home. You had to have opened doors. If this … Ouellette did not die of natural causes, we'll be looking for a killer who had to have passed through those same doors. Any prints we might have obtained from those doors will likely have been lost."

Ty slumped in the chair. "You're right, of course, Chief Inspector. However, I'm reasonably sure of two things. I think these prints I've given you, on the metal cup and on the steno-pad, will match those found on the bottles in that refrigerator at Saint-Sauveur. And I'm certain that you'll find that Ouellette did *not* die of natural causes."

Cousineau unclasped his hands and leaned over his desk. "Why would you say that?"

Ty decided to drop his bomb. "Because, your officers will find an antique hair comb under the embalming table where Ouellette's body was found. I know who it belongs to."

"Who? What hair comb?"

"I didn't touch it. But, I'd seen it before. The comb belongs to an Yvette Comtois, She's the proprietor of La Petite Perle, an antique store on Rue Principale … directly opposite the house where Jacqueline Morissette's body was discovered. In fact, Chief Inspector, Yvette Comtois was the witness who telephoned police to report the girl being carried *into* that house. She was the witness, interviewed by Montreal Police Sergeant Alain Robichaud. I conducted an interview with her, myself. I have her on film."

Adrien Cousineau ran the fingers of both hands through his hair and leaned back in his chair. "And you say this … comb … was near Ouellette's body?"

"He was lying on the table. The comb was underneath the table."

Cousineau picked up his telephone. "Get me dispatch," he said.

He gestured to Ty, to remain seated and began speaking to the QPP dispatcher. "First," he said, "get a couple of cruisers over to La Petite Perle on Rue Principale in Saint-Sauveur. Pick up the owner … Yvette Comtois, for questioning. Next, get in touch *now* with the officer in charge investigating the death of a funeral home operator in Sainte-Agathe. Tell him to call me direct. As quickly as possible *s'il vous plaît.*"

29

"THERE WERE AGREEMENTS of cooperation between the Université de la Sorbonne, in Paris, and the University of St. Gallen in Switzerland." Jason Moore was standing next to the vending machine outside CKCF's sports department. Clyde Bertram was in the process of buying a coffee, black with sugar. He was bent over, retrieving his change from the coin return.

"So, Yvette Comtois was educated. So what?"

"More than just the four year diploma, Clyde. She graduated summa cum laude from the Sorbonne. Her family lived in the south of France. Apparently quite wealthy, according to my research. She then went on to St. Gallen where she obtained a doctorate in dentistry. From the faculty of general dental practice, she immersed herself in the medical sciences ... dental surgery ... anesthesia, that sort of thing."

Bertram straightened up, dropping his change into his pants pocket. "Question is, how did she wind up in Quebec, running an antique store? With those qualifications?"

"That," Moore replied, "is where the story gets very interesting. It seems she married while doing post-graduate work. She established a dental practice in Zurich and was successful at it. Good reputation, or so the area newspapers reported."

"Why was this covered in the newspapers? Lots of people become dentists."

"Well, like I said, her family was wealthy and powerful ... and there was a court case."

"What sort of court case?"

Moore had been saving the best for last. "She was accused of *murdering* her husband."

"Ah-hah."

"Everything played out in Zurich. The husband was an older man ... an academic connected to the university apparently. The papers ate it up. That's partly why I was so successful in getting the low-down on Comtois. There was widespread publicity in both France and Switzerland, and I have a very good contact at Immigration Canada who clued me in on a lot of this stuff."

"I'm impressed." Bertram walked into the newsroom, with Moore trailing behind.

"What about the court case?"

"Eventually she was acquitted. All charges dropped. No one else arrested. It's a cold case."

"And she crossed the pond. She settled here."

"Right. There was some sort of falling out with her family. I'm not clear on that. She emigrated to Canada … became a citizen and settled in Quebec. Actually, she has dual French and Canadian citizenship."

Bertram paused outside his office door. "She set up a dental practice here?"

"No. On the surface it would appear her objective was to drop out of sight."

"Out of sight of what?"

"There's the sixty-four-thousand dollar question. Maybe just the publicity."

"When did all of this take place?"

"Mid-fifties."

"So, she's been here for roughly seventeen or eighteen years."

Moore nodded. "Running that store in Sainte-Agathe. Right."

"And never got back into dentistry. Interesting."

"Not so far as I can tell."

"Okay, Jason. Good work on all of that. I don't know where it leads, but give the background to Ty when he gets in. He can update the Morissette story for the six o'clock and we can mention Comtois is being questioned by police in connection with a suspicious death in Sainte-Agathe. Stay *away*, and I mean *completely away* from this whole fingerprints thing. We don't want to go there until we know how Cousineau reacts to it."

Moore started heading for his own office and turned back toward Bertram in mid-stride. "What if Ty was right?"

"About what?"

"What if forensics gets a match on the prints of this Ouellette character and the ones found on the Saint-Sauveur bottles?"

Bertram shrugged. "Then, we'll report it. *Until* then, it's just speculation."

QPP Sergeant Roger Tremblay pulled up outside *La Petite Perle* at quarter to six on Wednesday evening. Orders had come down from on high. He wasn't clear on the reasons a Chief Inspector would be directly involved, but he knew it had something to do with the funeral home. He'd waited until the body of Fernand Ouellette was loaded into a morgue truck and had intended to eat his evening meal in Sainte-Agathe before going home to his wife and kids in Morin Heights.

Tremblay knew Ouellette's body would be transported to forensics in Montreal. He had not been aware, until ordered to the Saint-Sauveur antique shop, that the funeral home operator's death might be connected somehow to the triple homicide on Rue Princi-pale. Yvette Comtois said she'd spotted eleven-year-old Jacqueline Morissette being forced out of the Chevy station wagon. Instantly, his mental picture of the little girl in the freezer drove his appetite away. He thought of his own daughter, watched a second police cruiser pull into a lot next to the church on the corner, and shivered in a cool evening breeze out of the northwest.

Art Bradley never liked sharing the spotlight, much less the six o'clock lead story. Not unless it involved *only* a field report. That way, all of the drama could be his alone. He resented the fact that Clyde Bertram frequently seated his star reporter next to him on the *Flash News* anchor-desk. "Another sonofabitch after my job," he thought.

Studio-Director Steven Collyer was counting him out of the newscast theme. "Take Camera one. Cue Art."

Bradley inhaled and began reading the script. He had a unique ability to glance down at his copy only occasionally, memorizing whole paragraphs and maintaining eye contact with the viewing audience. "Good Evening," he said, keeping a sober expression. "On this April first, *Flash News* looks back at a tragic story … the death of eleven-year-old Jacqueline Morissette after she was abducted here in Montreal, and whose body was found in a freezer at Saint-Sauveur on March 13th.

Collyer called on the *switcher* to "take camera two." Bradley and Davis were on a two-shot. Bradley continued. "Reporter Ty Davis is here with me in studio to bring you up to date on developments ... Ty."

"Take camera three," Collyer shouted.

Ty turned simultaneously to the camera, on a close-up. "Thanks, Art. For those of you who haven't been following this story ... some background."

A script assistant began counting Ty down to film "Voice-over in ten, nine ...."

"The little girl and a friend were returning to school from their lunch hour. Morissette was forced into a Chevrolet station wagon that later turned up at *this house*."

The fieldstone house on Rue Principale came up, full-screen. The station wagon was parked in the driveway.

"But, before police were able to locate the girl's body in the basement of the house, *two other* bodies were found in the living room."

A long-shot of the bodies was shown.

"It is now believed by police that forty-three-year-old Francis Duguay and twenty-two year old Marlene Brannigan were responsible for the Montreal abduction and ultimate murder of young Morrisette."

Some general scenes of the living room were on screen. Bertram had been adamant about avoiding any close-ups of the naked bodies. Ty kept talking.

"At first, police were calling their deaths a murder-suicide. Now, however, it's clear that Duguay and Brannigan were fatally shot by an unknown attacker."

The scene shifted to the Jacques Cartier Bridge.

"On the same day all of this was happening, a man identified as Serge Blouin committed suicide by jumping off the Jacques Cartier Bridge in Montreal."

Now, a full screen exterior shot of the Centre Hospitalier Laurentien.

"Then, exactly a week ago today, Dr. Denis Desjardins who was affiliated with the Centre Hospitalier Laurentien in Sainte-Agathe des-Monts, was shot at *his* home on Lac des Sables in that Laurentian community. *Flash News* was able to establish a definite link between Dr. Desjardins and suicide victim Serge Blouin. Blouin was the personnel manager at the *same* hospital."

Ty heard the script assistant's voice in his earpiece. "Sound-up in ten seconds."

"I talked with a Donald Quesnel at Centre Hospitalier Laurentien. He works in the hospital morgue, where Desjardins' body was initially taken."

Quesnel appeared on camera.

"I saw them, *de temps en temps*, eating lunch together. In the hospital cafeteria."

Collyer ordered the *switcher* to a one-shot on camera three. Ty stared into the lens.

"And the story doesn't end there. Police are now investigating the possibility that Dr. Desjardins might have been killed by the same person, or persons, who murdered the Morissette kidnappers ... Francis Duguay and Marlene Brannigan.

"Two shot on camera two," Collyer's voice echoed in Ty's ear. He and Art Bradley were back on screen together. There was no film footage of the Ouellette funeral home. Ty, Greg and Jerry had been in too much of a hurry to get out of Sainte-Agathe. Ty glanced at the anchorman.

"And, Art, just this morning ... yet another body turned up."

Bradley tried to look interested. Ty addressed the camera.

"That of Fernand Ouellette ... a funeral home operator in Sainte-Agathe."

"How does that tie in with everything else?" Bradley asked.

"In a previous report, I mentioned that Duguay, Brannigan and Desjardins all had a strange mark ... precisely the *same* mark or puncture wound on their right lower hip. It remains to be seen whether Ouellette has a similar wound .. but Dr. Desjardins' body was cremated at the Ouellette funeral home. I have confirmation that Desjardins *knew* and had past dealings with Fernand Ouellette."

Bradley cast a startled glance at camera-two. "Do police have any idea, at this point, whether this … Ouellette … died of natural causes?"

"Well, Art, all I can tell you in answer to that is that police are currently in the process of rounding up an antique store owner in Saint-Sauveur. Viewers might recall an interview I did with her on March 13th. Yvette Comtois was the same woman who alerted police to the fact that eleven-year-old Jacqueline Morissette was being held in the house on Rue Principale. When Provincial Police officers were investigating the funeral home operator's death, this morning in Sainte-Agathe … an article belonging to Yvette Comtois was found next to his body."

Bradley had no trouble, at this point, displaying an expression of complete surprise. "So, it looks like it could have been another killing?"

Ty shook his head. "The Comtois-Ouellette connection could be a coincidence. I think we have to stress that no charges have been filed against this woman. Police are referring to her as a person of interest."

"And it's a compelling and" … Bradley searched for a word … "*horrifying* story, Ty. Thank you for bringing it up to date and I'm certain we'll be hearing more about it."

The on-set debriefing with Ty was over. Bradley moved on to his next story.

30

BEFORE LEAVING THE TELEVISION station, Ty called Sarah and Charles and was reassured that Catherine and Robin were fine. The children had come home from classes, full of enthusiasm about the annual school play. Catherine was to have a small part in a presentation of "Goldilocks and the Three Bears" put on by grades two through six. Sarah told Ty she had gone into the Reddy Memorial that afternoon to visit with Elizabeth. Ty was suddenly seized with guilt. "You and Charles have been so great," he said apologetically. "I'm on my way, now, to see Liz. Did you happen to run into Dr. Nelson?"

"No, Ty. He was off on some kind of emergency. But Elizabeth was talkative and her color was back. She seems on the mend. She asked about you."

Ty choked up. "I, uh … I wish I didn't have to work."

"I know, Ty. But your job is important and, as I say, Liz understands. So do we."

"Thanks, Sarah. I'm really grateful for everything you're doing. I'll check in at the Reddy on my way home. Do we need anything at the store? I can pick up some groceries."

"Already done," Sarah replied. "I stopped by Steinberg's earlier today."

Two QPP Constables accompanied Sergeant Roger Tremblay through the front door of La Petite Perle and Tremblay jumped, involuntarily, as the entranceway bells chimed. He realized his hand had automatically grasped the handle of his side-arm. One of the constables, who'd followed him into the antique shop, gave him a concerned look. "Easy, Sergeant, this is pretty routine."

Tremblay nodded, embarrassed by the fact that he was spooked by a couple of bells. The three men proceeded into the dark interior of the store. Tremblay nearly tripped on an old spinning wheel and, in avoiding it, banged his knee on the edge of a counter. "Goddamn it!

Look for a light switch." He stood in one position until an overhead fixture clicked on and the shop was bathed in a soft glow.

They were literally surrounded by antique chairs, tables, bureaus, a butter churn, several spinning wheels of varied size and a grouping of carved picture frames leaning against each other. A glass-encased counter displayed coins, jewelry, wrist and pocket-watches, pewter steins and an expensive-looking silver tea-set. Numerous mirrors hung on the walls, reflecting each other and creating the illusion of a much bigger interior space.

Tremblay spotted a closed door at the rear of the shop. "Hello," he shouted, moving slowly toward it. There was no reply from beyond. One of the constables remained near the entrance and the other followed the Sergeant. "Doesn't appear to be anyone around," he told Tremblay.

The two men entered the room at the back of the shop. It contained a pull-out couch that was made up as a bed, a desk and two, large chairs. A television set stood on a small table and scattered around on the floor were a wicker basket with a pillow in it and several plastic bowls. There was a small kitchenette and a second door led into an adjoining bathroom.

"Looks like she *lived* here," Tremblay remarked.

The Constable pointed at the bowls on the floor. "And she had pets."

"One thing's certain," Tremblay added, "she was in one hell of a hurry to get out. I'll radio it in. Dispatch will probably keep the place under surveillance, but I have a feeling Yvette Comtois won't be coming back. She's left all of her belongings. She didn't even lock the front door."

Liz was sitting up in a chair beside her bed. Her face was flushed and she smiled broadly as Ty walked into the room. "Freedom tomorrow," she said excitedly.

"Wonderful," Ty replied. "Has that been confirmed?"

"It has. Dr. Nelson was in here a few minutes ago. He says I'm fit as a fiddle and good to go."

Ty unfolded a metal chair, which had been leaning against the wall, and placed it next to hers. He tried not to show the concern that gnawed at his insides. "Any idea what time you'll get your walking papers?"

Liz folded her legs underneath her body in the big recliner chair. "Sometime after breakfast I think. I told Dr. Nelson you'd be coming in after work this evening. He's somewhere around and he said he wanted to see you. My mother visited this afternoon. She says Catherine and Robin are doing great and Catherine is going to be a baby bear in her school play."

"So I understand. I spoke with Sarah earlier."

"Well, you'd better check in at the nurses' station. That's where Dr. Nelson usually hangs out, unless he's wrestling with one of us ... *crazies*."

Ty was about to say she wasn't crazy, but Liz was staring at him with an odd intensity.

"Just remember what Nelson said, Liz. You're fit as a fiddle and good to go."

She looked away toward the room's west-facing window. "I'm sorry about all this," she said in a subdued tone of voice. "Sorry to have put everybody through it."

Not knowing precisely how to respond, Ty stood up and walked toward the corridor. He turned, at the door, and realized that Liz was tearful. "No need to apologize," he said. "You've just been through it like all the rest of us. And you've had a much harder time than we have. Just keep in mind that you're on the road to recovery ... and, Liz, you're coming home tomorrow."

She wiped at her eyes and tried to smile. "I love you. Please go see Dr. Nelson."

A young intern nodded at him and opened the locked door of the psych-ward for Ty. There were two nurses behind the circular counter. He asked one of them whether the doctor was available to see him and was directed to Nelson's office. He'd barely knocked on the door, when Nelson invited him in. "Good to see you, Mr. Davis. Come on, then. Have a seat."

Ty sat down on the comfortable couch he'd been directed to on the first occasion he'd been in Nelson's sanctum. He tried to avoid looking at the wall mural and it's patient-produced alien landscape. "How's she doing, Dr. Nelson?"

"Well. She's doing well. But I do have some thoughts going forward."

"Please. That's my biggest worry … that, somehow, this isn't over yet. Know what I mean?"

Nelson rested his elbows on his huge desk. "I do indeed, Mr. Davis. And it would be irresponsible of me to say that Elizabeth is, shall I say, completely out of the woods?"

"So, what now?"

"To begin with, Elizabeth is to be discharged tomorrow. You and I have discussed her *disthymia* … her depression. We've ruled out physical causes for this but I've decided that lithium is *not* the way to go."

"Then what?"

Nelson rested his chin on one hand. "Remember, Mr. Davis, I told you I think Elizabeth is quite treatable. We talked about her lumbar puncture and the spinal fluid revealing elevated levels of *creatine phosphokinase* or CPK?"

"I remember asking you to explain that in English."

Nelson laughed. "I also emphasized that your wife is not generally psychotic and that she might suffer from a *unipolar* or major depressive disorder. I still believe this to be the case. I'm not convinced, however, that my initial diagnosis was entirely accurate, when I told you I believed her psychotic behavior might have resulted from a momentary lapse into a bipolar state."

Ty sat forward on the couch. "Now," he said, "I *am* confused."

Nelson leaned back in his chair. "I've had the best part of two days to observe Elizabeth. We've run certain tests, as I told you, and I'm now of the belief that all of the symptoms Elizabeth has exhibited are due to something we call dissociation."

"What's *that* mean?"

"Full blown dissociative disorder provokes mood swings, general depression, suicidal tendencies, sleep problems. It can trigger alcohol and drug abuse, which you tell me led to her post-partum experience of three years ago. It can also cause psychotic-like symptoms, including auditory and visual hallucinations."

"So, is that what you think Liz *has*? This … dissociative disorder?"

"*Dissociation*, yes. Not the disorder itself, which would be much more serious. But I believe Elizabeth has suppressed something in her past. When she took the valium, she had no memory of doing so. It was a kind of … out of body situation. You've told me that, when she got rid of your living room furniture, she behaved like a different person … like someone you couldn't even recognize or reason with."

"Yes, that's true. But what do you mean about suppressing something in her past?"

"I'd like to put Elizabeth under hypnosis, Mr. Davis. With you present and with both of you approving the procedure, of course."

"Hypnosis! Why?"

"Because whatever it is that underlies the outward behavior, hypnosis has the potential to reveal it."

"If you say so. I suppose we'd both agree."

"Good. In the meantime, I've prescribed an antidepressant for Elizabeth. Not lithium. *Mianserin hydrochloride* has a positive track record in the treatment of depressive illness. There are no adverse effects on the cardiovascular system as in the case of *tricyclics* like *amytripyline* or *imipramine*."

Ty stood up off the couch. "There you go again, doc. And my response, *again*, is … if you say so."

Nelson rose out of his chair and extended his hand. "Alright. We'll start her off with a mega-dose. I'll administer that here." He handed Ty a prescription. "This is for 0.5 milligram tablets. Once a day, until we see how she reacts. I'll see you and Elizabeth tomorrow morning and the three of us can discuss a mutually convenient date for the hypnosis."

Ty shook hands with Nelson. He left the office and headed back to the psych ward to say good night to Liz.

31

AN URGENT CABLE REACHED Werner Hochstrasser at the University of Basel, early on Thursday morning. Laurent Picard had watched a Montreal telecast on the previous evening. The cable was brief and to the point. Quebec Provincial Police were investigating another murder, likely connected to the breakaway sect in the Laurentians. What knowledge did Hochstrasser of the current whereabouts of Yvette Comtois—a woman they hadn't seen in years?

Hochstrasser read the cable as he walked through a five hundred-year-old university corridor toward the Biozentrum department. Hairs stood up on the back of his neck. He knew a great deal about Comtois. She had been initiated by the Order more than twenty years ago when she had been a gifted young student at the Université de la Sorbonne in Paris. She had proven to be a dedicated proponent of the organization's ritualistic ceremonies, displaying a native talent for Talmudic-like insights.

He had allowed her to incorporate *Shemhamphorash* into the rituals ... a term of power said to possess the seeds of creation itself. Although Hochstrasser did not fully believe in such things, Comtois was convincing in her argument that there is a natural and intimate connection between words and the things signified by them. "If one repeats the name of a supernatural entity," she insisted, "it is possible to summon that entity to *do one's bidding* for goodness or for evil. All things," she had said, "are in sympathy .. acting and reacting upon one another."

Hochstrasser was impressed. In fact, to some extent, his scientific endeavors in the Biozentrum reflected the axiom that the *visible* is, to human perception, merely a proportional measure of the *invisible*. Two paths ... science and mysticism ... led from the *known* to uncover the *unknown*.

His work at the university focused on a greater understanding of the mechanisms of life. The Biozentrum, virtually a new department in 1972, had attracted scientists from all over the world. All of them were engaged in an investigation of biological processes on a molecular basis. The collective aim was to discover what a human cell consists of and how it works ... how, for example, a cell knows whether to become a leg or an eye. Hochstrasser had been fascinated with the similarities between his perennial interest in the field and Comtois' occult approach to the same questions.

Based on the idea that all worldly things act in sympathy with each other, Comtois firmly believed that transmutation was possible. She claimed that every individual possessed an animal form that could be entered, at will, through a process of magical incantation. "Once achieved," she emphasized, "the animal could be cast off by piercing the skin with a sword or by consuming the living petals of a rose."

Hochstrasser had rejected this, but the idea of introducing it into the Order's initiation ritual proved popular. The Council gave its consent and Comtois' reputation as a spiritual leader had grown. The Order financed her pursuit of a doctorate and subsequent postgraduate work at St. Gallen University in Switzerland. Despite Comtois family objections, she set up a lucrative dental practice in Zurich. Her parents wanted her to return to France and threatened to disinherit her if she refused. She remained in Zurich.

Then there was her affair with a much older professor at St. Gallen. Hochstrasser recalled that the Order had instructed her to end it. Comtois agreed to do so and had subsequently accepted considerable sums of money from the Order to establish and fully equip her Zurich office. She had lied. The professor sought and obtained a divorce. Yvette Comtois and he were married.

The Council, accustomed to strict obedience among its followers, had employed an *elder* by the name of Ueli Berlinger to mete out lethal punishment for the betrayal. The professor had been found shot to death in the newly-wed couple's Zurich apartment. There had not been sufficient evidence to convict her, but Comtois was charged with the murder and ultimately ... with the Order's financial and political support, she had been acquitted of the crime.

Hochstrasser entered his lab in the Biozentrum. He chastised himself for not following up on Yvette Comtois, over the years. She had been an embittered woman when she'd folded her business in Zurich. She had warned the Order that forgiveness was out of the question. Then, she had simply disappeared. Hochstrasser later traced her to Canada, but had ultimately lost track of her movements. Years ensued with no consequences, either for the professor's murder or as a result of Comtois' promise to avenge her husband's death. He placed his cane on the back of his chair, folded the cable from Saint-Félix-de-Sébastien and sat down at his desk in the Biozentrum. The past had crept up on him.

On some days, chasing stories was like finding a needle in the proverbial haystack. Jason's day file on Thursday April 2nd offered up several needles, and the call from Montreal Police Lieutenant Peter Loughlin complicated matters further. There were three reporter-camera teams available to him, presuming Ty was able to make it in. If not, only two teams were on tap. Jason would have to cherry-pick.

Mayor Drapeau had called a press-conference for ten a.m., at city hall. That was a must, even though the Mayor hadn't revealed a topic. Hospital administrators were entrenched in their opposition to a Common Front contention that management personnel could provide essential services during an April 11th general strike. More than 200,000 civil servants, teachers, hospital and social services workers were poised to walk out in ten days. Union attempts to negotiate with the Bourassa government were fruitless. The March 28th warning strike had brought about no positive effect at the bargaining table.

"So Jason," Loughlin sounded upbeat for a Thursday morning, "this Chief Inspector Cousineau has been keeping me in the loop. Anything that can be connected to the Morissette kidnap case is still shared information."

Moore chewed on the end of a toothpick. He'd given up cigarettes. The toothpicks and numerous packages of lifesavers satisfied the urge. "Something new?" he asked.

"I take it you're up-to-date on the Ouellette funeral home matter."

"We are. At least we *were* as of yesterday."

"Then you know about Yvette Comtois."

"Yeah. Yeah, I know she's in the wind."

Loughlin chuckled. "And she's likely to stay that way. Cousineau called me this morning. Apparently there's a warrant out, now, for Comtois' arrest."

"*That's* new. Yesterday, she was only a person of interest."

"Right. Well it's a murder warrant, according to the Chief Inspector. Forensics pulled an all-nighter on Fernand Ouellette's body."

"And?"

"They found some interesting things in his blood. Not sure I'll pronounce it properly. Cousineau called it *Bupivacaine*."

"What the hell is that?"

"Some kind of anesthetic. Used in the management of pain after dental surgery."

Moore nearly dropped the telephone. "Is Cousineau … are *you* aware that Comtois is, or *was*, a dentist?"

"Cousineau got into her background. Yeah, that's come out. Forensics found a needle mark on Ouellette's neck. An injection of this stuff, which by the way is soluble in water and colorless, acts as a nerve block. Good for pain. But, too much of it results in a systemic toxic reaction. Shuts down the central nervous system, respiratory and cardiac functions."

"Jesus! So Ouellette was definitely murdered."

"Beyond a doubt. Poor fucker probably smothered when his airways closed down. Maybe cardiac arrest. They're still working on official terminology for cause of death."

"But Comtois is *it*."

"Cousineau is pretty much convinced she did it. And, you'll be pleased to know, he's not planning any charges against Ty."

Moore decided to play dumb. "Ty? What'd *he* do?"

Another round of chuckling. "Don't play coy with me, old buddy. I know about the fingerprints."

"Oh yeah. The fingerprints."

"Ty was taking one hell of a risk."

"Well, he's a reporter."

Loughlin paused for a moment. "And a good one. The hair comb was damned important to Cousineau. And here's the topper."

"What's that?"

"The fingerprints matched the Saint-Sauveur bottles. Dr. Denis Desjardins and our dead funeral home operator were in cahoots. They had their source for the human organs. God only knows what they were planning for Jacqueline Morissette."

"God," Moore replied, "certainly had nothing to do with it."

32

JERRY POIRIER WOKE UP THURSDAY morning with an excruciating headache and a mild fever. He realized, casting off the mantle of sleep, that he'd been dreaming about ice-cream, and the memory of Greg Peterson's double-scoop in Sainte-Agathe sent a chill through his body. He pulled his blankets up over his shoulders and resolved to call in sick.

The big house on Côte Sainte Catherine Road in Outremont was silent. Jerry listened for any sound that might indicate his father hadn't left for work. There was only the rhythmic ticking of an alarm clock beside his bed. He rubbed at his eyes and reluctantly sat up. The clock was always set fifteen minutes later than the actual time … a trick he'd used at Ryerson Institute to get him to classes on time. The initial shock of thinking he was late always made it impossible to go back to sleep. That was the case now. Jerry found himself fully awake and uncharacteristically alert for such an early hour.

Slowly, he swung his legs off the bed and slid his feet into slippers he'd left on the floor the night before. The headache persisted as he walked out into the hallway, intending to use cold water from a bath-room faucet to freshen up. He stood still for a few moments outside his father's room, but there was no sound of running water or any hint of movement from within. He knocked on the closed door and waited for a response. "Dad? You there?" Nothing from beyond. Jerry decided to use his father's bathroom, the nicest of three in the house.

Sunlight streamed through east-facing windows along one side of the master-suite. He squinted in its brilliance, shielding his eyes with one hand as he pulled the drapes closed. His head was pounding when he backtracked toward the bath-room. On his way, he spotted a leather-bound booklet on his father's side table. He'd seen it before. It contained a list of appointments and was something Jean-Jacques always carried in his briefcase. It was almost never out of his sight. It was decidedly private … none of his business … yet he found himself unaccountably drawn to it.

There was an accompanying sense of guilt as he began to thumb through the pages. No out of the ordinary appointments were indicated for this Thursday, the second. He flipped to the next page. A marginal note for April 3rd read "Call Laurent Picard. Our Lady of Lourdes." There was nothing listed for the fourth but, under Sunday the fifth, his father had written two words in red ink … "FULL MOON." The same red ink and block-form letters highlighted Wednesday the eighth. Again, there were only two words … "*THE BIDDING.*"

Yvette Comtois had been meticulous in her planning. The loss of her mother-of-pearl hair comb was extremely careless, but she began to look upon it as a sort of blessing in disguise. It forced her to make a decision she'd been thinking about ever since Laurent Picard established his *lodge* in Saint-Félix-de-Sébastien. She would leave the Laurentians and move closer to the target. Comtois' obsession with the idea of exacting revenge on the Order, an obsession of nearly two decades, was drawing closer to an end.

Her intention to move was delayed when Picard's arrogance caused Francis Duguay to rebel. She watched, with interest, as the Corporation Énergie executive coincidentally moved into an old house opposite her shop on Rue Principale. The fates had smiled. The Order had come directly to her.

It was a simple matter to befriend Duguay, who was easily swayed by her long-term background with the Swiss Council and her intrinsic knowledge of its history and its rituals. Duguay introduced her to Marlene Brannigan. Brannigan, in turn, was a patient of Dr. Denis Desjardins in Sainte-Agathe. Desjardins worked with Serge Blouin and, because of his role at the Centre Hospitalier Laurentien, had sometimes frequent contact with Fernand Ouellette. Hospitals and funeral homes were, by their very nature, inclined to cooperate.

Comtois soon realized that her ability to manipulate others to her own ends would provide her with an opportunity to bring down Laurent Picard and, by extension, provoke international police interest in the Order as a whole. The breakaway sect in Saint-Sauveur was born. Duguay and his ilk were spiritual sponges, soaking up her promises of rejuvenation and mystical powers. The secret room in Duguay's basement was built.

In spite of Desjardins' initial resistance to the prospect of cannibalism, Comtois was able to convince him that it was essential to the process of *transmutation*. An accident on the Autoroute provided the ingredients for an *elixir* which, she explained, would give him and the others access to animal strength and vitality and even prolong their lives. The concept ran contrary to his science background, but Desjardins had already rejected religious orthodoxy and was starved for alternatives.

He worried about harvesting organs from the unfortunate accident victim. Comtois was able to persuade him to let her consult with Fernand Ouellette about cremation of the body. The funeral home operator proved susceptible to her wiles and was recruited into the group. He too, it seemed, was disenchanted with blind faith and was in search of proof that life was not some kind of cosmic accident. His professional preoccupation with death underlined his deeply-ingrained fear of mortality.

A ceremony was held and the *elixir* tested. Comtois prepared the solution, including minute portions of the accident victim's liver and a hallucinogenic drug. Duguay became putty in her hands, believing his strength in general and his vision in particular had markedly improved. Not long after the ritual behind the false wall in his basement, Comtois advised him that the ability to literally transform into an animal depended on obtaining the organs of a young virgin. "This" she told him, "would increase the potency of the solution and ensure the transfer of youthful energy and longevity."

Acting on Comtois' instructions, Duguay abducted Jacqueline Morissette. Brannigan helped him to smother the girl and hide her in the secret room. On that same day, still influenced by the rituals in Saint-Sauveur, Serge Blouin leapt from the Jacques Cartier Bridge, believing he possessed the ability to fly like a bird. His death only attracted more police attention. Stage one of Comtois' plan was complete. An official investigation would inevitably be traced back to the *lodge* in Saint-Félix -de-Sébastien.

The Autoroute accident was one thing. Murder, so far as Desjardins and Ouellette were concerned, was unacceptable. Comtois, however, reminded them of the crime they had already committed and emphasized their complicity in the Morissette killing. The trap was sprung. The dye was cast. She knew Laurent Picard would have kept close tabs on Duguay's activities after his defection from the main *lodge*. It was only a matter of time, before he and Werner Hochstrasser enrolled Ueli Berlinger in the equation. She would have the man who killed her husband all those years ago in her sights.

Comtois looked over her new home. Her dogs, Pearl, Max and Mike had already staked their claims. Pearl curled up on a couch near the windows, fronting onto Route seven, and growled authoritatively at Max when he tried to share it with her. Max and Mike settled in opposite corners of the small living room.

The hair comb incident was inconvenient, but Yvette Comtois was now only a few miles from Our Lady of Lourdes Church. She would have preferred to have more time to pack her things, instead of moving into a furnished house, however she hadn't forgotten to take three important items from the tiny shop on Rue Principale.

She had an inward sense of satisfaction as she set about the business of cleaning the slender, sharply pointed rapier sword she had used in the *transmutation* ritual. All of the Saint-Sauveur initiates, from earlier years, bore the mark of the seventeenth-century weapon. Since emigrating to Canada, Comtois assumed another sword had been employed for subsequent ceremonies in Basel. She was picturing Ueli Berlinger's face in her mind, when she loaded her .32 calibre pistol and hung the red cloak in a closet … the cloak she had worn proudly nearly twenty years ago … the one with the words *Münsplatz, Zurich* inscribed on the collar.

33

ELIZABETH STARED AT HER REFLECTION in the bathroom mirror. She had been under suicide-watch ever since her arrival at the Reddy Memorial Hospital but today she was going home. For the first time, she had been allowed to bathe, apply makeup and shampoo her hair, without the presence of a nurse overseer. Dr. Nelson had issued the order and told her he no longer considered her a threat to herself.

Elizabeth did not share his confidence. She was transfixed in front of the mirror. Despite the makeup, there were dark circles under her eyes. She felt completely unsure of herself, and the prospect of seeing her parents ... of simply behaving normally in front of her family seemed a monumental challenge. Whether she remembered it or not, she had tried to take her own life. Her hands were trembling as she brushed her hair and tried to recall Nelson's attempts at reassurance.

"You've experienced an emotional trauma," he'd said. "Not unlike a physical injury, it requires healing. The human brain is very compli-cated, but it's part of your body. It gets sick. It *will* get well. The medication I've prescribed will put you on that road and we'll all work together to see that this never happens again."

Elizabeth was fully dressed and sitting in the recliner chair next to her bed, when Ty walked into her room. She had not been able to convince herself that swallowing all that valium was *not* something she could have prevented. "Damn it," she thought. "If only I could remember."

"You all packed?" Ty asked, turning on his brightest smile. "Let's blow this popsicle stand."

She was grateful to him for making light of the situation. "We're not going on a Caribbean cruise you know." She tried to match his joke with one of her own. "I'm really quite scared, Ty."

"Scared of what? There's nothing to be scared *of*. If I were you,

I'd have been more frightened of wearing those stupid Johnny-coats that show your butt to the world. Now, you're in your favorite jeans, ready to jump into the arms of your number one guy and put this place in the rear-view mirror." He pulled her to her feet and hugged her. "Liz, whatever this was all about, we'll get to the bottom of it. All you have to do, now, is come home." The makeup around her eyes began to run. Elizabeth was crying.

Interpol's constitution was clear. The International Criminal Police Organization was constitutionally forbidden from involvement in political, military, religious or racial crimes. Nearly two-hundred member countries received color-coded notices, on a regular basis. Quebec Provincial Police had to access the information through appropriate federal channels. Chief Inspector Adrien Cousineau was familiar with the protocol.

The color-coded notices ranged across the spectrum. Cousineau took it upon himself to contact Interpol's main head-quarters in Lyon, France, believing that "code-green" applied to Yvette Comtois. He was on the phone with a ranking officer. "Then go ahead and *ask* Fischer," his voice underlined his resentment that he might be required to go through Ottawa to get additional information.

"I am required to do so," the Interpol agent replied. "Let me get back to you."

Cousineau hung up the phone and lit a cigarette. He had read about Paulinus Fischer, the Interpol President. He was winding down a four year tenure with the organization after a sterling career with the German Federal Criminal Police (BKA.) His earlier years had been overshadowed by a Nazi background. Under Hitler's government, he had been a member of the *Sturmabteilung* ... a para-military group referred to, in infamy, as the "brownshirts." When Hitler took control of Germany in 1933, the SA was superseded by the *Schutzstaffel*. Fischer had then become part of the SS ... the Führer's Praetorian Guard and the Nazi party's Shield Squadron.

"Quite the resumé," Cousineau thought. "And I have to ask this dog for favors." He was startled by his telephone ringing.

The Interpol officer was back on the line. "Paulinus says what do you want to know?"

His abruptness caught Cousineau off guard. "As I told you," the Chief Inspector began, "Yvette Comtois' murder case was a cause célèbre in France about eighteen years ago. We think she's done it again, here in Quebec."

"And, as I told *you*, Chief Inspector, she was acquitted of the crime."

"Yes. Yes, that's true. But it appears to us that she could be connected to *several* murders and our investigations point to cult activities."

The Interpol officer hesitated. "You're familiar," he finally said, "with our constitution?"

"I have a copy on my desk as we speak."

"Cult activities are considered religious, by nature. We are not permitted … "

"Yes, I understand that *monsieur*. Your code-green, however, allows you to share criminal intelligence if crimes involve more than one member-country and if those crimes might be repeated. All I ask is a bit of information, on someone we suspect could be involved in a series of murders. These crimes *could* be connected to a cult. We just don't know."

"As the President asked, Chief Inspector, what do you want to know?"

Cousineau grabbed a pen and prepared to take notes. "How was Comtois acquitted of this killing in Switzerland? Who represented her?"

"Hers is a wealthy French family."

"So they paid the legal fees?"

"No *Monsieur*."

"Who, then?"

Cousineau heard the officer breathing into the telephone. "We, that is to say, Interpol has known for many years about an international and very powerful organization called the Order of the Sword."

"In other words … a cult."

"You could call it that, Chief Inspector. We really don't have any idea *what* it is."

"Comtois was a member?"

"*Oui*."

"And this ... Order ... paid the bills?"

"It's difficult to establish a money trail *Monsieur*. This is, essentially, a secret society. As I said, it is international. There are branches in several countries. Precisely *how* it's bankrolled is an internal matter, the details of which are not disclosed. Numbered Swiss accounts you understand. However Comtois *was* represented by a lawyer whom we believe had connections to the Order. That is correct."

"You have a name for this lawyer?"

"Picard. Laurent Picard."

Cousineau wrote it down. "Why did Comtois emigrate to Canada?"

"A mystery *Monsieur*. Perhaps to escape the notoriety?"

"Well, she's our problem now. Are you still investigating this ... cult?"

"We watch. The scrutiny is, shall we say, unofficial?"

"Understood. Thank you for talking with me. Thank your, uh, President."

Rush-hour traffic had virtually evaporated by the time Ty left N.D.G. and headed along Jean Talon for the station. It was 10:45 Thursday morning. Liz was safe at home, yet he was haunted by an unsettling concern that her stay at the Reddy Memorial had marked only the beginning of their troubles. She had been so very frightened.

Charles and Sarah greeted her at the door. Liz was glad to see them ... glad to be home ... but her underlying sense of guilt made it an awkward reunion. When Sarah mentioned that Catherine and Robin would be home from school for the lunch hour, Liz inexplicably burst into tears and retreated to their bedroom. Her mother cast an exasperated glance at Ty, who found he could react only by shrugging his shoulders. Charles stood by, watching helplessly. "It'll be alright, Ty," he said, trying to sound reassuring. Let her rest a while. We'll look after things here. Don't worry. We'll call you at work if there's any problem."

Now, as he walked into the newsroom at CKCF, Ty felt the word *problem* grossly understated the seriousness of Liz's condition. He spotted Jerry Poirier, sprawled in one of the chairs near the boardroom table. "Well you look like crap," he said.

"Got a fever." Poirier didn't bother straightening up in the chair. "Wasn't planning to come in at all."

Ty sat down on the opposite side of the table, where *Flash News* production meetings took place twice a day. He kept his distance, not wanting to share a virus. "Then why *did* you?"

"Why did I what?"

"Come in. Why come in if you're sick? Just spreads it around."

Jerry finally sat erect. His face was flushed and there were beads of perspiration on his forehead, but his eyes were alert. "Something's gonna happen," he said. "I don't know *what*, but I think it's big."

Ty put on a puzzled expression. "Like what?" He wasn't sure if Poirier's fever was doing the talking. He most certainly wasn't behaving normally.

The junior reporter appeared agitated. He leaned his elbows on the table and began speaking in hushed tones, as though he didn't want anyone to overhear him. "I found my father's appointment book at home. He always carries it with him, but he went to work. Left it on his night table."

"Yeah?" Ty wished he'd get to the point. "What are you trying to say, Jerry?"

"Some strange shit in that book, Ty. First of all, Dad reminded himself to call someone named Laurent Picard."

"So?"

"So, right beside Picard's name he wrote Our Lady of Lourdes church."

"Ah-hah." Ty was pleased the conversation was finally going somewhere.

"That's not all. I have no idea who Picard *is*, but obviously he has something to do with whatever goes on in that place … whatever was *going* on that night in Saint-Félix-de-Sebastien."

"Okay. That makes sense. We can do some checking on the name. What makes you think something *big* is going to happen?"

Poirier proceeded to tell Ty about the two references in Jean-Jacques' appointment book to a "FULL MOON" on the 5th and "THE BIDDING" on the 8th.

Ty couldn't explain why the words triggered the images. He was suddenly put in mind of the peculiar markings in Francis Duguay's secret room, of the Key of Solomon bookstore on Place D'Armes and of the old man who'd told him the object of a conjuration was to call upon a supernatural entity to "*do one's bidding.*"

34

LA VOIX POLICE-REPORTER Réal Gendron was impressed. He tele-phoned shortly after noon, as Ty was playing catch-up on the Dra-peau news conference. Jason Moore's shortage of reporter-camera teams had left him no alternative. The assignment-editor made a deal with one of the French stations to ask the Mayor for an English clip. It was a tit-for-tat arrangement. CKCF often reciprocated when CTMF TV was short staffed.

Gendron was his usual, bubbly self. "Allo my frien'. Pretty sneaky. You're learning some of my tricks, eh?"

Ty was sitting at his work station, staring at his typewriter and trying to script a report on Drapeau's ten o'clock announcement. "Hey, Réal, how're they hanging? Whatta ya mean … learning your tricks?"

Gendron laughed heartily. "I know what you've been up to," he said. "Just got off the phone with our Chief Inspector Cousineau. Nice work on the fingerprints."

"You mean Ouellette?"

"*Exactement.* Cousineau didn't know whether to shit or steal third. At first, he was really pissed. Said you'd messed up a crime scene … tampered with a dead body." Gendron made a *tsk-tsk* sound into the phone.

"Got him the goods on Yvette Comtois, though."

"That bit with the hair comb. Very nice. Very nice. I'll make a police reporter out of you yet."

"Ha ha, very funny."

Gendron's tone changed. "Seriously though, I think this Comtois is key to a lot of other things. Maybe we should exchange notes, eh?"

"Shoot," Ty replied. "I'm all ears."

"Well, for starters, how much do you know about her background?"

"Okay, I'll agree to give you what I have. What're you giving *me*?"

"You know how this funeral home operator died?"

"I do. An anesthetic. *Bupivacaine*, shot right into the neck."

"*C'est vrai.* You also know this is something dentists use in pain management?"

"Yep."

"And you're aware that Comtois was … *is* a dentist, by profession."

"That too."

Gendron chuckled. "You're a hard man to impress."

"Look, Réal, I know that there's a murder warrant out on Comtois. Cops are keeping a close eye on her shop in Saint-Sauveur, but she's been a no show. Here's a couple of things *you* might not be aware of. The fingerprints I stole from Ouellette matched up with the ones found on the bottles that contained the human organs. So far, there are six people dead … the little girl, Jacqueline Morissette, Marlene Brannigan, Francis Duguay, Dr. Denis Desjardins, Serge Blouin and the funeral home guy, Fernand Ouellette."

"Right. Okay, I knew about the connections. I *didn't* know about the fingerprint match. Interesting. Then Ouellette and Desjardins were cutting up bodies."

"And, certainly, the whole bunch of them were consuming *parts* of them."

"Question is … why?"

Ty wanted to be cooperative, but he was reluctant to reveal what he'd learned about rituals and conjurations. "Something to do with that basement hideaway in Saint-Sauveur, I guess."

"No doubt. Probably the Morissette girl was on the menu."

Ty decided to change the subject. "Looks that way. What are you hearing from Cousineau?"

"Okay. Fair enough. You filled me in on the fingerprint match. Cousineau has got Interpol involved."

"Really! So, there's a much broader picture than just a bunch of wackos in the Laurentians."

"No question about it. The cannibalism and the Morissette girl aside, the Chief Inspector thinks Ouellete's murder was the *only* one of the four that Comtois actually committed herself."

"Meaning what?"

"That we're looking at some sort of international influence. Comtois got her dental training in Switzerland. Brannigan, Duguay and Desjardins were professional hits. What we have to find out is *who* wanted these people dead? And for *what reason*?"

Ty realized that, despite his good relationship with the Chief Inspector, Gendron was not aware of Comtois' Swiss murder trial. Cousineau, it seemed, had not been entirely forthcoming. Ty thought that providing the *La Voix* reporter with *that* information would compromise Moore's source at Immigration Canada. "See you in the newspapers, Réal." He experienced a twinge of guilt for not confiding all he knew about Comtois. Gendron would have to do some more digging, on his own.

Gendron clicked his tongue. "We'll talk again my frien'."

Supper wasn't sitting well and rush-hour traffic on the Swiss expressway was crawling. Frankl Anderegg left Sandoz labs at four-thirty, grabbed some fast food on the way and turned off the expressway at the blue sign marked *Kantonsspital*. As he passed through a tunnel and crossed the viaduct he reviewed his concerns about the drug. He intended to warn Werner Hochstrasser that even a mild dose of the *Rivea corymbosa* produced intense hallucinogenic results.

On the main street, just west of the University of Basel, Anderegg stopped near the massive *Spalentor Gate*. The gate, flanked by two fortified towers, had been part of a stone wall that had completely surrounded Basel's old town at the beginning of the fourteenth century. The Spalentor Hotel, on *Schoenbeinstrasse* stood directly opposite. He found parking in front of the hotel and gathered his notes and the plastic container in which he'd placed the pills and a quart jug of the fluid.

Hochstrasser's room was on the third floor. Anderegg refused help from a bellhop, but tipped the young man anyway. He took an elevator, despite his claustrophobic tendencies, and knocked on the door of room 311. Werner Hochstrasser swung it open, greeting him with an enthusiastic handshake. "Come in. Come in, Frankl. We were just talking about you." He turned around, using his cane for support, and preceded Anderegg into the suite. There were five other men inside scattered about the room in a variety of chairs.

Anderegg recognized Linus Blosch, one of the Order's other Council members, who served under Hochstrasser—five in all, including himself. The fifth member had only recently been named and he'd never met him. Hochstrasser pointed his cane at the tall, lanky individual with the weatherworn face. "Frankl, this is Ulrich Sennhauser. He, as you, is now a full member of the Council. He's also an archeologist, who has made the most incredible discovery on Cathedral Hill. Ulrich, meet Frankl Anderegg of Sandoz Labs."

The two men shook hands, as Anderegg awkwardly held the plastic container and his notes under one arm. Hochstrasser continued. "I believe you know everyone else here. Gentlemen, I thought we could all enjoy some privacy here at the *Spalentor*." They all nodded their approval. "Frankl, why don't you put that picnic basket, or whatever it is, down on the desk over there. I presume it contains the … correct me if I'm wrong … the *Ololuhqui?*"

"That's what the natives call it. Actually it's *Rivea corymbosa* and I …"

Hochstrasser cut him off. He had expected Anderegg would re-emphasize the inherent dangers of the drug and he wanted no interference in his plans for the ritual. "Come sit down, Frankl. You look tired." He addressed the group. "Frankl has brought us pills and a liquid form of this drug."

Anderegg stood his ground. He was determined to make his point. "Two-hundred pills," he said. "A quart of the fluid. I cannot emphasize enough, however, that this is an extremely powerful hallucinogen."

"Yes. Yes." Hochstrasser swiveled his body around and sat down in the room's most comfortable chair. "*You* have used it?" he asked.

"I've conducted numerous, clinical tests. Yes. I have used it, Werner."

"And you're showing no ill effects. You appear quite healthy."

"True, but these tests were under strict conditions. I was very careful to …"

Hochstrasser scowled. "Should we use the pills or the liquid, Frankl?"

"To be quite clear, I'm not sure we should use *either*."

"Pills or liquid, Frankl? It's a simple question."

Anderegg realized there would be no dissuading the *Supreme Leader*. "Then, if you're absolutely determined … the pills. It's much easier to regulate the dosage. If we were to mix the liquid into some sort of drink, some people could conceivably consume more than they should."

"The pills then. It's settled. Thank you, Frankl." He turned his attention to Sennhauser. "Ulrich, what can you tell us about preparations?"

The archeologist stood up and stretched. "It's been very difficult, but I believe the temple is ready."

"According to everything we discussed?"

"Everything."

"Perhaps you'd like to explain, Ulrich."

"There were technical problems. This is an ancient ruin, you understand. Celtic in origin. Located directly behind the Basler Münster church. My men have been excavating on Cathedral Hill for several years. We've uncovered two Roman roads near the church, and the remains of numerous Roman fortifications … all destroyed in the earthquake of 1356." Sennhauser's eyes were blazing with excitement. "You must understand that our ceremony, on the eighth, will be a one time only event. I cannot keep the temple under wraps any longer. It has the utmost historical significance. It actually pre-dates the Romans by several hundred years and somehow survived the quake."

Hochstrasser interrupted. "This is all very interesting, Ulrich. But you mentioned technical problems?"

Sennhauser sat down again. "I'm sorry. I go off on tangents. Yes. Technical problems, but nothing my team couldn't handle."

"And this … team … They are all members, correct?"

"The temple is buried beneath the *pfalz* very near our older excavations. No one, but these select few has seen the tunnel leading into the ruin, much less the ruin itself. Yes, the team is made up entirely of senior members of the Order."

"Good. There is electricity in the temple?"

"A generator is located in the tunnel."

"And the lighted torches?"

"All assembled. All electronically synchronized, according to your specifications."

"Excellent. What about *The Bidding* itself?"

"Quite the work of art." Sennhauser was beaming. "The circle and triangle are in white chalk. The triangle and all the names of power are in vermilion red."

Hochstrasser clapped his hands together. "Then we are ready, gentlemen. A little show-biz for the faithful. The perfect location. The junction of three roads, two of them Roman by design." He chuckled. "The site overlooks water ... the Rhine River, of course. And we meet between the hours of midnight and two, three days after the full moon. All according to the ritual of transmutation."

He looked around the room for reactions. Everyone but Frankl Anderegg was smiling. "I might add that our initiate is a young lady who works with me at the Biozentrum. Her name is Julia Bragger. She is quite brilliant and most anxious to join the Order. As to our *Lodges* at locations around the globe, I've taken time-zones into account. Their rituals will coincide with Swiss time. The power of collective energy."

[35]

THE NEWS-CLIP FROM CTMF TELEVISION typified Mayor Jean Drapeau at his autocratic best. Ty found it difficult to script a lead into a topic like wastewater treatment. Drapeau had sidestepped questions from the French language reporters about the impending Common Front strike. His ten o'clock news conference was about an Executive-Committee decision to create a technical plant division at City Hall. It would be responsible for preparing construction plans and specifications for the treatment of wastewater from the western and southwestern sectors of the Island of Montreal and Ile-Bizard. By-law 27, adopted the year before, had authorized the city to make a three hundred million dollar loan for the project. Drapeau refused to talk about anything else.

"Bo-o-o-ring," Ty said out loud, as Jason passed his work station.

Moore grinned. "Just write an inspirational lead to the story. We'll let Bradley talk about it. What did Réal Gendron have to say?"

Ty slapped the top of his typewriter. "I hope you have other plans for me. There are no words in my Underwood to describe how excited I am about fucking wastewater. Gendron will be coming out with pretty much the same stuff *we* have on Fernand Ouellette and Yvette Comtois."

Moore sat down in the work station next to Ty's. "We'll get the jump on him though. *La Voix* won't go to print with the story until tomorrow morning's edition."

"Actually," Ty replied, "we have more than time on our side."

"What do you mean?"

"Gendron gave me something we *didn't* know, but he's weak on details about Comtois."

"How so?"

"First of all, Chief Inspector Cousineau is talking with Interpol. Gendron fed me that information and is all hot to trot about the

174

idea of an international cult operating here in Quebec. Cousineau *didn't* clue him in on the whole bit about Comtois' murder trial."

"Does Gendron know about the *Bupivacaine*?"

"Yeah. He does. He also knows that Comtois is ... *was* a dentist."

"So he's aware of the warrant out on her for Ouellette's death."

"He is."

"What did you give *him*?"

"I told him about the fingerprint match. He'll be writing about Dr. Desjardins, Fernand Ouellette and their involvement with the human organs found in Saint-Sauveur."

Moore popped a toothpick into his mouth and secretly wished it were a Mark Ten cigarette. "Okay. See if your Underwood can churn out an update on the story. Use the Interpol angle. Dig up some visuals on the antique store. I think it's time we paint a true picture of Yvette Comtois."

"You taking me off this wastewater shit?"

Moore stood up and started walking toward his office. "You're capable of doing two things at the same time. I just know you'll prepare a gripping lead on Drapeau."

Ty watched the assignment-editor close his office door. He pulled the page he'd been working on out of his typewriter. Drapeau could wait. He picked up his phone and began dialing the number for Chief Inspector Adrien Cousineau.

Jerry Poirier went home. After his brief meeting with Ty his fever spiked and the headache became unbearable. When he arrived in Outremont, he fished in his pocket for the house keys and realized that, in his hurry to leave, he'd left them in his bedroom. He parked the Volkswagon bug in the driveway, stared at his father's two-car garage and the windows of their family room above it. He hadn't climbed out of those windows since his pre-teen years, when he'd decided his parents were being unfair to impose a school-night curfew on his social life. He had not been permitted to visit friends after ten p.m. The windows provided an easy exit from the house. He prayed, now, that they weren't locked from the inside.

Jerry shimmied up a maple tree beside the garage and hoisted himself on to the roof … trying to ignore the fact that he was considerably less agile than he had been at age twelve. It was a peaked roof over the garage and the pain in his head made him unsure of his balance as he carefully made his way toward the wall. The family room extended halfway out, onto the garage below. The driveway and front lawn were on a steep incline down to Côte Ste. Catherine Road, giving him the impression he was scaling a much higher structure. For one, frightening moment, he thought he might fall.

Jerry closed his eyes and reached for the window. When his hands gripped the frame, he braced his feet on either side of the peaked roof and pulled upwards. It slid open easily. He slowly slipped through into the darkened room beyond. His breaths were coming in short gasps as he traced his fingers along the wall in search of a light switch. He found what he was looking for and, suddenly, the family room was illuminated by the overhead Tiffany lamp his mother had insisted on buying so many years ago.

The room itself had been a huge project. His father, he recalled, had made a bank loan to accommodate its construction. He'd told Jerry and his brother Yvan that this would be *their* hangout. A television set had been built into one wall and a ping-pong table still occupied a corner of the big room. Jerry sat down in an easy chair in front of the TV. He realized it had been weeks since he'd spoken to his older brother. Thoughts of their early days growing up in Outremont saddened him. Theirs had been a happy family. Yvan's success as a Bay Street lawyer had overshadowed his own career aspirations. He'd always wanted to be a journalist but, somehow, being a lawyer and pulling in a six-figure salary seemed to trivialize his decision to attend Ryerson Institute.

Jerry eventually got control of his labored breathing. He walked over to the window, closed and locked it. Leaving it unlocked was a burglary waiting to happen. Out in the hallway he paused outside the room his father used for an office. The door was never ajar and, unless he had particular reason to enter, Jerry always asked permission. Jean-Jacques was … always had been … extremely territorial. "This," he'd said of the family room, "will be *yours*." It was made abundantly clear to him and Yvan that the office was out of bounds to them and their friends.

The door, to his surprise, was partially open. Jerry pushed on it and stepped into the space beyond. Again, to his surprise, his father's desk-lamp was on. He felt like a trespasser as he gave into curiosity and slowly walked deeper into the study. There, on the desk, was the appointment book he had seen that morning. Jean-Jacques had apparently returned from work, perhaps to retrieve it, and had moved it from his bedroom into the office. "But why?" he asked himself.

He opened the book to the page marked April 3rd. There was a new notation below the words "Call Laurent Picard. Our Lady of Lourdes." It read ... "*deliver the cloaks*." Jerry looked around the room. Could Jean-Jacques be referring to the cloaks at Venise-en-Québec? He didn't think so. His eyes darted about, looking for an answer, and came to rest on the walk-in closet. He'd come this far in the invasion of his father's privacy. His heart was beating fast, as he opened the louvered doors. At least twelve of the mysterious cloaks ... exact duplicates of the ones found in Saint-Sauveur and those at his family's cottage ... hung inside.

36

It was a dilemma. Ty had two reasons to call Chief Inspector Cousineau. The second one was a problem. He didn't know how to broach the subject of the old church in Saint-Félix-de-Sébastien, without calling attention to Jerry Poirier's father. On the other hand, he was more sure than ever that Réal Gendron was right … that the goings-on in the Laurentians had wider implications. Gendron had suggested some sort of international organization.

First, he had to find out why Interpol had been consulted. While Cousineau's phone was ringing Ty played his favorite game … connecting the dots. Francis Duguay had worked for La Corporation Énergie, the same company where Jerry's father was a Vice-President. Jean-Jacques Poirier possessed Swiss-manufactured cloaks, like the ones found in Duguay's house. He attended a church in the Montérégie that was no longer a church. Jerry had described bizarre sounds coming from the building on the night he'd followed his father's car. Why had Duguay moved to the Laurentians and was there a connection between the Morissette killers and whatever was going on in Our Lady of Lourdes?

Cousineau picked up his phone on the ninth ring. His tone indicated he wasn't pleased to hear from another reporter. "*Oui Monsieur* Davis. You and your friend Réal Gendron should really be going through public relations."

Ty pressed on. "Réal tells me you are talking to Interpol."

"It's true."

"About what, Chief Inspector, if I might ask.?"

"Come come, *Monsieur* Davis, you must know that we are looking for Yvette Comtois."

"I *do* know that, Sir. What I do *not* know is why the Quebec Provincial Police are talking to Interpol about a Sainte-Agathe murder."

Cousineau seemed to be thinking it over. There was a long silence.

"Chief Inspector? Are you still there?"

"*Oui.* You must appreciate, *Monsieur* Davis, that this is an open case. Anything I say to you has the potential of helping Comtois evade my officers."

"Not if I don't put it on the air. Your officers wouldn't even be *aware* of Comtois, if I hadn't recognized that hair-comb and given you the name."

"And, if I agree to give you certain information, you will not use it on television?"

"You have my word. Whatever I report … I'll clear with you first. For example, Gendron told me you believe Comtois was responsible for Ouellette's murder but you think someone else was behind the killings of Dr. Denis Desjardins, Francis Duguay and the Brannigan woman. I *will* be using that in my next report. So will Gendron."

"What is it, then, that you want to understand?"

"Why Interpol? Look, we know about Comtois' background. We know she's a dentist, trained in Switzerland. We're aware of her family in France. *And*, Chief-Inspector, *I'm* aware that you held back information from Gendron about Comtois' acquittal in a Swiss murder trial."

Cousineau cleared his throat, obviously taken aback. "This is why I'm reluctant to talk to the press. Did you tell Gendron about *that*?"

"Nossir, I did not. These are details my assignment editor picked up from his own sources."

"You wouldn't be talking about Montreal Police Lieutenant Peter Loughlin, would you?" Cousineau was obviously on the edge of anger.

Ty realized he was in danger of compromising Loughlin. "No. my assignment editor found this out from a longstanding contact at Immigration Canada. Comtois' story was all over the papers in France and Switzerland, at the time of her acquittal. Not too hard to find."

Cousineau seemed to buy the explanation. Ty was careful not to mention the fact that Loughlin had also filled Moore in about the *Bupivacaine*, used in the Ouellette murder. He wasn't sure how Gendron had found out about that. "It still leaves me wondering, Chief Inspector, what Interpol has to do with all of this."

Another pause on the line. Cousineau was lighting a cigarette.

"Alright. You can use this if you wish *Monsieur* Davis. The acquittal you refer to was brought about by a skillful lawyer. That lawyer was hired and paid for by a very old organization, with branches in several countries."

"A cult?"

"Interpol wasn't officially confirming that. It's called the Order of the Sword."

"And I can use this in my report?"

"I don't see how it would help Yvette Comtois avoid arrest. Yes, you can use it."

"Just one more thing, Chief Inspector, if you can. What was the name of this lawyer?"

"Laurent Picard."

A charge of adrenalin coursed through Ty's body. That was the name in Jean-Jacques Poirier's appointment book. "Thank you, Chief Inspector. You've been a big help." He hung up the phone and headed for Jason Moore's office.

Packages were sent special delivery to Montreal, London, Paris, Frankfurt, Melbourne and Martinique. The return address, written on the brown wrapping, was a Post Office Box in Basel, Switzerland. For customs purposes, Werner Hochstrasser labeled each of the boxes "Chocolates. Refrigerate on receipt."

Laurent Picard expected to pick up the package at the post office at Cathcart and University Streets. He would park in the underground parking lot at the Queen Elizabeth Hotel and walk back to the post office, according to the pattern he followed every time the Order wished to communicate with him.

Picard enjoyed his visits into Montreal, and was looking forward to a steak dinner at Gibby's Restaurant on Youville Square. The restaurant was contained in the old Youville stables, built in 1825 on land owned by the Gray Nuns. Picard found it relaxing. Ueli Berlinger would meet him there.

He had received a brief note from Hochstrasser the week before, informing him that the package would be sent out "next day delivery," on Thursday the 2nd. It was to contain the very best Swiss chocolates.

Picard was told that, beneath the layer of candy, would be the product of Sandoz Labs. One tablet for each member. There had been only three words on the note from Hochstrasser. "Find Yvette Comtois."

Flash News, at six o'clock on Thursday evening, led the hour with the latest on the Morissette kidnapping and murder. The main focus of Ty's report, however, was the killing at the Complexe Funéraire Ouellette, the police search for Comtois and her ties to the Order of the Sword.

"Provincial Police," Ty told anchor Art Bradley, "have been in contact with Interpol headquarters in Lyon, France. They are now looking into the possibility that what happened to young Jacqueline Morissette in Saint-Sauveur and the subsequent deaths of five people may be linked to a secret society based in Switzerland. Comtois is suspected in only *one* of these deaths. The outstanding question, now, is who is responsible for the killing spree in the Laurentians? Was the Order of the Sword choosing the targets and if so … why?"

For the first time since March 13th, Clyde Bertram had okayed using the cannibalism angle. Ty went into great detail about the human organs and how fingerprints found in Duguay's refrigerator had matched those of both Fernand Ouellette and Dr. Denis Desjardins. He mentioned Serge Blouin, the Jacques Cartier bridge suicide and the startling discovery made on Blouin's autopsy table. Bertram vetted the report before it went to air, after Moore made it clear that *La Voix* would headline the story in Friday's edition.

Shortly after Ty's debriefing on set with Bradley, Jerry Poirier telephoned Moore from Outremont. It was Ty's habit, when asked to do a live hit on the evening news, to carry his coat and briefcase to the studio so he wouldn't have to return to the newsroom. That way, he could make a quick exit from the station and head home. Poirier asked Moore to stop him. He had urgent news.

Jason all but ran down the stairs to studio two. He caught Ty as he was checking out at security. "Got a call from Jerry Poirier," he said, breathlessly. "Phone him back. He says it's important."

"What'd he want?"

"Didn't say. But he sounded pretty wound up."

Ty did an about turn. "Okay. I've gotta get home to Liz, though. If this turns out to be something that needs a follow-up, I'm not available for overtime."

Moore grinned. "I'm not *authorizing* overtime. Bertram's already over budget." They walked back in the direction of the building's rear staircase. "Thanks for not mentioning the *Bupivacaine* on the air. Loughlin would've had my ass."

"No problem. I nearly fucked that up with Cousineau. Told him you'd got your info about Comtois' murder acquittal in Switzerland from Immigration Canada and from newspaper records. The *Bupivacaine* didn't come up."

Ty sat down at his work station at a quarter past six. When Poirier answered the telephone, in Outremont, the junior reporter was actually whispering. "My father got home a few minutes ago," he said. "I'll make this quick. There's a dozen of those cloaks, hanging in Dad's study."

"Wha-a-a-t?"

"*At least* a dozen. I didn't count 'em. Some blue. Some red. I told you I thought something *big* was going to happen. What the hell do we do now?"

Ty quickly thought it over. "We have options. If we go to the police about the cloaks, your father's in deep shit."

"Yeah, but what if he knows about all these murders? What if he's involved somehow?"

"He's *your* father, Jerry. Is he a news junkie? Would he even *know* about the murders?"

"Maybe not. He never watches English television, even though I work in the business. I've never seen a copy of *La Voix* in the house. But he added another reminder in his appointment book for tomorrow. Next to Picard's name and the reference to Our Lady of Lourdes, he wrote *deliver the cloaks*. By the way, what do you mean we have options?"

A plan was beginning to formulate in Ty's mind. "If we get the police involved, Jerry, we both know they'll descend on that old church. Picard will be pulled in for questioning. Your father too. We might never know the significance of *The Bidding*. Whatever is in the works for Wednesday the 8th ... even its connection to this Order might be lost."

"So what are the options."

"*Steal* one of those cloaks."

"What?"

"*Steal* one of those cloaks. Put it away somewhere, where your father won't find it. Maybe he's just a messenger boy for Picard. Maybe they were sent to him so he could distribute them among other members of this cult, or whatever it is. It's possible there are others, like Francis Duguay, who work with your father at Corporation Énergie."

"That's possible. But *steal* one? What if he misses it?"

"He probably will. Maybe he never counted them. We'll have to take the risk."

"Why?"

Ty hesitated. "Give the cloak to *me*, Jerry. And those options I mentioned?"

"Yeah?"

"I'm not sure of this, but I think the ones you found at Venise-en-Québec belong to your father and possibly that lady friend you said he had. Blue cloak for men. Red for women would be my guess. I need a blue one. I'll explain later."

37

THE PAPERS WERE SIGNED. The six month lease bore a false signature. Yvette Comtois had introduced herself to the landlord as Nadine Parent and she had not been asked for any personal documents to prove her identity. The tiny, furnished house on Route Seven would serve her purposes adequately, until she could make other arrangements.

She was sure the police would be aware of her transaction at the Royal Bank in Saint-Sauveur. A $50,000 withdrawal would not go unnoticed. Eventually, she would have to use her real name to access the mutual fund she had established upon arrival in Canada. But that could wait. She had much more pressing business to deal with. It would be a full moon on Sunday. Three days later, she would stand vigil at Our Lady of Lourdes church. Yvette wasn't sure that a ritual was planned. If it were, she did not intend to miss it.

Pearl sat in her own chair at the kitchen table ... mouth open in anticipation as she watched her mistress eat. Yvette had found a convenient market in St. Jean sur Richelieu and purchased a substantial order of meat, vegetables, fruit and dog food. Pearl was getting on in years and her arthritis made it difficult to stand over her dish on the floor. The dish was in front of her, on the table, but she was more interested in the pork chop on Yvette's plate.

Max and Mike were also aware of the pork chop, but they sat patiently beside the table hoping that sad eyes and the occasional, forlorn whining would send some of it their way. Comtois chewed slowly. An eighteen-wheeler rumbled past on Route Seven, but she hardly noticed. The volume was still turned up on the old black and white TV set in the living room. Art Bradley's voice echoed through the house and she was thinking about the young man who had interviewed her on the day Jacqueline Morissette was murdered. He had been so very polite. His report, which had led the *Flash News* hour, showed that he was also a very clever young man. "Perhaps," she thought, "too clever for his own good."

The sun was low in the sky by the time Ty drove Mobile 14 into the laneway next to his Oxford Avenue flat. He felt indebted to Liz's parents for looking after things, and this was accompanied by an underlying sense of guilt for having to report into work every day. He remembered Dr. Nelson saying that "physical environment is a very important part of patient rehabilitation." Nelson had warned him that Liz would be particularly sensitive to his attitude toward her.

Ty turned off the ignition and began walking around to the front of the building. He wasn't at all sure that he *had* the correct attitude. What if he said something or even conveyed a negative emotion? His stomach growled as he walked up the front stairs. He had felt hungry when he left the television station. Now, faced with uncertainty about the future, he believed he might have to be sick. The events of the past few days were like nothing he'd ever experienced before.

Sarah greeted him at the door. "We're all in the kitchen," she said. "Catherine and Robin had a snack when they got home from school, but it got to be six-thirty and they couldn't wait for supper. I've got yours in the oven."

Ty's face reddened. "Sarah, I can't tell you …"

"I know. I know, Ty. We're just glad to be here when you need us. Charles and I wouldn't have it any other way."

"Thank you. How's Liz doing?"

"Having a cup of tea. The kids are listening to one of Grandpa's war stories."

"War stories?"

"Well, you know Charles. Loves to talk about the good old days. I must admit, he has a talent for entertaining children."

Ty smiled. "He *was* a teacher, after all."

"A *professor*, but he seems to be able to embellish his tales of growing up in Montreal just enough to appeal to the younger set. By the way, Liz is doing fine."

They walked down the hall and into the kitchen. Catherine was laughing out loud at something Charles had just said. Robin was making engine noises, pushing a red plastic race-car back and forth on the table top. Catherine spotted him first. "Da-a-d-d-ee!" she screamed, catapulting herself off her chair and running into his arms."

"Hi Punkin', how's my girl?"

"I'm gonna be in the school play," she gushed.

"So I've heard. Congratulations. That's wonderful."

Robin suddenly realized he wasn't getting any attention. "She's gonna be a stupid bear."

Charles raised one finger in the air. "Bears are very smart, Robin. Especially the three bears in Goldilocks."

Robin didn't seem to want to argue the point. He resumed making engine noises and Ty kissed him on the head. Elizabeth sat, quietly sipping her tea, taking it all in. "How was work?" she asked.

"Work is work," he replied. "More importantly .. how are *you*? It must be great to be home."

Liz gave him a wan smile. "Okay. I'm okay. Yes, it's a huge relief to get out of that place."

"Don't blame you there. What a loony bin." The words were out of his mouth, before he realized what he was saying.

"What's a loony bin?" Catherine wanted to know.

Ty glanced at Charles for help. "Hospitals, Catherine," he said. They're so busy all the time. Everybody's running around. People are yelling at each other. Loony bin is just an expression your father used to describe where your mom went when she got sick."

Robin stopped playing with his race-car, momentarily. "Mommy went in an am-blee-ance."

"That's right, Robin. And now she's all better."

Both children seemed quite satisfied with the explanation. Sarah looked at Liz, sympathetically. "Kids. Why don't you guys head into the living room with me. I'll bet there's something good on television. Ty, don't forget your supper. It's hot in the oven." She started walking toward the front of the house, with Catherine and Robin trailing close behind.

"Sorry, Liz." Ty said. "I was just referring to those very bizarre people who kept peering into your room."

"Loony about describes it," she replied, letting him off the hook for his insensitive remark. "Dr. Nelson called. He wants to see us, Monday, for the ... hypnosis."

"Really. That soon?"

"He said there's no time like the present."

Jerry waited until after midnight. His father had finally gone to bed around eleven, after a late supper and a couple hours of mindless TV shows. On two occasions during the evening Jerry made futile attempts at conversation. Jean-Jacques had been distant and preoccupied. Now, standing outside his father's bedroom, he listened for any indication that he was still awake. There was only the sound of snoring.

Jerry was torn. He loved his father and part of him felt obligated to confront him about Our Lady of Lourdes ... to tell him the truth about the night he'd followed him to Saint-Félix-de-Sébastien. He wondered whether he was in denial, because yet another part of him didn't *want* to know the truth. Was his father even *aware* of the murders, or was he simply an innocent member of a secret society ... a kind of bizarre social club? If Laurent Picard and the Order of the Sword were behind the bloodshed in the Laurentians, did they share that information with the membership? He hoped not.

"*Steal* one of the cloaks," Ty had said. Jerry tiptoed past the bedroom and eased open the door of his father's study. It creaked, slightly, on its hinges. He hesitated, silently praying he hadn't awakened his father. When there were no telltale noises from down the hall, he went inside. The room was in darkness. The sweet aroma of his father's pipe-tobacco hung in the air.

Jerry switched on the desk lamp and proceeded toward the closet. The cloaks hung inside. He reached for a blue one, lifting it off the hanger, and then it occurred to him that an empty hanger might call attention to the fact that one of the cloaks was missing. He snatched it off the rack and, after closing the closet doors and shutting off the desk lamp, retreated into the hallway ... like a thief in the night.

38

Laurent Picard tipped a car-jockey in the Queen Elizabeth Hotel's parking garage to keep his Mercedes-Benz 250CE near the hotel doors. He would be only a few minutes at the post office and he didn't want to have to wait while someone fetched the vehicle from the sub-floors. The parking attendant pocketed the twenty dollar bill and assured him he would find the Mercedes right where he'd left it.

Friday morning had dawned bright with sunshine. Picard went up the escalator to the hotel's ground floor and headed for the exit on to Dorchester Boulevard. He thought a brief walk in the spring air, around the corner to University and Cathcart, would help his appetite. Ueli Berlinger had agreed to meet him at Gibby's for lunch. Berlinger was a seafood enthusiast. Picard preferred Gibby's specialty—a medium-rare sirloin, baked potato, a mixed vegtable, and a side dish of Portabello mushrooms.

Thoughts of the meal to come accompanied him to the Post Office. Hochstrasser's note had assured "next day delivery," and the chocolates had been dispatched the day before to the Order's Regional Commanders in several cities around the world. He had no doubt they would be waiting for him.

Picard ignored a homeless man in a ragged coat, who asked for bus fare and started to tell a story about a job waiting for him in Hawkesbury, Ontario. He waved the man off, without responding. He wasn't about to underwrite a trip to the nearest tavern. "Besides," he thought, "the lazy bastard probably hasn't worked a day in his life."

A few minutes later proved he was right about the package. When Hochstrasser made a promise, he kept it. On the upper left corner of the brown wrapping was the P.O. Box number, in Basel, Switzerland, he had often used to communicate with the Supreme Leader. On the lower left were the words "Chocolates. Refrigerate on receipt."

"Chocolates, indeed," Picard chuckled to himself. He tucked the package under one arm and returned to the hotel to retrieve his car. Less than one hour later, he sat at a table in Gibby's staring at the chiseled jaw of Ueli Berlinger. There was no humor in that face and, if the eyes are a window to the soul, Berlinger's eyes were coal black and empty.

"Good to see you again," Picard said, sounding less than sincere. "You're aware of developments?"

Berlinger was looking over the menu. "The scallops look good. What're you ordering?"

"Steak. *Are* you up to date on this Sainte-Agathe business?"

"Bit of a cluster-fuck isn't it?"

Picard was reminded of the reasons he'd never liked his luncheon guest. He was crude and lacked respect for the Order's hierarchy. "You could say that, Ueli. Of course Fernand Ouellette was *your* responsibility."

Berlinger did not appear to be insulted by the remark. "And *you* let Francis Duguay defect from your *lodge*. I wouldn't be here if you'd dealt with that little problem in the first place."

"Spilled milk, Ueli. Now, it's mopping up time."

Berlinger's smile looked more like a snarl. "Another contract?"

Picard nodded. "Yvette Comtois has resurfaced."

"I got a cable from Hochstrasser. So?"

"And Werner is well aware that we failed to keep track of her. The police are on her trail and we want to make sure the trail doesn't lead to us."

"And neither you, nor the police, have any idea where she is … do you?"

"No idea at all."

"And you want me to do *what*?"

Picard paused, as a waiter approached their table. They placed their orders, asking for coffee while they waited. The waiter disappeared through a door behind the salad bar. "There's a choir loft at Our Lady of Lourdes," he finally replied. "A perfect location for you to be able to spot anything unusual."

"You expect Comtois to be there?"

"Impossible to say. Eighteen years ago, she vowed revenge on the Order. She killed Ouellette. It's anybody's guess what's on her mind."

"Why would she have done that? Why kill Ouellette?"

"Look, all I know ... all Hochstrasser knows, is that she's a loose cannon. Before she reappeared, after all these years, we were content in the belief she was just a dirty little secret from the past."

"And you're hoping I'll ... *remove* the problem."

"If you can find her. There's a murder warrant out on her. According to this TV reporter I listen to, police are investigating the possibility she had a hand in everything that's happened in the Laurentians."

Berlinger shrugged. "That's a good thing, don't you think?"

"It temporarily takes the heat off us, but she could lead the authorities right to our doorstep. And don't forget, Ueli. *You* ... killed her husband."

There was a hint of annoyance in Réal Gendron's voice, when he called Ty shortly before noon on Friday. "I'm going to have to keep a closer eye on you," he said. "You've been holding out on me, eh?"

The morning edition of *La Voix* contained a full background of the Morissette kidnapping and murder, including all of the details about Interpol, the police search for Yvette Comtois, the anesthetic used in the killing of Fernand Ouellette and the fact that Comtois had studied and practiced dentistry in Switzerland. It did *not* include anything about her acquittal on a previous murder charge. Nor did it refer to a shadowy organization called the Order of the Sword.

Ty had a great deal of respect for Gendron. At the same time, he felt he had good reason to have kept certain information to himself. "You mean the bit about her marriage to a professor and the fact she was accused of his murder?"

Gendron chuckled. "You're getting to be almost as sneaky as me, my frien'. Yes ... *that* bit. Also this cult you talked about on the air last night. You knew I couldn't go with my story until this morning. You were going to scoop me anyway."

Ty felt a trifle guilty. "You're right, Réal. But here's the deal. I didn't get that information on Comtois' acquittal from my *own* sources. Jason Moore got it from *his*. After you and I spoke yesterday,

I got on the blower with Cousineau. He was pissed off when he found out I knew about the Swiss trial, but I managed to convince him that Moore got the inside stuff from Immigration Canada."

"So he thought … what?"

"That Moore got it from the cops, I guess. Somebody's head was gonna roll."

"So where did Moore get it?"

"From the cops. That's why I couldn't talk about it with you."

"Where'd you hear about the cult?"

Ty took a deep breath. "Cousineau told you all about Interpol. What he *didn't* tell you is this Order of the Sword picked up the tab for Comtois' legal expenses. Got her *off*, in fact."

"So no one was ever convicted of her husband's murder?"

"No one. And, by the way, I wasn't able to use anything about the *Bupivacaine* either."

"How come?"

"Because Moore got that from the cops as well. Cousineau would have known where it came from. I knew *you* would use it in your piece, this morning. Now that's it's gone public, I'll be able to blame you."

Gendron laughed out loud. "I think I've underestimated you, Ty. You *are* as sneaky as I am. And I'm going to have a little conversation with our dear Chief Inspector. He's been holding out on me too."

"Maybe," Ty replied, "you didn't ask him the right questions."

39

Liz stared at the mural on Dr. Barry Nelson's office wall. During her three-day stay in the adjacent psych ward, she had not been outside of the locked-down section. "That's scary," she said. Nelson only smiled, quietly studying her reaction to the wild colors and contorted images.

Ty sat in a chair on the opposite side of the room. He would be an observer only. The weekend seemed to have dragged by, through multiple conversations with Charles and Sarah Walkley and his frustrating sense that time had slowed down. Catherine and Robin seemed content with the idea that their mother had fully recovered from whatever illness she had experienced. Ty hadn't been able to convince himself. He watched Liz sleeping, but couldn't sleep himself. On Sunday evening, during one of his bouts of insomnia, he'd wandered into the living room and his attention was drawn to a spectral light filtering through the front windows. A full moon hung above the trees on Oxford Avenue. He thought of the notation in Jean-Jacques Poirier's appointment book and was overcome by a wave of foreboding.

Now, a silent observer to Liz's hypnotherapy session, he felt as though he was being pulled helplessly out to sea by an invisible riptide. In his mind's eye, Liz and the children stood on the shore frantically waving as he drowned.

"This might well be the first of several sessions," Dr. Nelson explained. "If we're lucky, however, age regression might take you back to some of the highlights in your life, Liz. The good ... *and* the bad."

"Why would that be lucky?" Ty asked. "I mean, if she focuses on the *bad* things?"

"The purpose of clinical hypnosis, in Liz's case, is to find out why she experienced depersonalization. Why, on the day she swallowed those pills, she perceived the external world to be unreal or somehow fundamentally changed."

Liz was frowning. "I don't understand, Dr. Nelson. Why can't I remember taking the valium?"

"I believe you experienced dissociative amnesia, Liz. By that I mean an acute form of hysteria ... brought on by stress. Ordinarily, an individual's stream of consciousness is unified. Everything makes sense. With stress, you would continue to function but would gradually become isolated from conscious awareness and voluntary control."

"In other words," Liz replied, "I was nuts."

Nelson smiled his reassuring smile. "I'd prefer to say that your suicide attempt was a hysterical accident. Your loss of memory was, in my opinion, clinical dissociation."

"So what now?" Ty asked.

"I'm hoping to put Liz into a trance-like state. Basically, this is a natural state during which your attention, Liz, will be narrowly focused by my voice and you can become relatively free of distractions."

"Alright."

"Good. Shall we begin?"

Both Ty and Liz nodded in the affirmative. Nelson placed his chair directly in front of hers. Ty looked on, from a darkened corner of the room.

"Elizabeth," Nelson said, "I want you to look into my eyes and concentrate *only* on my voice. There is nothing but my-y-y voice in your mind. My-y-y voice. You are very relaxed. Ver-r-y comfortable and your eyes are getting heavy. Look into *my* eyes, Elizabeth. All you can see is *my face*. The room is growing darker and dar-rr-ker around the edges of my face. The room is slowly evaporating. Now, you see *only* my face. You hear only my-y-y voice and you are ver-rr-y sleepy. *Close* your eyes, Elizabeth. Set your mind free-e-e. Let your mind wander-r-r."

Liz closed her eyes.

"As you listen to my voice," Nelson continued, "you are very comfor-table ... completely relaxed. Free-e-e of all worries ... all distrac-tions ... as if floating on a sof-f-t cloud."

Liz's eyes fluttered. Her face was expressionless.

"Can you hear my voice, Elizabeth?"

She nodded.

"Take a deep breath. Ride the clouds wherever you wish to go. My voice will guide you. Move the forefinger on your right hand if you understand."

Her finger spasmodically rose and fell back into her lap.

"What do you see, Elizabeth?"

"Clouds." Her voice was husky.

"Good. Now, Elizabeth, look down *through* the clouds. As you descend toward the green earth below, you will also be traveling backward through time. Are you floating down Elizabeth?"

"Yes."

"Good. Take your time and listen to my voice. I'm going to count backwards from ten. When I reach one, you will have landed on the ground and you will be much younger. You will feel invigorated. Free of all stress. Ten, nine, eight ..."

Ty watched, as Nelson counted down, marveling at the changes in her face. Wrinkles around her eyes and above the bridge of her nose seemed to fade away. She looked, for all intents and purposes, like a younger version of herself.

"Two, one," Nelson stopped counting. "Where are you now, Elizabeth?"

"At McGill. I've passed the exam. I'm walking."

"*Where* are you walking?"

"To the Roddick Gates. I'm going to meet my boyfriend."

Nelson glanced over at Ty and smiled.

"How do you feel?"

"Excited. I'll be graduating soon."

"Congratulations, Elizabeth. I'm going to ask you to walk out on to Sherbrooke Street. When you get there, you will be younger still. With every step, you are going farther back in time. Younger ... and younger. The years are slipping away."

"Slipping away. Yes-s-s."

Ty jerked upwards in his chair. Liz sounded like a little girl.

"How old are you now, Elizabeth?" Nelson asked.

"I'm ten years old. My daddy calls me Lizzy-bits."

"Alright. Where are you, Lizzy-bits?"

"On the school bus."

194

"What do you see?"

"My brother, David."

"Is he on the bus with you?"

"Yes, but I'm sitting next to my friend, Margaret."

"David is alone?"

"Across the aisle."

"I want you to describe how David feels about being alone. Can you do that?"

"He's scared."

"*Why* is he scared, Lizzy-bits?"

"Because, he has to get off the bus by himself today. I'm going to Margaret's house."

"How old is David?"

"Five. He's five years old. Mommy says I'm in charge."

"In charge of David?"

"Yes-s-s."

"Does he usually get off the bus without you?"

"No."

There was an underlying note of fear in her response.

"Why are you going to Margaret's today?"

"To do our homework."

"Alright. I want you to take a deep breath, Lizzie-bits. Tell me when the bus stops."

Elizabeth's chest rose and fell. The little girl's voice continued, but now it was tinged with terror. "It's stopped. David is getting off. No David, no-o-o! The car! He doesn't see the car!" She began waving her arms and tried to stand up.

Nelson remained calm. "It's alright, Elizabeth. You're not *on* the school bus any more. You're floating in the clouds again. There's a blue sky and the sun is warm. I'm going to count to ten, Elizabeth. When I reach ten, you will awaken. You will remember nothing of your journey through time and you will feel refreshed and very calm. One, two …"

Liz slumped in the chair. Nelson finished counting and her eyes opened. "W-what?" She searched the office for Ty. "Are you still there?"

"Over here, Liz. I never left."

She appeared slightly disoriented.

"When are we … I mean, did you hypnotize me already, Dr. Nelson?"

"All done, Elizabeth. How do you feel?"

"I don't remember being hypnotized. Did it work? Did you learn anything?"

Nelson crossed his legs and waved at Ty to come over and join them. "I think it was very successful," he replied. "You had mentioned that your parents are still here in Montreal?"

"My parents? Yes, they're staying with us for a little while longer."

"Good. Good. It's rare, in only one session, but it's possible we may have pinpointed the trigger in all these episodes of depression you've been experiencing. I'd just like to clarify some things with your father and mother, if that's alright with you. Ty, you were a silent witness to the hypnotherapy. I'd appreciate if you'd keep the details to yourself until I've spoken with Mr. And Mrs. Walker. Perhaps, after that, we could have another session here in my office."

"I shouldn't discuss anything with Liz?"

"Best if you don't, until we all get together again. Elizabeth, you did extremely well, however, I'd prefer it if you'd refrain from asking Ty what actually transpired while you were under. I promise, you will know soon enough. When I think it has the most value therapeutically. Understand?"

"Okay. I'm curious though. Did I do or say anything … unusual?"

Nelson smiled. "First," he replied, "let me discuss that with your parents."

[40]

Jerry Poirier folded and wrapped the blue cloak, disguising it as a gift. His father was at the breakfast table when he came downstairs. "Somebody's birthday?" he asked.

Jerry had hoped Jean-Jacques would already have gone to work. When he spotted him at the table, he was glad he'd gone to the trouble of preparing the package. "Yeah. One of the guys I work with." He poured himself a coffee and tried to act nonchalant.

"Since when do you buy birthday presents for … a guy you work with?"

"He's turning thirty. Bunch of people at the station are planning to take him out to lunch."

His father still seemed to think it was peculiar. "Everybody's buying this guy presents?"

Jerry put his coffee and the package on the table and sat down. He realized he'd begun to perspire. It was as though Jean-Jacques suspected him of something. "No," he replied, carrying on with the lie, "but he's been damn helpful to me in getting acquainted with everything at CKCF. Put in a good word to the news director on my job performance. He's the union president and, as such, has quite a bit of clout. Besides, with the shift I'm on, I won't be able to go to lunch with the rest of them … so I thought …"

Jean-Jacques changed the subject. "Jerry, I won't be home tonight. Going to take a break and head down to the cottage for a few days."

An icy chill ran up Jerry's spine. He knew precisely *why* his father was taking a break, and why he was taking it at Venise-en-Québec. "That's nice. Kind of bleak, though, this time of year on the lake."

"Weather's supposed to be good for the rest of the week. I just need the peace and quiet."

Suddenly the shoe was on the other foot. It was Jerry's turn to ask the questions. He studied his father's face. Jean-Jacques had never been a good liar. "Well, enjoy yourself. I'll hold the fort 'til you get back. There's a full moon, you know. It'll be a clear view in the country, without all this city pollution."

Jean-Jacques' expression gave him away. He swallowed some coffee and simply nodded in agreement. Jerry didn't know the meaning of the full moon, but his father had silently confirmed that the notations in his appointment book were significant.

Charles Walkley answered the phone. Sarah had said she was planning to go food shopping after seeing Catherine and Robin safely to their school. It was shortly after eleven on Monday morning and he'd been expecting Ty to call from the Reddy Memorial. It *wasn't* Ty. "Mr. Walkley," the caller began, "this is Dr. Barry Nelson. I've been looking after your daughter, Elizabeth."

It felt, to Charles, like his heart had skipped a beat. "Has something happened? Is everything alright?"

"Yes, yes. Sorry, Mr. Walkley. I didn't mean to give you a fright. Everything is fine. Elizabeth and Ty have just left my office. I wanted to take the opportunity to introduce myself to you and, if you have no objections, to ask you some rather delicate questions."

"About Elizabeth?"

"Well, yes. Indirectly. Mr. Walkley, I'd like to ask about your *own* recollections of a tragedy your family experienced years ago. Under hypnosis, Elizabeth became quite agitated when this came up."

"You're talking about our son, David."

"Yes. That's right. I apologize for dredging up sad memories, but I believe David's, uh, accident may be a root cause of at least *some* of your daughter's emotional distress."

Charles sat down at the little telephone table in the hallway. "She was very young when this happened."

"Under hypnosis, she said she was ten."

"That's correct. There was a five year age difference."

"If you don't mind, Mr. Walkley ... "

"Charles. Please call me Charles. And Dr. Nelson, anything my wife and I can do to help, we're at your disposal."

"Good. That's great to hear, Charles. Above all else, Elizabeth needs family support. Can you tell me, then, what *you* recall about the accident?"

"It was twenty years ago. Elizabeth and David were together on their school bus. I was at work at Loyola College and my wife had taken on a voluntary role at the NDG Library for boys and girls. During that time, Elizabeth was given the responsibility of walking her brother from the bus to our home. We had a housekeeper at the time. She stayed with the children until their mother was free, usually around 4:30."

"Uh-huh. And what happened, as you remember it, on the day of the tragedy?"

Charles paused before answering. "According to the police report, nothing out of the ordinary. They got off the bus and ... "

"Wait a moment, Charles. *They* got off the bus?"

"That's right. That's when the driver of the car failed to stop. David was hit. Killed instantly."

"I see. Mr. Walkley, this is *not* the way Elizabeth described it during the hypnotherapy."

"What do you mean?"

"Please understand. There are ethical issues involved here. Doctor-patient confidentiality and ..."

"I'm her father. We all want what is best for Elizabeth, Dr. Nelson."

"Yes. Certainly. Ty was witness to everything that happened in my office this morning. I asked him not to discuss it with your daughter, until I'd had the chance to speak to you and your wife."

"What? Discuss what?"

"This might come as a bit of a shock to you, Charles. I *am* concerned about your reaction to it because Elizabeth's full recovery from her depression, even her thoughts of suicide, might be at stake."

"Ethics aside, Dr. Nelson, you *must* tell me. Rest assured, Sarah and I will follow whatever advice you might have."

"Very good, then. Charles, under hypnosis, Elizabeth revealed that she and a little girl by the name of Margaret were planning to go to Margaret's home on that day to do their homework. The way

Elizabeth described it, she did *not* get off the bus until *after* the car hit your son."

"Good God! David was alone?"

"I have to assume that this was a real memory, on Elizabeth's part. Something she has suppressed for twenty years. A massive burden of guilt, because you and your wife had put her in charge of David."

"Oh Lord!"

"That's right, Charles. I warned you this would come as a shock."

"And you think this ... suppressed memory might be causing all of Elizabeth's problems?"

"Because she never told you and Sarah, did she?"

"No. No, she didn't."

"So, in her mind, that part of the tragedy was buried. If she could rule out the fact she had shirked her responsibility to David, she could forgive herself for having failed him."

"But, in reality, she never *did* forgive herself."

Nelson's voice took on a deeply serious tone. "The subconscious doesn't forget, Charles. The point is ... can you ... can you and your wife forgive her?"

"My God, she was ten years old. *Of course* we can forgive her. She was just a little girl. It might have been unfair of us to give her that responsibility in the first place."

"That's all I wanted to hear, Charles. Leave it with me, then. I'll be seeing Elizabeth again on Wednesday. Talk this over with your wife, and with Ty if you choose to, but let me deal with this, professionally."

"You want us to keep this to ourselves?"

"Until I've talked with Elizabeth. Yes. And something else I think is important. Elizabeth didn't experience a postpartum depression with the birth of her first child."

"No. No she didn't."

"It was coincidental with the birth of a *male* child."

"Robin. That's right."

Nelson paused briefly before speaking again. "It's possible that bringing a boy into the world could have been a trigger, in and of itself."

"In what way?"

"In that, deep in her subconscious, Elizabeth was aware she'd failed in her responsibility to David. Now, she had another young boy to care for."

"I see."

"When Robin turned five, the very age that David was killed in the accident, the depressive behaviour began again."

Charles Walkley felt his stomach churn. He thought he might burst into tears. "Poor Elizabeth. Poor, *hurt* little girl."

"Knowing all of this, now, I'm convinced we can begin to really bring about a full recovery."

"Thank you, Dr. Nelson. Very much. Of course, we'll cooperate in every way possible."

41

MONDAYS WERE ALWAYS CHAOTIC. Jason pored over his dayfile records, trying to separate the "must-covers" from the softer stories of the day. Clyde Bertram had urged him to do a followup on the Common Front strike plans. He knew that Ty would be anxious to report the latest on Yvette Comtois and her, so far successful, flight from the law. Greg Peterson was already on the road, shooting a teachers' protest outside the headquarters of the Protestant School Board of Greater Montreal, on Fielding Avenue. He had two camera-men available to him, besides Greg, and Sports was asking for one of them.

When Ty walked into his office at noon Jason was fighting off an overwhelming desire to start smoking again. The life-savers and toothpicks weren't cutting it. Ty appeared drawn and slightly under the weather. He plopped himself down in a chair next to the police radios and began tapping his fingers on the desk.

"Rough morning?" Jason asked.

"Un-fucking-believable."

"How'd it go at the hospital?"

"It *went*, and I think it took me *with* it." Ty shared his experience in the hypnotherapy session. He'd been forbidden to talk about it with Liz. He needed to get it off his chest and Jason was a good friend.

"Wow. So what happens now?"

Ty leaned his elbows on his knees. "Jason, I've pretty much *had* it. I know this is a bad time to spring this on you, but I think I'm going to have to book off for a few days. Liz has to see Nelson again on Wednesday. That's going to be pivotal in her recovery process and I'll need to be there. I'd like to spend the rest of today and all day tomorrow with her. She's ... fragile as hell. Charles and Sarah have bent over backwards for us and the kids, but Liz and I have had *no* real time together, even on the weekend."

Jason wrinkled his brow. "I understand, Ty. Let's go clear it with Bertram. I'm sure there'll be no problem."

"I've got some vacation days coming to me, going all the way back to last Summer."

"Let's see what Clyde has to say. I'm betting he'll just *give* you the time off."

Jerry drove into the parking lot, behind CKCF, at 12:35. His shift didn't begin until three but he had a gut feeling that Ty wouldn't be around any later than necessary. Jerry found himself torn between confiding in his father and pursuing the mystery of the blue and red cloaks. Ultimately, he decided to hand off the package to Ty. Jean-Jacques had been less than truthful about his planned visit to the family cottage. His involvement with Laurent Picard and whatever went on behind closed doors at Our Lady of Lourdes was, apparently, not open to discussion.

Ty's work station was empty when Jerry walked into the newsroom. Clyde Bertram's office door was closed but, through the glass windows, he spotted Jason and Ty seated opposite the news director's desk completely enveloped by a cloud of cigar smoke. Jerry dropped the package next to Ty's Underwood and sat down to wait. Eventually, the door swung open and the blue smoke swirled into the newsroom proper.

"Hey, Jerry. I see you brought me that *gift* we were talking about," Ty winked.

Jerry stood up and said hello to Jason, as the assignment editor headed for his own office. "Yeah. The gift."

"What say we take a walk down to the coffee machine?" Ty asked, picking up the package and heading for the corridor. Jerry followed.

"What's it for?" he asked in a whisper. "If you're thinking what *I'm* thinking, you're about to take news reporting to a whole new level."

"Why not?" Ty replied. "The cloak is my ticket in. Look, Jerry, *you* told *me* you thought something big was going to happen. If that's true, it's probably going to happen on Wednesday night, and it's going to happen *in that church*."

"Shouldn't we be talking to the police?"

"The cops know about the cloaks in Saint-Sauveur. We're already out on a limb, by not telling them about the ones in Venise-en-Québec."

"Because that would implicate my father."

"Exactly. We know that all of them were manufactured in Switzerland, but that doesn't necessarily mean your father is connected, in any way, to the murders up north. The cops are already on to this Laurent Picard and the fact that he was the lawyer who represented Yvette Comtois at her murder trial in Zurich. So, it's not as though we are deliberately withholding evidence."

"True. But they might *not* be aware of this meeting at the church … this "*Bidding*," or whatever, that was mentioned in my dad's appointment book."

"And we have no idea what it's about, either. That's why I need the cloak. I want to get into Our Lady of Lourdes to find out. If the cops turn up, so be it. Meantime, this is our story … yours, mine and Greg's."

"So, what do you want from me. Or, for that matter, from Greg?"

"You'll be my safety net. If I'm successful in getting into the meeting, you guys can wait outside. If I'm in trouble, or if anything untoward happens, you have my permission to call the police. Greg can shoot some exteriors of the church, and if you're well hidden behind cars in the lot, or bushes near the building, you might even get some shots of people arriving and going in."

"Jeez, Ty, these people could be dangerous."

Ty smiled. "Remember, I'm the guy who stole fingerprints from a dead man. Since when do we back away from a dynamite story?"

"My father's already *at* the cottage."

"Really?"

"Left after breakfast this morning."

"Okay. See, I agree with you Jerry."

"About what?"

"Something big … *is* going to happen."

42

"WE HAVE THE WHOLE DAY to ourselves. What would you like to do?" Ty had awakened Tuesday morning with the strong feeling that he and Elizabeth had to get out of the house. "I thought maybe Old Montreal? Something like that?"

Liz had only picked at her breakfast. She glanced at her father. "Do you and Mom mind looking after homework? The kids'll be home …"

Charles smiled. "In case you hadn't noticed, sweetheart, your mother and I have been handling things for several days now. You and Ty go and do something fun. We'll be fine."

Liz took a swallow of coffee. It seemed to take a great deal of effort to appear cheerful. "I know, Dad. And it's been a great relief to me that you're here. Maybe Ty and I could just go out to lunch or something. We could be back by the time Catherine and Robin get home from school."

Sarah, who had been busy washing dishes in the kitchen sink, chimed in. "Lunch s-munch," she turned toward the table holding a dish-rag in one hand. "You need to get away for a few hours. Dad and I will look after the kids. Just give us a call this afternoon, and let us know what you're up to."

"What *about* Old Montreal?" Ty repeated his question. "We could just walk around by the waterfront. Find a nice restaurant for lunch and then maybe head down to the old Expo 67 site."

Liz pushed her coffee cup aside and stood up. "It's a beautiful day," she pointed at the window. "I think I'd rather hike around Mount Royal. Beaver Lake and the Lookout."

"Deal," Ty replied. "Fast food at the Chalet. Maybe a horse and buggy ride around the mountain. Sounds good to me."

Liz finally smiled and disappeared down the hall and into their bedroom. Ty lowered his voice and addressed Charles. "Did Dr. Nelson call?"

"He did."

"And?"

"And Sarah and I know about Elizabeth staying on that school bus. All these years ... blaming herself for David. It's hard to believe."

"You didn't *say* anything!"

"Absolutely not. This ... Nelson ... was insistent."

"Same for me," Ty replied. "I saw the whole thing. She was hypnotized and she just about went berserk when this came up. Nelson swore me to secrecy, as well."

Sarah sat down at the table and Charles appeared very concerned. "I hope the doctor knows what he's doing. There's no telling *how* Elizabeth will react to having something like that yanked out of her subconscious. She's kept this, even from herself, for such a very long time."

Ty nodded. "I just don't know enough about psychotherapy, Charles. But I *do* have confidence in Dr. Nelson. Looking on the positive side, if Liz can finally put it all behind her, he's reasonably sure it will be her first significant step toward full recovery."

"Well," Sarah said, "we'll know *tomorrow*, if Nelson's on the right track, *won't* we."

Greg Peterson hated Tuesdays. He dropped off his film, on yet another protest, at the lab for processing and decided to leave the sound camera in Mobile 7. Greg knew that Jason would have another assignment for him as soon as he got back to the station.

It had been a disappointing weekend. Suzie had telephoned on Saturday, to say that she was down with a cold and wouldn't be driving in from Ottawa. Greg spent most of Sunday cleaning his photo studio in Old Montreal. What with Ty's preoccupation with the Morissette murder and subsequent events, he was beginning to wonder whether he'd ever have time to book new, commercial shoots. The rent for the Suzie-Q Agency was killing him. He'd sat for the longest time on the wide-plank floor taking mental inventory of his cameras, lenses, tripods, backdrops, props and lighting.

Sunlight streamed through the studio windows, cutting a swath between low-rise buildings along St. Paul Street. Over the three years since Suzie had bankrolled the business, he'd managed to pay her back the ten-thousand dollars. They'd shared in the meager profits ever since, but lack of time had eaten into his ability to attract new business.

Now, sitting in Mobile 7 behind CKCF, Greg began to fashion a plan. If he sold everything off to another Montreal freelancer, he'd split the proceeds down the middle with Suzie, pay off some outstanding bills and absorb the monthly rent into his strained monthly budget. His mother was frequently reminding him that Suzie wasn't going to wait forever. Marg Peterson wanted grand-children. "You're getting on, you know. Time to move out and move on. Get your own place. Marry the girl."

It was just one more reason to hate work. Greg realized that, essentially, he lived for the weekends and the wonderful feeling that life actually made sense when Suzie was in town. He slammed the car door in his frustration and walked toward the rear entrance of the television station. He was wondering whether he could make enough of a profit from selling his studio equipment, to buy an engagement ring.

"Greg. I'm glad I ran into you." Jerry stood in the corridor outside the photo department. "I have to discuss something with you. It involves working *off the clock*." He told Greg about Ty's plans for Wednesday night.

Seagulls wheeled into the wind above Beaver Lake on Mount Royal, diving every now and then for scraps of food. A group of school children on a field trip scattered bits of dried bread on the surface of the water under the watchful eye of their teacher. Ducks paddled around them, making pleasurable duck noises of pleasure at the bounty.

Ty held Liz's hand as they headed up a paved walkway toward the Chalet at the top of the mountain. For the first time in weeks, Liz seemed to be relaxed and enjoying herself. "Do you think it's over?"

Ty hadn't been expecting a serious question. "Over? You mean, your depression and everything?"

They walked slowly, hand in hand, stepping to one side of the road as a calèche driver maneuvered his horse down the steep hill.

"Yes. And everything. My crazy moods. The memory lapses. Thoughts of suicide. Everything."

He squeezed her hand and carefully considered his reply. "With any luck, Liz, it *will* be over. Nelson seems to be on top of it. The medication you're taking will kick in over a period of time and we may find out something more when we go to the Reddy tomorrow."

Liz's face took on a worried expression. "Like what? Can't you tell me ... anything?"

"Nelson has to handle it, Liz. I gave him my word. He did have a talk with your father. *You* were there. You gave him permission to discuss it with your parents."

"I know. It's just that I'd like some idea of what I'm in for. Whatever happened during that hypnotherapy session *must* have been pretty revealing. It *scares* me."

Ty rested his hands on her shoulders and looked squarely into her eyes. "Liz, you know I love you. I understand that you're frightened. So am I." He pulled her towards him and hugged her tightly, whispering into her ear. "Let this thing play out the way Nelson wants it to. I'll be there, every step of the way. And I promise, we 'll get through it together."

A single tear ran down Liz's cheek. Ty kissed it away.

43

DR. BARRY NELSON'S OFFICE was absent of sound. The colors in his wall mural seemed to ebb and flow, as though somehow alive. Ty bit his lip nervously. "More hypnosis?" he asked, breaking the silence.

Nelson invited Liz to take the same chair she'd sat in, for the hypnotherapy session.

"No. No, not this time. I think Elizabeth and I will simply work on being as relaxed as possible. How do you feel this morning, Liz?"

"A little edgy."

"Well, that's to be understood. Tell you what. Ty, you sit over there." He waved at a chair in the corner of the room. Now, Liz, it's unconventional that Ty is here with us or that you wanted him here for our earlier therapy. Is it still your wish that your husband observe our conversation today?"

"Yes. Absolutely."

Nelson took the chair opposite hers. "Then, if it helps you … makes you feel more secure … I have no objections."

"Thank you."

"Before we begin, I'd like to explain what I think is going on with you. We all retain things in memory. Some of these things are routine and relatively unimportant. Some of them are significant in terms of our daily lives. Ordinarily, we can summon up memories at will. Names of people we've known. Events. Music we enjoyed years ago. The titles of motion pictures. Historical data. You name it. Sometimes it seems impossible to consciously recall a tidbit of information, because it's been stored in the subconscious, then hours after we've tried to remember it we suddenly blurt it out."

Liz nodded in agreement. Ty watched from the corner shadows of the office, as Nelson continued. "Look upon it as a kind of file-drawer, Liz. You try to find a file and, at first, you can't. Remarkably, inexplicably in fact, the file you're after is easily accessed at a later point."

"Okay. That's happened to me before."

"It's happened to all of us. But there's another category of file that we need to discuss today. One that, perhaps, hasn't been put into alphabetical order. One that, no matter how hard we try, we simply cannot retrieve. This would be what is commonly referred to as a repressed memory … information that continues to elude us … buried deep in the subconscious for whatever reason."

"You think that's the case with me?"

"Ordinarily, it takes several hypnotherapy sessions to uncover a memory that would seem to be significant. But, yes, something came up last week that seems to fit into this category."

"What, exactly?"

"I'll get to that. First, however, this is *not* hypnosis. But I'd like you to close your eyes and for just a few moments, listen to my voice. Good?"

"Okay." She closed her eyes.

"Now, Liz, I want you to breathe in through your nose and out through your mouth. Deep breath … *in*. Out through your mouth. *In … out. In … out.* That's it. You're body feels heavy in the chair. You are becoming more and more relaxed. *In … out.* I'm simply going to ask you some questions and, between the two of us, we might be able to draw that hidden file out into the open. That is to say, *into* your conscious stream of thought. Understand?"

"Yes, I understand."

"I'd like you to tell me about your little brother."

"David?"

"Yes, David. What do you remember about him?"

"I … loved him."

"I'm sure you did. But what sort of boy was he?"

"Full of energy. Always excited about things. Very active."

"Apparently it runs in your family. In fact, I understand that your parents felt *you* were hyperactive as a child."

"I was tested."

"I'm aware of that, Liz. I'm also aware of the conclusions reached by your family at the time, that you were extremely bright and that your, uh, hyperactivity was the drive behind your need to achieve."

"I won a scholarship to McGill."

"Yes. So you think David's energy levels were similar?"

"He was a great kid. It's like he went off in a thousand directions at the same time. He collected marbles, for example. Had hundreds of them. He was enthusiastic about school. He was able to *read* at the age of three."

"You were *proud* of him?"

"He was my baby brother."

"Of course. What can you tell me about ... the *accident*, Liz?"

She suddenly opened her eyes. Nelson smiled reassuringly. "I'd like you to keep your eyes closed. Try to go back to that terrible day, if you can."

"He was hit by a car."

"Are you still feeling relaxed?"

"I guess so. Yes, I'm relaxed."

Nelson paused for a moment, before speaking again. "I want you to open your mind to it, Liz, as difficult as that might be. What do you hear?"

"What do I hear?"

"Yes. When David was hit by the car, what are you hearing?"

"Screaming."

"Are *you* screaming?"

"*Everybody* is. The bus driver. All the kids. *Everybody*."

"Can you tell me what you see?"

"David isn't moving. There is ... blood on his face. The man who was driving the car is kneeling beside him. People are running."

"To call the police?"

"Someone went to telephone for an ambulance."

"Where are *you*, Liz."

"The bus driver is holding me back. I want to go to David."

"You feel ... responsible?"

"I was supposed to look after him."

"What can you tell me about your little friend, Margaret?"

All the color seemed to drain from Elizabeth's face. Ty leaned forward in his chair as she began to reply. "She was my best friend in the fifth grade."

"Yes. Was she there on that day?"

"On the bus."

"She was *on* the bus when the car hit David?"

"Oh-h-h-h!"

"It's alright, Liz. I know this is very hard for you. Try to relax. What are you recalling about Margaret that made you so upset?"

"I … I don't know. I can't. I can't remember."

"Was Margaret a smart girl?"

"Very smart. We were good friends."

"Did you sometimes do your schoolwork together?"

"Oh God!"

"What is it, Liz? What do you see?"

"Margaret is sitting *next to me* on the bus! We're coming to my stop!"

"What is David doing?"

"I can't. I don't want to."

"It's okay, Liz. This was twenty years ago. Nothing can hurt you now. It's a sad, sad memory. That's *all* it is. Now, try to tell me. What is David doing?"

"He. He's waving goodbye."

"At you?"

"Please. Please. This is *too much!*"

"*Why* is David waving, Liz?"

She began to rock back and forth in her chair. "Because he's getting off the bus."

"By himself?"

"I see the car! It's not stopping!"

"*How* do you see the car? Where are you?"

"Through the window. David is outside and the car isn't stopping! I … I can't warn him! It's too fast! Too fast!"

Nelson glanced over at Ty and back to her. "Elizabeth. You can open your eyes now. Let's talk about this."

Perspiration rolled down her forehead. Nelson handed her a damp, cold cloth. "How do you feel?"

"I stayed on the bus. I … *killed* David."

"Why would you say that?"

"Because I was *responsible*."

"You were ten years old. Do you think you'd done a good job of looking after David all those times *before* the accident?"

"Yes."

"If you had tried to cross the street with David on that day, do you think you could have prevented what happened?"

"I don't know."

"Think about it, Liz. You said the car was going too fast."

"It was."

"Then how could you have stopped it?"

"I guess that's true. I *couldn't* have."

"What do you feel guilty about?"

"My parents. I never told them."

"Told them what?"

"That I let David get off the bus alone."

Nelson rested his elbows on his knees and stared into her eyes. "If you had stepped out around the front of the bus *with* David, what might have happened?"

Her lower lip was quivering. "I imagine the car would have hit *both* of us."

"And do you think that would have made your parents happier?"

"No."

"Alright. Then let's look at what you're saying. First, you said you *killed* David. You *know* that's not true don't you?"

"The *car* killed David."

"That's right. And you also said you thought you'd been doing a good job looking after David. Isn't that right?"

"Not on *that* day."

"That day could have ended *both* your lives."

"It didn't."

"No, it didn't. For just a moment then, Liz, let's examine this deep sense of guilt you've been living with all of these years, without even knowing *why*."

"Okay."

"When I asked why you feel guilty, you said it was because you never told your parents you'd allowed David to get off the bus alone."

"Yes."

"Yet, you also agreed that had you been *with* your brother, that car probably would have hit both of you."

"So what are you saying?".

"I'd prefer *you* to come to your *own* conclusion. Other than not telling your parents … what else would have embedded itself so deeply in your subconscious? What else could have caused so much guilt over so long a time?"

Liz looked off into the corner of the room, thinking. "Because I survived? David *died* and I'm still alive?"

Another smile from Nelson. "Good. *Very* good, Liz."

"But how do I live with *this*?"

"Before today, you didn't even know what *this* was. Now, it's possible to deal with it consciously and logically."

"My parents will never forgive me."

"What about forgiving *yourself* … Can you do that?

"I don't know. I can try, but *how*?"

"We'll work on that together. As to your parents, I've already spoken to them … as I told you I would."

"You mean, they *know*?"

"Not only do they *know*, Liz, they're having a hard time forgiving *themselves* for imposing such a great responsibility on you. You're going to have to help *them*."

She began to sob. "I … I don't know what to say."

"This was a terrible, tragic accident, Liz. An accident you could *not* have prevented. Thankfully your parents didn't lose *two* children on that day. Go home and talk to them. They love you very much."

44

Basel, Switzerland, Wednesday, April 8: 11:30 p.m.
Paris, France, Wednesday, April 8: 11:30 p.m.
Frankfurt, Germany, Wednesday, April 8: 11:30 p.m.
London, U.K., Wednesday, April 8: 11:30 p.m.
Fort-de-France, Martinique, Wednesday, April 8: 6:30 p.m.
Melbourne, Australia, Thursday, April 9: 8:30 a.m.
Saint-Felix-de-Sebastien, Quebec, Canada, Wednesday,
*   April 8: 5:30 p.m.*

WERNER HOCHSTRASSER's instructions, to the Order's Regional Commanders in each city, had been clear. "It is imperative that the *transmutation* rituals begin simultaneously."

In each location, around the world, followers would gather at 11:30 p.m. Swiss time, ninety minutes in advance of their respective ceremonies. "The rituals," Hochstrasser emphasized, "must begin precisely at 1:00 a.m. Swiss time." That would be no problem for Paris, Frankfurt and London. They were all on the same clock. Members in Canada, Martinique and Australia would simply have to cope accordingly.

Regional Commanders were instructed to provide their Elders with the *Rivea corymbosa*. The Elders, in turn, would distribute one pill to each member in attendance. The last pill would go to the *initiate* in each city. Frankl Anderegg had indicated it would take at least thirty minutes for the recipient to experience the drug's full, hallucinogenic properties. "Be warned," he'd told the recent gathering at the Spalentor Hotel, "the effects can last up to twelve hours. There's no predicting how each individual will react." Hochstrasser hadn't been concerned.

It was well after one o'clock in the afternoon when Jerry Poirier finally reached Ty on the telephone. There were no new developments in the police search for Yvette Comtois. The day's news run had been dull at best. Jerry was less worried than he had been about the stolen cloak. "My father took off for the cottage about ten o'clock this morning," he told Ty. "I checked. There are still seven cloaks hanging in his study."

Ty sat at the small table, down the hall from his kitchen. Liz and her parents were sitting at the kitchen table in deep conversation. He kept his voice low. "Good. Maybe he's some sort of recruiter for this Order. It must be there's only a handful of members at his corporation. He probably only needed the ones he took with him."

Jerry agreed. "Anyway, he won't miss the one we filched. At least, not today. What's happening your end? When do you want to head to Saint-Félix-de-Sébastien?"

"Is Greg willing to go?"

"You mean … off the clock?"

"Yeah. I want this to be strictly voluntary. We may or may not get a story out of it, and I'm pretty sure Jason wouldn't be able to authorize the overtime."

"No problem. Greg's planning to use his mother's car."

"Good idea. A marked news car would stick out like a sore thumb. Also, even if we parked it a mile away, it would be just our luck if your father spotted and recognized your Volkswagon."

Jerry chuckled. "It's easy to recognize. Front end's all bashed in on one side. Dad's been trying to convince me to buy a new one. If he *saw* it, he'd *know* it. What time do you want to leave?"

Ty glanced at his watch. "It's nearly one o'clock, now. I've got to stick around for a while longer. Liz and I just got back from the hospital an hour ago. A pretty intense mood here at the house. When are you and Greg off duty?"

"We lucked out there. Greg's on the seven to three shift. When he checks out I don't think Jason'll have anything more for me. I've been teamed up with Greg."

"Perfect. I'll leave Mobile 14 at the station. Meet you at Greg's mother's house, say, around four o'clock? This will probably be a fairly long stakeout. The moon won't be up 'til after supper and your father's appointment book indicated the full moon had something to do with this meeting at Our Lady of Lourdes. Can't hurt to just get there and wait."

"You're still planning to go inside?"

"Just me and the blue cloak."

Dogs are always atuned to human emotions. Such was the case on Wednesday afternoon, as Yvette Comtois prepared to leave her newly-acquired home on Route 7. Max and Mike were aware that something was up. They weren't sure what it was, but they had a sense that their mistress was about to go out and, even for a short period of time, they didn't like to be abandoned. Max hovered around Yvette's feet, tongue lolling out of his mouth, trying to smile a doggie smile. "Maybe," he thought, "she'll take us with her." Mike had been watching from his assigned corner of the small living room. His food dish was empty and he worried she might forget to fill it.

Pearl's dark eyes surveyed Yvette's actions. Her perception of events to come was much more complex. Pearl could sense tension and reach conclusions that were well beyond the native intellect of her canine companions. She was, after all, nearly nineteen years old. She had a European background and drew from a rich life experience. Whatever was in store, it involved the bang-stick. Pearl had seen the .32 calibre pistol fired at least twice before. She wasn't frightened by it. The bang-stick was exciting and it always meant she was about to share another adventure.

Now, Pearl's olfactory glands were reacting to an unfamiliar odor. She watched, as Yvette worked over a wooden salad bowl, which contained the foul-smelling substance. Her mistress was smiling as she crushed and ground potassium chlorate into granules that resembled ordinary table sugar. She then mixed equal volumes of the granulated chlorate with sugar and poured the bowl's ingredients, carefully, onto a dry sheet of paper folded at the edges. After measuring six tablespoons of the mixture and depositing the powder on to a second, very thin paper, she folded the works into a tight packet.

There were more sulphurous odors from another source. Yvette used a pair of pliers to grind the heads off several handsful of safety matches. When she had a sufficient quantity of this material she went to her purse and pulled out a length of firecracker fuse, inserting one end of the fuse through the paper packet and into the mixture she'd prepared in the salad bowl. Pearl had no way of knowing what any of it meant. She was able, only, to sense the excitement and was convinced that something important lay ahead. As she worked, Yvette Comtois was humming.

45

THE RHINE FLOWED DARKLY NORTH ... a black ribbon cutting through Basel's Old Town and becoming all but invisible in the night-shrouded distance. From his vantage point on the *Pfalz*, high above the river and behind the cathedral, Werner Hochstrasser couldn't make out the massive pine trees of the Black Forest in Germany. The Vosges Mountains appeared as a smear on the horizon.

He glanced at his watch, noting that Ulrich Sennhauser was late. The archaeologist had agreed to meet him at nine-thirty, to give him a tour of the Celtic temple concealed below the modern terrace since the first century. Hochstrasser had spent the earlier part of the evening in the *Marktplatz*, where he'd munched on fresh fruit and a pretzel he'd purchased from a street vendor. He'd walked up cobbled streets and through a maze of ancient alleys, from the *Marktplatz* along the *Rittergasse* to *Münsterplatz* ... the cathedral square.

Sennhauser finally emerged from the cloisters, adjoining the *Münster* to the south. He was out of breath. The massive arches of the cathedral's *Choir* behind him, displaying carved elephants and grotesque creatures, were now mere shadows against a star-filled sky. "Sorry." Sennhauser bent over forwards, with his hands on his knees. "Not as young as I used to be."

Hochstrasser waited until the archaeologist had fully recovered. "I had no trouble with security, whether you were here on time or not," he said, in a scolding voice. "Tourist hours for the *Münster* are long over."

"Didn't think you would have. I told them you'd be coming." Sennhauser mopped his forehead with a handkerchief. "They also expect the others, around eleven o'clock."

"And?"

"And *they'll* have no problems. My crew has done a lot of digging on this hill. The security people all know and trust me. But, if it's a concern, I'll station someone here on the *Pfalz* to usher them to the tunnel."

Hochstrasser frowned. "How have you kept this a secret ... this area being one of Basel's most popular tourist attractions?"

Sennhauser was finally breathing normally. "It's *not* a secret, at official levels."

"What?"

"I had to notify government officials that a discovery had been made. I simply told them, and this is standard practice, that my team was still in the process of uncovering what appeared to be a significant find. They agreed to follow my lead, on when to go public with it."

"How'd you find it in the first place?"

Sennhauser smiled broadly. This was his favorite subject. "Well, as you know, I've done a great deal of work at the Roman settlement of *Augusta Raurica* to the east. As you also probably know, there was a castle where the *Münster* now stands. There were Roman fortifications here that were destroyed in the devastating quake of 1356. Two Roman roads converged right about where we stand and traces of the road were found, running underneath the cathedral itself."

Hochstrasser nodded, somewhat impatient with the history lesson. "Yes, yes. These roads are part of the reason I decided to hold the ritual here. *Transmutation* must occur between the hours of midnight and two, three days after a full moon, at the junction of three roads, on a cliff or hill overlooking water. The site is perfect."

Sennhauser looked skyward. An orange colored moon was just beginning to rise. "To get back to your question. In recent years there has been very little archaeological attention paid to Cathedral Hill. However, I've never lost interest in what might lie beneath this ground. The *Keltenwall* ... the Celtic wall which can be seen through skylights on the *Rittergasse*, has always led me to believe there was more to discover. So, I come up here fairly regularly to, shall we say, humor my curiosity."

"So?"

"So, one day I was digging around about ten metres from the stairs leading down to the *Münster fähre* ... the ferry ... when I pulled something out of the ridge that intrigued me. Just a vitrified piece of what appeared to be a glassy substance. I recognized it for what it was, but I had to be sure."

Hochstrasser had reached the limits of his patience. "For God's sake, man, what *was* it?"

"Something that had been exposed to extreme heat. Something that had been fused, as a result. We had it carbon-dated. It was from the first century ... no doubts, it *was* Celtic. The heat was generated by the earthquake."

"And that's when you began a full scale operation?"

"About six months ago. We were some ten feet into the hillside before we found what *has* to be one of the most important archeological finds since *Augusta Raurica* ... a perfectly intact, Celtic temple."

"Is it safe?"

Sennhauser smiled again. "As solid as the day it was built. We've punched holes to the surface over there," he pointed at a clump of trees toward the end of the *Pfalz*. "Air circulation below is excellent."

"Nobody's spotted these, uh, holes?"

"If they have, they might have thought some animal had been at work. There's no hint of what they really are."

Hochstrasser clicked his tongue. "Good. Good. Shall we?" He began walking in the direction Sennhauser had pointed. By now, the orange tinted moon had turned a mustard color and occupied a sizable portion of the eastern sky.

Marg Peterson was insistent. "You boys will need *something*. It's already past four."

Greg's mother had made and wrapped several sandwiches. She placed them on the kitchen table. "What about drinks?"

Greg picked up the brown paper bag. "Thanks Ma, we'll stop for something along the way."

Ty and Jerry both agreed. Ty gave Marg a hug. "No wonder Greg's getting a little pot belly there, Mrs. Peterson. You feed him too well."

She raised an eyebrow, glancing briefly at Greg's midsection. "I think Greg can blame most of that on Molson's Ale."

Ty laughed. "Anyway, thanks for this. We'll certainly make use of the sandwiches. And thanks for letting us borrow the car."

"That old Ford doesn't owe me anything. Been driving it for years. There's a full tank of gas, by the way." She shrugged. Her face wore a worried expression. "I don't know what you three are up to, but be careful." She handed Greg the keys.

Laurent Picard had no truck with the supernatural. It was his firm belief that the human race was a cosmic coincidence and that life, in general, was entirely owing to happenstance. He was a lawyer and businessman and, as such, felt he was an effective Regional Commander. The Order, after all, required the talents of someone whose mind wasn't cluttered by existential theories.

Hochstrasser was, he knew, the sort of scientist who kept an open mind. The mumbo-jumbo surrounding this so called *transmutation* ritual was, in Picard's opinion, a stretch even for the Supreme leader.

"Show-biz for the faithful," Hochstrasser had emphasized. "Gives the initiates a sense of spiritual belonging. For those who truly believe," he'd added, "the Order offers an alternative to orthodoxy. The main attractions, of course, are money and power."

Picard's initiate was a young woman whose university major had been African history. Maya Hopkins' post-graduate work had brought her from Harvard to McGill and she had distinguished herself in all her academic pursuits. He doubted she would be impressed by Hochstrasser's idea of "show-biz." Hopkins was also a knockout. Picard thought he'd rather get her into the sack than behave like some sort of mad magician in sorcerer's robes.

He watched through leaded windows in the Our Lady of Lourdes rectory, for the first cars to arrive. He was entirely at peace with his atheism. His role tonight would be strictly play-acting. "God," he often told himself, "was the product of weakness and fear. "Evil," he was convinced, "sprang from human imagination and *neither* was an entity unto itself."

46

CHIEF INSPECTOR COUSINEAU tapped his fingers on his desk pad. It was a nervous reaction to an ongoing battle with tobacco. He'd tried to quit on more occasions than he cared to recall and *this* time seemed to be the worst. Twice, during the course of the afternoon, he reached into his coat pocket for his beloved pack of Gitanes cigarettes. Twice, he came up empty. His tapping fingers were doing nothing to relieve the tension.

Sergeant Roger Tremblay's report, on the search of Yvette Comtois' shop in Saint-Sauveur, lay open in front of him. Bank account cleaned out. Antique store abandoned. Tremblay and two other officers had found a Land Rover, registered in her name, parked behind the building on Rue Principale. For all intents and purposes, Comtois had evaporated. Cousineau instructed Tremblay to check for possible car rentals in the area. None had turned up. Had she hitch-hiked? Cousineau thought that was unlikely. No one would pick up a middle-aged woman with pets standing on the side of the Laurentian Autoroute.

The urge to leave his office and buy another pack of Gitanes became almost overwhelming. He knew he was missing something, in connection with the recent murders, that could provide a clue as to Comtois' whereabouts. But what was it? His mind was racing almost as fast as his heart was beating. He'd have to accompany tobacco withdrawl with a change in his dietary habits. Cousineau loved to eat and, even now midway through the afternoon, his stomach growled.

The Chief Inspector re-examined the Tremblay report. Comtois allegedly murdered funeral home operator Fernand Ouellette. Ouellette was linked to Dr. Denis Desjardins in the illegal harvesting of human organs, but how did *that* relate to the fugitive? He held the folder in front of his huge stomach and leaned back in the chair.

Ouellette, Desjardins, Brannigan, Blouin and Duguay formed the puzzle. All were involved in some sort of cult. All, directly or indirectly, were complicit in the killing of young Jacqueline Morissette.

Cousineau recalled a mental exercise used to stimulate a child's deductive reasoning. It was usually entitled "*what doesn't belong in this picture*?" Then, it hit him. The only individual among the five murdered adults, who had not been long-term residents of either Saint-Sauveur or Sainte-Agathe, was Francis Duguay. He had rented the old house on Rue Principale and, along with Marlene Brannigan, appeared to have been directly responsible for Morissette's abduction. The secret room in that house belonged to *him*.

Cousineau felt a twinge of excitement. To the best of his knowledge none of the others, including suicide victim Serge Blouin, had any history of cult-leanings. *Ergo*, Duguay must have imported the madness when he moved into the area from Montreal's south shore.

The Chief Inspector put the Tremblay report back down on the desk. He would issue orders to his men to find out everything they possibly could about Duguay's movements and acquaintances before he moved to the Laurentians. The Order of the Sword, Interpol had told him, had tendrils that extended far and wide. He'd just about made up his mind to celebrate the discovery with a cigarette purchase when his phone rang. Apparently, a 1970 Buick had been stolen from a private home along Saint-Sauveur's main street, at just about the time Yvette Comtois disappeared from sight. It was, only now, coming to his attention.

The old Ford pulled to the left and the engine valve-lifters made clattering noises as Greg maneuvered around the back roads of the Montérégie region. "Ma's done it again," he said, yanking at the wheel to avoid a cat that suddenly darted across the road. "She meant well, by gassing-up the car for us. It's just that every time she fills the gas tank, she tops off the oil. I don't know how many times I've told her."

Ty grinned. "Think we'll make it all the way to the church, or is this serious?"

"Nah. Too much oil in the crankcase is all."

"So that's what's making all this noise?"

Greg shook his head. "Her mechanic's told her too. If you overfill the damn oil, the crankshaft churns it up causing air bubbles in the lubricating system. The bubbles get into the lifters."

Jerry Poirier chimed in from the back seat. "Nothing to worry about until the engine begins surging and doesn't respond to the accelerator."

"A-hah," Ty leaned over and made eye contact with him. "So you *know* about these things?"

Jerry nodded. "Not a whole lot. But I have to keep my Volkswagon going and I've learned out of necessity. When those bubbles get into the hydraulic lifters, they can mess up the valve train."

"Then what?"

Jerry shrugged. "We walk."

Farm country flew past as the trio moved closer to Saint-Félix-de-Sébastien. Greg had to come to a full stop along the dirt road between Route 7 and the town's main street. A bearded man wearing a Wirthmore seed-hat, bib-jeans and rubber boots was driving his Jersey cows from a pasture on the left to the barn and milk-house on the right. One of the cows, with an udder that appeared ready to explode, was stubbornly refusing to move. She turned her sad brown eyes toward Marg Peterson's Ford and ignored the farmer's prodding.

Ty glanced at his watch. It was just after five o'clock. "C'mon Bessie. Places to go people to see."

The cow mooed. The man in the bib-jeans slapped her on the hind-quarters and shouted. Eventually, Bessie followed her sisters along the trail toward the barn and Greg eased his foot on to the gas pedal. The car *clacketty-clacked* toward Our Lady of Lourdes.

Father Jean-Marc Laframboise wasn't actually buried in the small cemetery by the church. A memorial stone had been erected, however, after the parish's first serving priest died of consumption in 1776. The American Revolutionary War was a year old. New Hampshire had already become the first post-colonial sovereign nation in the Americas when it broke off from Great Britain and was one of the original thirteen states that founded the United States of America just six months later.

Father Laframboise, whose remains were dispatched to his birthplace in the Gaspé region, was much revered in the small farming community. He had served the spiritual needs of local families for thirty-four years, and area residents collectively agreed to erect the stone. The cemetery had grown around the memorial, accommodating deceased members of some of the more prominent parishioners. The last, actual burial in the tiny lot was in 1910.

Ueli Berlinger had no interest in the history. He stood concealed behind the Laframboise monument and noted every car and every individual arriving in the adjacent parking lot. Some, both male and female, were already wearing their cloaks. Others carried small packages, brief-cases or duffle-bags. Berlinger supposed they would change into the cloaks inside the church.

He had told Laurent Picard that he was prepared for any eventuality. If anything seemed out of the ordinary as the ceremony began he could react quickly and effectively. He had brought a lightweight kit containing components which, when assembled, became a fully functional rifle. It was easily put together and entirely stowable and the kit included fifty rounds of small calibre ammunition. Berlinger did not believe he'd need to use the rifle, even if the Comtois broad showed up, but Picard had insisted he take it to the choir loft.

He also carried a World War Two fighting knife. It was originally standard-issue to the Royal New Zealand Airforce and Berlinger had found it lethally handy in the past. He thought the knife would be his weapon of choice as the evening unfolded. He could spot a threat from the choir loft, then make his way down the stairs and into the crowd below. A quick thrust into the kidney would resolve any problem much more quietly than the rifle. Berlinger had counted eighteen cars entering the parking lot. Some contained two or more people. It was going to be a busy night.

47

THERE IS A LARGE PLATE-GLASS *window in the Farmers' Co-op, front-ing on to the main street in Saint-Félix-de-Sébastien. Yvette Comtois is staring through it at the Buick LeSabre she's parked opposite the church. She has switched license plates on the 1970 car, removing the old ones and replacing them with plates from a Ford pickup she spotted near her small house on Route 7. Comtois is buying time. She doesn't want the Buick to be identified as stolen. It will be some time, she figures, before the Ford owner realizes his original plates are missing. As a further precaution, she would move the car to a more distant location and walk back.*

No one in the Co-op seems to mind her presence. If anyone asks, she will tell them she wanted to get out of the sun while waiting for a friend. Cars have been entering the Our Lady of Lourdes parking lot across the street since five o'clock. She is ready. The red cloak is in the Buick with Max, Mike and Pearl. She will leave the car windows cracked open for the dogs. It is a warm afternoon. In a large purse she is holding in one hand, Comtois has stashed six incendiary devices and the .32 calibre pistol.

She is about to leave the Co-op and circle around to the right of the church rectory when she hears the noise. It sounds like someone is having car trouble. An old Ford Fairlane, with obvious engine problems, pulls up about fifteen feet behind the stolen Buick. Comtois instantly recognizes the three young men who step out on to the sidewalk.

Four by four tunnel support beams and horizontal boarding between the verticals shored up Ulrich Sennhauser's tunnel. Anyone taller than five-foot-eight had to bend over to access the ancient temple that lay some four meters into the hillside below the *Pfalz*. It was not a place for the claustrophobic.

A portable 5500-watt Coleman generator provided nearly ten hours of electric power. It was noisy. Sennhauser had enclosed the machine in a three-sided plywood wall. Sound absorbing eco-tiles, composed of light peat, crushed limestone and wood-fibers were then applied, all but eliminating the sound of the five gallon gas engine.

The Order's elite began arriving, as Hochstrasser had instructed, around eleven o'clock. Among them were Council members Frankl Anderegg with the *Rivea corymbosa* and Linus Blosch from the Ministry of Tourism, several Elders, including two from Sennhauser's archaeological team, and a petitely-built initiate, Julia Bragger, from the Biozentrum. Sennhauser dispatched one of his men to the *Münster*, to guide the others to the tunnel opening.

"My God!" Hochstrasser exclaimed, when everyone was assembled, "it's fantastic!" The end of the tunnel was curtained off from the Celtic ruin. The immediate impression of it's splendor was made on two levels of perception; size and majesty. Sennhauser was beaming. "This entire structure," he told the gathering, "is a religious building called a *Cella*. It was likely constructed in the late first century A.D. for ancestor worship, the monitoring of certain celestial events and for the celebration of the Celtic Festival of the Dead."

There were appropriate "oohs and ah-hs" from the cult members. Sennhauser continued. "This walled area is 35 metres across, in the shape of a polygon. It has at least twenty sides. You'll notice a mound, in the center. My team has established that it is a bronze-age burial mound, pre-dating the temple by at least a thousand years and converted into the mausoleum you see before you. This was probably for a local tribal chief. Temples were often built on the site of earlier religious or ceremonial structures and many of them, in modified form, were used into early Christian times."

"And ceremony, as you are all aware, is the nature of tonight's meeting," Hochstrasser interrupted. "Note the circle and triangle on the floor of the temple." Everyone did.

"These will be our focal points for the ritual of *transmutation*. I'd like all of you to greet our initiate, Julia Bragger. Julia works with me at the university and has shown great promise in our work at the Biozentrum. According to tradition, after tonight Julia will become the beneficiary of all the Order's resources, both political and financial. A portion of her income will be assigned to the treasury and

228

her future success in all her endeavors will be assured."

In unison, the members shouted, "Welcome, Julia."

Ty was in no hurry. He, Greg and Jerry spent roughly fifteen minutes on the opposite side of the street from Our Lady of Lourdes, walking up and down the sidewalk and observing the arrivals. They stayed behind parked cars to avoid being in sight of the church. It's main doors did not front on the Main Street, but were on the side of the building next to the driveway that led into the parking lot. Despite some initial barking from Pearl, Mike and Max in the stolen Buick, none of them took any notice of the dogs. They were too intent on the task at hand. A man, dressed in a white cloak bearing some sort of symbol on the left of his chest, greeted cult members on an exterior staircase as they streamed in from the parking lot behind the church. Although none of the three had ever met him, Ty assumed this had to be the infamous Laurent Picard. The white cloak, he guessed, was probably a mark of his rank in the Order.

"If he's who I think he is," Ty remarked, "that means the adjacent rectory is unoccupied. Let's wait for those side doors to close. I think I'll be able to slip into the church through the back."

Jerry was about to respond when a white 1972 Cadillac drove up Main Street and pulled into the parking lot. There was an undertone of sadness in his voice when he said "my father's here." He stood behind Greg, in case Jean-Jacques glanced to his right.

Greg turned and patted him on the shoulder. "It's not as though you didn't expect him," he commented.

Jerry nodded. "Still," he watched the Cadillac as it disappeared behind the church, "I guess I was hoping he'd just stay at the cottage. The worst thing about this whole nightmare is my father's involvement."

Ty began strolling back to Marg Peterson's Ford. "Question is," he addressed Jerry, "involvement in what? Remember, we have no proof that your father is even aware of the murders in Saint-Sauveur, or any of the other crap that's going on."

The reassurance didn't seem to offer any consolation to Jerry. "So what now?" he asked Ty.

"We wait. Greg, you grab the Bell and Howell out of the car and we'll gradually work our way into the parking lot by way of the rectory. You guys can conceal yourselves behind some of the vehicles in the lot. Get some shots, if you can, of faces. Shoot an establisher of the church itself. When everyone's inside. I'm going to break into Picard's residence. It's attached, so there'll be access to the church. Then, we'll see won't we?"

Greg appeared puzzled. "See what?"

"Whether Yvette Comtois turns up. I've got a strong feeling she'll be here, if she's true to form. Something about a settling of accounts." He was completely unaware that Comtois had witnessed their arrival and remained concealed in the Farmers' Co-op.

"Yeah, well," Greg replied, "whoever killed those people in the Laurentians could *also* be here. I'm beginning to think we should be calling the cops."

Ty, momentarily, displayed an expression of concern. "Maybe you're right. Too late now, though. We're going to have to let this play out. And, if I know our favourite Chief Inspector, the cops may show up on their own. Cousineau's no dummy."

Greg fished the Bell and Howell out of the Ford. The trio walked up the street, past the church, and crossed into a field about a hundred yards beyond the rectory. From their new vantage point, they spotted the old cemetery. "Perfect," Ty said. "Clear view of the parking lot from there," he pointed at the headstones. "You can shoot from behind one of those, without being seen. I can scoot over to the rectory and put the cloak on once I'm inside."

"What if you don't come out?" Greg wanted to know.

"Give me an hour. If I haven't rejoined you by then—call the cops."

48

A MOOD OF ANXIOUS expectancy descended on the now thirty-four people, assembled below the *Phalz*. The tunnel entrance lay camouflaged, despite the unliklihood of anyone wandering about Cathedral Hill after midnight. The orange-tinted moon had dropped below the horizon and, on the surface, the ancient temple revealed nothing of its two-thousand year old secrets. Negligible light filtered upwards through the air-vents.

Cult-members carefully hung their street clothes in metal lockers Sennehauser's crew had brought in when the archaeological excavations first began. They now wore the red and blue cloaks and many of them wore little else. Werner Hochstrasser was in white. Council leaders were in purple. *Regional Commanders*, in the various *lodges* around the world, were entitled to wear white as official representatives, in their respective countries, of the Supreme Leader. The Swiss *lodge* was Hochstrasser's home. No Regional Commander was needed here.

The Supreme Leader raised his arms. "All gathered here," he said, in a commanding voice, "are familiar with the proceeding. I will take the first pill as the clock strikes twelve-thirty. This drug has not been used in our past ceremonies, but I'm assured by the Council that it is not unlike the hallucinogens we have employed before." Hochstrasser glanced at Frankl Anderegg, who was shifting nervously from one foot to the other. "The drug, *Rivea corymbosa*, has been clinically tested by Council member Anderegg and has proven to have no ill effects. It should provide a pleasant, if not spiritual journey for all of us, reaching its highest degree of intensity in about thirty minutes from the point of ingestion and lasting for several hours."

Anderegg said nothing. Hochstrasser continued. "Form a line, if you will, brothers and sisters. After I have taken the drug, it will be passed to the Council *members*, to you and so on to our initiate Julia

Bragger. Julia's initiation and the ritual of *transmutation* will begin sharply at one."

Hushed conversations began, as the cultists lined up. No one was entirely clear on the meaning of the ritual that would follow Bragger's official entry into the Order.

Ty, Greg and Jerry stepped over a low wrought-iron fence surrounding the tiny graveyard. As they did so, two other cars arrived in the parking lot. Ueli Berlinger had already entered Our Lady of Lourdes, carrying the rifle-kit and wearing the two-edged fighter-knife in a sheath attached to his belt. The trio was alone in the cemetery.

"I'm going to make a dash for the rectory," Ty said, "while Picard is greeting people at the church entrance. I don't think there will be that many more cars coming in. From here, Greg, you might get a few shots of new arrivals. But stay put until you think the coast is clear. If you can't get some close-ups of people, maybe it would be an idea to shoot license plates. That way, at least, we could do some cross-checking back at the station and begin to identify some of these cult members."

Greg gave a thumbs-up. "I'll bet the cops'd be interested in seeing these plates."

"Sure," Ty agreed, "first, we get the stuff on the air. Then we talk to Cousineau and company. Remember, if I'm not out of there in an hour, call in the troops."

"Will do." Greg checked his watch. It was six-forty.

Ty tucked the blue cloak under one arm and stepped over the fence into the parking lot. There was only one light on in the rectory next to the only apparent door. He headed for both, listening for any sound of approaching cars out on the Main Street. In spite of his rubber-soled shoes, his quick but scuffing movements seemed to reverberate off the field-stone walls of the old priests' house.

A small screened-in porch faced the parking lot, obviously someone's idea of a less formal greeting area and certainly a fairly recent addition. Ty pushed open an outer door and stepped in onto a pine-plank floor, taking every precaution to make as little noise as possible. The boards squeaked in spite of his efforts. The main door to the rectory was glass-paneled. He approached it cautiously and stared through into what appeared to be an entrance hall off a living room to the left. He slowly turned the door-handle, which was unlocked, but early spring humidity had swollen the wood frame and he had to use his shoulder to get the door open. It made a *chuffing* noise as it swung inwards.

Ty's eyes darted around the room. To his right, a corridor led into pooled darkness towards the church. Immediately in front of him a heavy wooden banister curved upwards along a carpeted staircase. The living room, lit by only one lamp, contained a large couch and several comfortable looking upholstered chairs surrounded a huge coffee table. Two rockers were arranged in front of an open fireplace. On the coffee table, there were two glasses and a half-empty bottle of Glenlivet single-malt scotch. He made a mental note of the fact that Laurent Picard had not been alone in the rectory prior to the events of the day.

Ty was momentarily unsure of what to do first. He decided he'd better get into the blue cloak in case he was discovered prowling around Picard's residence. At least he could then simply say he had entered the building through the parking lot and was looking for a way into the church. He stepped into the shadows below the staircase. There was no sound in the house, other than his own breathing.

The fireplace gave off a smokey odor, leading him to believe the house-guest, whoever he was, had enjoyed a log fire the night before while consuming Picard's scotch. There was too much of a dent in the bottle for day-time drinking. April temperatures were high by noon and continued to drop off into the fifties and sixties during the night … cool enough for a fire.

Ty slipped the cloak over his head and stepped out from under the stairs. Slowly, he made his way down the darkened corridor towards Our Lady of Lourdes. An archway, fashioned out of the same fieldstone that made up the building's exterior façade, was at the end of the hallway. He walked into an office space he assumed was once used by the priests as a vestry to hang vestments and store sacred vessels and parish records.

Unknown to Ty, Picard had auctioned off most of the church's contents and had surrendered the records to the Village of Saint-Félix-de-Sébastien. However, some of the church linens and communion equipment remained on shelves to the right of a second field-stone archway on the opposite side of the room. A heavy wooden door closed the vestry off from the church itself. He was about to open it and emerge on the other side as just another cult member when he heard a noise behind him. Before he had a chance to turn around, he felt a sharp stinging sensation in the side of his neck as he began spiraling downward into a black abyss.

Yvette Comtois tucked the syringe into her purse, along with the pistol and the half-dozen incendiary devices. When Roche Pharmaceuticals had synthesized *Flunitrazepam*, earlier in the year, she had obtained a one-time prescription for the *benzodiazepine* drug, telling her physician she suffered from severe insomnia. Using her knowledge of pharmacology, she had transformed it into an alcohol-based injectable solution popularly referred to in Europe as *darkene*. She'd initially intended to instruct Francis Duguay as to its uses for the purpose of abducting a young girl. In the end, she'd changed her mind. Duguay was bound to miscalculate the dosage and, in retrospect, the kidnapping of Jacqueline Morissette had been accomplished quite successfully without the drug.

Comtois had been certain, however, that it would come in handy at some point in the future. She stared down at the limp body of the young reporter who'd interviewed her at La Petite Perle. She calculated the sedative hypnotic properties of the *darkene* would wear off in two or three hours but, in the meantime, she'd have to hide him somewhere.

She began to drag Ty back down the corridor into the rectory. He was heavier than he looked and, by the time she reached what she assumed was a basement entrance, her breath was coming in short gasps. She didn't want to harm the young man. For just a moment she thought of simply rolling him down the staircase but ruled that out. In her own way, Comtois sort of admired the reporter's ingenuity. She had no idea where he'd obtained the blue cloak he was wearing, but she decided his plan to infiltrate the Order's meeting was in some respects not unlike her own.

"Smart kid," she thought, as her fingers searched for a light-switch that would illuminate the now darkened stairs. She found a three-switch panel on the wall. Her first attempt lit up an overhead fixture and she quickly flipped it off. The second attempt was a success. She grasped Ty under the arms and, moving backwards toward the basement, pulled him after her. His feet *clumped* against each stair as she eased him downward.

Once at the bottom, Comtois bent over with her hands on her knees. Her heart was pounding and perspiration had beaded on her forehead. "Now what?" she surveyed the unfinished basement area. Crates of stored materials were stacked against the far wall, on the Main Street side of the building. An oil-burning furnace which she guessed had been a replacement for the coal or wood of the past, was on her right. Nothing but open space to the left. More boxes. A long table with various tools spread out on it. Then, she spotted it. There was a door, in the wall behind the furnace. Laboriously she dragged Ty toward it.

The door opened on to a pitch-black space beyond. There was no window in the room and light from the basement stairs barely reached it. Comtois left Ty lying on the basement floor while she explored. There was a string-cord connected to a single light bulb on the ceiling of the room. She pulled it and found herself in an old root cellar. Shelves containing mason jars, now empty of the pickles or tomatoes they once held, lined the walls. Dried up parsnips and other vegetable remains had been swept into a corner. It didn't appear that even Laurent Picard had any use for the area. "Perfect," she said out loud, as she turned around and reentered the basement proper. She grabbed Ty around the arms and resumed dragging him. "Mr. Davis," she told him, "sleep well."

49

THE FIRST SIGNS the *Rivea corymbosa* was working were evident just before one a.m. Swiss time. Similar schedules were being followed simultaneously in Quebec, Germany, France, the U.K., Australia and on the island of Martinique. Beneath the ground of Cathedral Hill, several of the cult members had assumed the lotus position on the floor of the Celtic temple and were waving their hands in front of their faces. They seemed fascinated by the familiar, as though their hands had somehow transformed themselves into the miraculous.

Some were familiar with the LSD-like hallucinations. Others waited patiently for Werner Hochstrasser to begin the proceedings. The *Supreme Leader* leaned on his cane. In his other hand he held a rapier sword, much like the one Yvette Comtois had kept for herself after leaving Europe. The introduction of hallucinogenic drugs to the rituals had become a tradition and had served to elevate his role in the eyes of the followers to that of a true spiritual guide.

Hochstrasser sensed the mood and walked toward the circle and triangle prepared by Ulrich Sennehauser. "I would ask," he began, "that you all stand, please. Julia Bragger, if you will join me here."

The young woman from the Biozentrum obediently took up a position beside him. She was small and appeared lost in the folds of her red cloak. Hochstrasser had instructed her to wear nothing underneath. "You might notice," he continued, "that the circum-ference of the main circle and that of the circle within are not com-plete. This is a door, if you will, to be sealed by myself only after Julia and I are in the center." He surveyed his audience. "Once the portal is closed, Julia and I will be protected from the entity I intend to conjure into the triangle."

There were mumblings among the cult members. Hochstrasser ignored them. "The ritual of *transmutation*, which will follow Julia's initiation into the Order, will involve calling on this entity to reveal, to all of us, what must be the end and aim of all alchemy ... to enhance our bodily strength, to endow us with physical longevity, to renew our youth and to allow our animal natures to surface."

Frankl Anderegg interrupted. "Why do you need to be protected from this, uh, entity you wish to conjure?" Anderegg's concerns about the drug he had brought to the temple continued to mount. Several of the followers had begun moaning and crying out.

"This is an ancient ritual," Hochstrasser replied waving his cane. "Like you, I wish to adhere to its precise nature and to specific incantations. If there are, indeed, forces beyond our understanding ... if my words are powerful enough ... if all of you are sincere in your wish for the ritual's success, the results could be remarkable. And, to answer your question, Frankl, the entity might try to lure me or Julia out of the circle by playing on our fears. If that were to happen, we could be subject to possession. The experiment would, of course, have failed and our very souls could be at risk." He paused, gauging the reaction. Hochstrasser wasn't at all sure he even believed in the existence of the human soul. "Are you with me?" Are you prepared to see beyond the veil?"

All present shouted "yes-s-s-s!"

Limping noticeably, he directed Julia Bragger into the center of the concentric circles. She had begun to sway dizzily. Her pupils were dilated. Hochstrasser crouched and, using the vermilion-red chalk Sennehauser had given him, he drew in the missing sections. "The door is closed," he declared, setting the sword on the temple floor and reaching into his pocket. He withdrew an amulet on a chain. "Take this," he told her. "Wear it on these occasions, Julia, as a mascot to ward off the evil eye and as a symbol of your membership in the Order of the Sword."

The crowd shouted, "Hail Julia."

Hochstrasser smiled as she slipped the amulet around her neck. He retrieved the rapier from the floor. "Raise your cloak," he told her. Julia did so, revealing her right leg and hip. "With this sword," Hochstrasser said, "I enroll this woman, Julia Bragger." He pressed the needle-sharp point against her right buttock and pushed. Blood gushed out of the wound and she yelped in pain. "From this day forward," he added, "let this blood flow with the river of creation."

"The river-r-r," cult-members chanted. "The river-r-r of creation."

Julia was visibly swaying back and forth on her feet. She lowered her cloak and a stain, colored a darker red than the material itself, began forming on her hip. Hochstrasser, again, laid the sword on the temple floor. "The Order of the Sword welcomes Julia Bragger as its new sister."

"Sis-ster, Sis-ster, Sis-s-s-ter ..." the chanting continued. One of the cult-members, inexplicably, began running in circles. Another lay prostrate on the ground, extending his arms toward the burial mound in the center of the temple. Frankl Anderegg watched on, fearful that the *Rivea corymbosa* was much too powerful, but Hochstrasser paid no attention to the bizarre behaviour. He was too taken with his own sense of power and importance.

Two names were underlined on Chief-Inspector Cousineau's priority list ... La Corporation Énergie and Laurent Picard. Sergeant Tremblay's background investigation of the late Francis Duguay had produced both. Numerous personal telephone calls had apparently originated from Duguay's office at the corporation, to a number in the Montérégie region. It was an unlisted number but, with the cooperation of Bell Canada, Tremblay had traced it to a Laurent Picard in the tiny farming community of Saint-Félix-de-Sébastien.

That was on Tuesday. By Wednesday morning, Cousineau knew a great deal more about Picard and the church he'd purchased in 1967 from the Catholic parish. It seemed the townspeople in that community were more than willing to share information and opinions about the peculiar goings-on at Our Lady of Lourdes. It was *enough* information to prompt Cousineau to make a call to the Cowansville QPP detachment. Through the officer in charge, there, he made arrangements to place the church under round-the-clock surveillance. Cousineau had a gut feeling he'd found the Quebec *heart* of the cult Duguay had exported to Saint-Sauveur.

* * *

When the pills were distributed, in the manner of the host to the communicants, Yvette Comtois held hers under her tongue and spit it into her hand when no one was looking. She kept the cloak's hood over her head and as low as possible on her brow. Others, among the cult-members, also wore the hoods. She was satisfied that she didn't stand out and that her face was sufficiently obscured.

The initiation of Maya Hopkins began shortly after seven. Comtois listened to the smooth tones of Picard's voice and recalled the terror she had felt during her murder trial in Zurich. The voice sounded older but was essentially unchanged. Picard had made a good show, then, of her defense. He was making a good show now as he thrust his sword-tip into the right buttock of the young initiate. Hopkins, like herself and all the *Order's* followers, would bear the scar forever. Comtois gritted her teeth. If Picard suspected *she* might be here Ueli Berlinger couldn't be far away. She was determined to find him and she knew just what to do when she did.

A sort of wildness began to sweep through the gathering. Picard's voice droned on, as he tried to explain the meaning of the ritual of *transmutation*, but it was frequently drowned out by shouts and unintelligible mumbling. Comtois realized that the drug administered by the Regional Commander was responsible. She observed, however, that its effects were unlike any she was familiar with. LSD was predictable. The elevator ride, from the point of swallowing it to full out *tripping*, usually lasted about thirty minutes. Then, if relaxed, the user *peaked* and the hallucinations could be controlled … even enjoyed. *This* drug, whatever it was, appeared to be running away with reason.

"God is dead!" a hysterical man shouted. "His head exploded!" He was pushing his way through the crowd toward Picard and Hopkins.

Three people were sitting on the floor, rocking back and forth. Another had stripped naked and appeared to be masturbating. Yet another was repeatedly banging his head against the paneled walls of the church. Blood cascaded down his face. Laurent Picard, who had also taken the pill, was unrelenting. He waved his sword and began to chant. Images flashed through his brain like a fast-action movie sequence, dancing before his eyes. Picard had begun to think that demons actually *do* exist.

50

"Thou disobedient servant," Hochstrasser bellowed, "I command thee to *do my bidding*." He signaled Ulrich Sennehauser, who lit a brazier in the center of the triangle. The flame burned low and steady, jumping only occasionally in a cool breeze that crept like pestilence along the floor of the temple. Julia Bragger shivered. Her hip throbbed and a mucousy drool ran down her chin.

"I demand," Hochstrasser continued, "that you show yourself. Do not deny unto those assembled in this ancient place the gift of rejuvenescence. Give to us what is accorded to the beasts of the field ... an escape from the emptiness of senility. Let us assume the most gracious amenities of joyous youth, grace, power, perfection and beauty. *Do my bidding*."

The small flame in the brazier seemed to sputter, sending sparks upward toward the ceiling of the structure. Silence fell on the throng, now transfixed by the unfolding ritual.

Sennehauser stood by a small panel, connected by an extension-cord to the power generator. As per instructions, he had synchronized a battery of lights along the temple walls. At the appropriate moment, he was to press a button causing the lights to be extinguished one by one. "Show-biz for the faithful," Hochstrasser had repeated his favorite line. Now, with the *Rivea corymbosa* coursing through his body, the *Supreme Leader* wasn't sure that special effects were even needed.

He turned to Julia Bragger, who had sat down in the inner-circle and was making mewling noises. "Bestow *Kischuph* upon this woman, Julia Bragger. Give her perfect memory, sight and hearing. Reveal that nature of her soul that is one with animal kind. *Do my bidding*."

Sennehauser hit the button. The cultists began chanting "*Do his bidding. Do his bidding*." The first light went out. Then the second, third, fourth and so on. When the last one blinked and died, and the temple was in full darkness, something happened that neither Senne-hauser nor Hochstrasser had planned. The brazier flame suddenly stopped sputtering and momentarily became a pillar of fire at least three meters high, enveloping everyone in a blood-red haze. If he was hallucinating, Hochstrasser realized it was a shared hallucination. There were screams. Cultists fell to the floor, shielding their eyes against the brightness of it.

What followed was not scripted. Julia bared her teeth. She went from a sitting position to a crouch—her hands clenching and un-clenching. Her eyes rolled back and the drool from her mouth was now a white, foamy substance. Hochstrasser wasn't aware he had discarded his cane. For the first time in decades, his game leg supported him perfectly and the words that spewed forth from his mouth were not his own. "Behold, the power that glows in the flower, glides in the stream, moves in the ocean and shines in the sky. Thus is linked this outpouring from this body into another … the foun-dation and fountain of all life."

Yvette Comtois was sure of one thing. Ueli Berlinger was somewhere in the church, because Laurent Picard would have wanted the secur-ity. She moved easily through the crowd, glancing at faces, watching for anyone who did not appear to be drugged. It was an easy task. A collective madness had gripped everyone present.

"Such strange weather," someone remarked to her in passing. "Everything's purple."

A man and woman were having sex on the raised section of floor where the church altar had once stood. One man had decided that his arm had been barbecued. He was biting at it and loudly declaring how it "tasted like chicken." Four of the women were holding hands and dancing in a circle around one of two vertical beams, supporting the choir loft. That's when she saw him. Berlinger was *in* the loft.

She walked slowly back into the center of the church, where Picard was ranting on about demons and *transmutation*. Maya Hop-kins, the initiate, had wrapped her arms around the Regional Com-mander's legs and was singing "Some Enchanted Evening," from the Broadway musical *South Pacific*. Standing next to the so-called *magic circle*, Comtois had a clear view of the entire structure. She noted the fact that there was only one set of stairs leading up to it, and both the loft and the stairs were made entirely of wood.

Once she spotted him for a second time, confirming in her own mind that it was indeed Berlinger, she headed for the former vestry. After subduing the television reporter, she decided that the small room off the church was the perfect place to conceal the incendiary devices. She left them on one of the shelves and covered them with some of the old linens she found there. Comtois had waited nearly twenty years. She could not fail now.

Gradually she picked her way through the mayhem that now consumed Picard's carefully-planned ceremonies, pausing occasionally to sit down, roll over or wave her arms. If Berlinger was as good as his reputation, he'd be looking for anything unusual. In these circumstances, rational behavior would be out of the ordinary. Eventually, she managed to isolate herself from the others and was standing directly beneath the choir loft.

Comtois had inserted varying lengths of fuse into the half-dozen packets. The Potassium-chlorate, sugar and match-heads combination would provide a choreographed series of firey explosions, timed to trap Berlinger and spur on the already chaotic atmosphere in the church. If Berlinger tried to escape, she'd decided to shoot the sonofabitch.

"Time's almost up." Jerry was looking at his watch and Greg was still filming license plates in the parking lot. "Whattya think?"

"What do you make it?"

"Nearly seven-thirty."

Lights shone through the stained glass windows of Our Lady of Lourdes and the parking lot was bathed in moonlight. They'd heard some shouting in the church, but Jerry decided it was similar to what he'd experienced on the day he'd followed his father to Saint-Félix-de-Sébastien.

Greg shrugged. "You know what? Maybe we should be at least *thinking* about calling the police." He rested the Bell and Howell against his shoulder. "But he went into the rectory at six-forty." He paused, thinking. "How about this? I'll cut through the cemetery to the street. I need to get an establisher of the church from over by the Co-op anyway. Ty said to give him an hour, so let's hold off for another fifteen minutes or so. By the time I circle the building and get some long-shots of the place, we can think of trying to reach Cousineau's office."

"Think he'll be around this late?"

"Nah. I don't think Chief Inspectors work past five o'clock. But we'll get *somebody's* attention."

"We'd better."

Greg smiled. He'd worked with Ty for enough years to know that risk-taking was part of his character. "Remember, Jerry, this is the guy who stole fingerprints from a corpse. He loves this kinda shit. Let's just wait a while longer." He stepped over the wrought-iron fence into the tiny graveyard and his silent camera was rolling.

Main Street was a No Man's Land. No one in sight. Only one street light cast a dim glow on to the sidewalk outside the Farmers' Co-op. Greg was getting a long-shot of the church, when he realized he was being watched. Two Quebec Provincial Police officers were parked near his mother's Ford. It appeared he and Jerry wouldn't have to call the cops after all.

51

"I CAN FLY." THE TUNNEL below the *Pfalz* vomited out more than thirty people. Werner Hochstrasser watched in horror as Council member Linus Blosch perched himself on top of the steep staircase leading down to the Rhine and the *Münster Fähre*. "You *can't!*" he shouted. But the wind had come up and his voice was lost in it. Blosch was giggling like a school girl as he leapt from the top stair, throwing his body forward. It pounded against a metal banister several times, before coming to rest about midway down the incline. Hochstrasser knew there was no point in hurrying. Blosch's twisted and broken carcass wasn't moving.

The *Rivea corymbosa* hadn't let up. Followers who had watched the spectacle behaved as though it was all very natural. One woman, who had somehow cut off her right ear and whose blood had saturated her cloak, grinned at Hochstrasser. Two of her front teeth were missing. "Marbo nats," she said. "Foyne brik tannenblatz."

Two men ran past Hochstrasser toward the cathedral. One of them appeared to be carrying the gasoline can Ulrich Sennehauser had used to fill the power generator. Before he could object, they doused themselves in the fluid and, using a pocket lighter, self-immolated. Their subsequent screams were mixed with laughter. Several of the cultists had encircled them and seemed to find their frantic movements entertaining.

Hochstrasser knew what he had to do. He, Sennehauser, Anderegg and the Elders had to get *off* Cathedral Hill. What had transpired in the ancient, Celtic temple would be attributed to vandals. "Whoever survives this drug and this night," he told himself, "will have to be sworn to secrecy." He realized he was crying, as he backtracked toward the tunnel. He *had* to warn the others. The Order could not be implicated.

* * *

She wasn't intending on a massacre. Yvette Comtois figured the poor fools involved in Picard's ritual, would have to fend for *themselves* once the fires began. Those who tried to escape through the side doors of the church below the choir loft, would be forced to retreat. There were two other ways to exit the building. Emergency doors lay to the right of the former altar. To the left was the stone archway leading into the vestry. People who had presence of mind could escape through the rectory. Comtois realized, of course, that presence of mind was sadly lacking. Drug-induced madness prevailed.

Yvette kept a close eye on the loft as she made her way toward the front of the church. Berlinger had twice peered over the railing at the top of the stairs, but she'd managed to avoid attracting his attention. She placed the incendiary device with a six-minute fuse at the base of the huge wooden doors. She positioned the second, third and fourth packets, each with three-minute fuses, along the wall.

She estimated that by the time the fire had established itself in the wood paneling beneath the loft, the one-minute fuses on the two remaining devices would have had time to reach the crushed match heads and the potassium chlorate. The stairs and much of the loft itself would be entirely engulfed in flames. Comtois reached under her cloak and pulled out a lighter. The .32 calibre revolver tucked in the belt of her corduroy pants, gave her all the confidence she needed. She lit the first fuse.

Réal Gendron showed up at seven-thirty-five. He parked his four-wheel-drive jeep, with "*La Voix*" emblazoned on the doors, directly behind the QPP cruiser and climbed out. The officer behind the wheel of the cruiser opened *his* door and unwound his six-foot-four frame.

Greg, who was still shooting his *establishers* of the church, watched as the big man approached the newspaper reporter. "Câlice," the officer swore out loud, smiling at the same time. "Who invited the media to this party?"

Gendron, being his usual charming self, extended his hand. The cop shook it. "Chief-Inspector Adrien Cousineau filled me in," he replied. "How long you guys been in the area?"

"Cousineau set this up with Cowansville. We pulled a three to midnight."

"Anything happening?"

The officer pointed at the driveway into the parking lot behind Our Lady of Lourdes.

"Bunch o 'freaks in the church," he shrugged. "We been on stake-out four 'n a half hours, moving the cruiser from one location to another. Nothing illegal, as far as we can tell."

Greg walked back along the sidewalk and greeted Gendron. "Ty was wondering how long it would take you to catch up," he joked.

"I bet he was."

"How'd *you* get on to it?"

Gendron smiled. "Cousineau," he replied. I called him on the Comtois investigation. He thinks she might be in the area. What have you guys seen?"

Greg looked at his watch. He momentarily ignored the question and addressed the officer. "I was going to come and talk with *you* when I spotted the squad car. My colleague, Ty Davis, went into the rectory just about an hour ago. Another guy I work with, Jérôme Poirier, is in a small cemetery adjacent to the parking lot. But Ty left us with instructions to contact the police, if he wasn't outta there in an hour."

The officer shrugged. "Look, my partner and I have orders too. Be on the watch for this, uh, Comtois woman. We have only a description and a lot of people went into that church. If she's here, we haven't seen her."

Greg put on a worried expression. "All I know is that my friend hasn't come out of there."

Gendron began crossing the street. He shouted over his shoulder at the big cop. "If you guys needed a warrant to search the place before, you don't need one now. Look!"

"Jeezus!" Greg exclaimed.

Smoke billowed into the parking lot. The front doors of the church exploded in flames.

The two remaining incendiary devices sent a curtain of fire up the stairs to the choir loft. By now, the interior paneling along the side of the building, including the rear wall of the loft itself, was raging. Ueli Berlinger had been poised to escape down the stairs. His muscles tensed as he grabbed his rifle kit and stared down into the chaos below.

Laurent Picard had given up on the ritual and, in spite of drug-induced confusion, he realized something dangerous was happening. He helped his initiate, Maya Hopkins, to her feet and began dragging her toward the vestry. There was no point in trying to control the other cult members. Insanity ruled.

"Pret-t-t-y-y," one woman said. Her red cloak had melted and her hair had burned off.

Picard watched, briefly, as she began climbing the loft stairs. A man and woman, who had apparently been playing a bizarre game of tag, were running in circles. The man was carrying Picard's discarded rapier-sword. When he finally caught up to her, he ran the sword through the back of her neck and shouted "*You're it!*"

Berlinger calculated it was about twelve feet to the floor of the church. He swung his legs over the railing, holding the rifle kit under one arm and lowering himself with the other. His considerable strength allowed him to hang vertically from the railing, using only one hand. He looked down before letting go, anticipating a painful drop to the stone-tiles. It was the last thing he ever did. Yvette Comtois shot him three times in the back.

He opened his eyes to darkness so absolute that the room had no discernable dimensions. He had no idea where he was. He couldn't tell by staring into the satiny blackness whether he was in fact in a room or in some sort of container.

Ty took a deep breath. The air seemed clean enough, so it was probably not a closed container. He wracked his brain for answers. What was his last, conscious memory? Had he been asleep or in some sort of coma? Had someone knocked him out? He ran the fingers of both hands through his hair and across his forehead. There was no detectable injury; no lumps or lacerations. "Drugs," he thought. He had to have been drugged. An icy terror suddenly raced up his spine. The air he was breathing was no longer clean. Ty smelled smoke.

52

"CALL FOR BACKUP! Call for backup! The tall Provincial Police officer yelled at his partner, who had not left his seat on the passenger side of the cruiser.

"Wha-at?"

"Backup!" the officer repeated. "Church on fire!"

The partner leaned over in the car-seat and saw the smoke. "Yessir," he said. "Right away." He began shouting into a dashboard microphone.

Greg and Réal ran across the street and into the parking lot. "We've gotta get in there!" Greg exclaimed. "Something's happened to Ty. I'm sure of it. He'd have been out by now."

As they passed the charred side doors of the building, they suddenly burst open. Something resembling a human being stumbled out on to the stairs, his clothes entirely burned off and portions of his body still on fire.

Réal tackled him to the ground and began rolling him over and over, trying to extinguish the flames. The man's eyes focused briefly then glazed over. He stopped breathing. Greg had filmed the horrific episode with his Bell & Howell. "Let's go," he said. "Nothing we can do."

They turned the corner into the main lot. Jerry Poirier was crouched over two more bodies, that of a man and a woman. He was almost hysterical. "I tried to help them," he said, in a voice choked with fear. "I tried to help them, but they wouldn't stop running. Christ! Je-e-s-sus Christ!"

Greg took one look at the blackened remains and headed for the rectory. "Ty went in through that door," he pointed. "He's in there, somewhere." Greg and Réal followed him into the porch.

Inside the rectory, they were nearly trampled. A veritable tide of wild-eyed cultists flooded down the hallway, leading from the church. The man Ty had tentatively identified as Laurent Picard had an arm around the waist of a young woman, who appeared to be enjoying the mayhem. Her high-pitched laughter sent chills up Greg's back. He waved frantically at Jerry and Réal, leaping out of the way as the terrified people pushed past him and exited through the porch into the parking lot.

"Ty!" he shouted. "Ty Davis! It's Greg! Can you hear me?" He wheeled around, looking for the other two. They weren't in sight. It seemed both had been swept backwards by the onslaught, leaving Greg standing alone at the foot of a curved staircase. Two men walked past him toward the porch. One of them was naked from the waist up and someone had used a knife to carve the words *Alpha and Omega* into his chest. Blood had coagulated around the wounds, but the letters stood out quite clearly. Neither man seemed alarmed at the turn of events in the church. They were talking to each other in calm voices. One of them clapped his hands together, as though pleased with something the other had said. Greg couldn't make *anything* of their conversation, as they passed into the night.

In the parking lot outside, people were climbing into their cars. Jerry couldn't distinguish one individual from another. Most were still wearing their hoods as they scrambled to safety. By now the fire inside the main church had become so hot that stained glass windows began exploding outwards, raining colored shards on to the pavement. An easterly wind seemed to carry the distant sound of sirens.

Jerry squinted into the smoke, desperately hoping his father had been among those who had escaped. His heart sank when he realized that Jean-Jacque's white Cadillac was still parked where he had left it. He gestured at Réal and the *La Voix* reporter tried once again to gain entrance to the rectory.

There was only one thing to do … *move*! Ty quickly realized that he had to get out. His eyes were watering from the smoke and his head throbbed. He moved his legs, relieved to find no restraints. "Stand up!" he told himself. Gradually, fighting a nearly overwhelming urge to vomit, he got on his feet and stretched his arms out in front of his body. The ink-black room, if that's what it was, provided no clue as to its nature. He literally couldn't see his own hands.

Inch by inch, he edged forward. When his fingers touched a smooth wall, he began moving sideways along it, hoping to find a doorway. His forehead suddenly connected with some shelving and he winced in pain. Ty was aware that the smoke had to be entering the room through an opening from the outside. Although it was progressively harder to breathe, he continued along the wall through the thickest of it. Ty remembered, from his many experiences at fire scenes, that most fatalities resulted from smoke inhalation. Most people were dead, before being fried. The gruesome thought spurred him on.

"Ty-y! Ty-y Davis! You down there? Can you hear me?"

It was Greg's voice, coming from somewhere above him. "Here!" he tried yelling. "Down here. I'm in some kind of … room." He began coughing uncontrollably and his words came out in raspy tones. "Greg! It's me! I need help!"

There was silence for a few, frightening moments and Ty was sure he had been abandoned. Then he heard the pounding sound of boots on a staircase. "He-er-re! I'm in he-ere!" he managed to shout, before experiencing another coughing spasm.

"Gotcha! Hold on! It's hard to see down here," Greg replied. "Keep making noise, if you can."

Ty balled his fists and slammed them down on the shelves he'd hit his head on. One of them gave way and Mason jars collapsed to the floor and shattered. Greg responded.

"Okay! I'm coming! I *hear* you!"

Seconds later, dim light poured in through an open door and Ty nearly fell into the basement beyond. "This way!" Greg grabbed his arm and began pulling him across the room toward the stairs."

Réal Gendron was standing at the top. "Got 'im?" he shouted down.

"Got him." Greg replied. "We're coming up."

When they reached the main floor, it was instantly apparent that escape through the rectory porch was impossible. A river of fire had flowed through the vestry, down the hall to the living room. The staircase Greg had stood beside, just minutes ago, was in flames and the draft created by opening the basement door was rapidly drawing certain death in their direction.

"The bedroom!" Greg pointed. "We'll have to get out through the bedroom!"

Fire chased them along the corridor and into a large, master suite. "Close the door!" Réal warned. "If you smash a window, we'll burn up."

Ty slammed the bedroom door behind him and Greg threw a chair through the nearest window. One by one, the three men climbed through it, emerging in the small cemetery beside the building. Jerry Poirier, the tall Provincial Police officer and his partner were waving in the fire-trucks. Three other squad cars, their dome lights flashing, were in the adjacent parking lot. Jerry raced toward them, leaped over the wrought-iron fence and, adrenalin charged, he nearly fell flat on his face. "You made it!" he exclaimed. "My God. You *made* it! Did you see my father? My father's car is still here."

53

THE HORRORS OF CATHEDRAL HILL were repeated in cult *lodges* everywhere. Coded background information on the Order was dispatched by Interpol to local and federal police forces. Aggressive investigations were choreographed by its head office in Lyons, and arrests followed within days. The secret society that had wielded so much power in so many countries ... was no longer a secret. Media headlines unmasked a history of political and corporate corruption. Major players in both worlds were exposed.

Of the thirty-four people who'd participated in Werner Hochstrasser's ritual below the *Phalz*, only eighteen survived. Many suffered injuries or, as in the case of initiate Julia Bragger, spent months in psychotherapy. The Supreme Leader was arrested at his office in the Biozentrum. During his ensuing court case, he did not require the use of a cane.

Frankl Anderegg, who was led from Sandoz Labs in handcuffs, later admitted to possessing and distributing a dangerous hallucinogen. Ulrich Sennehauser's archaeological discovery near the *Basel Münster* was overshadowed by his now public association with the shadowy Order of the Sword. Others would eventually take credit for uncovering the first century Celtic temple. The battered body of Council member Linus Blosch was retrieved from the staircase leading to the *Münster Fähre*.

In all, fifty-four died in Switzerland, France, Germany, the U.K., Canada and Fort de France, Martinique. Jerry Poirier's father was one of them. Funeral services for Jean-Jacques Poirier were held a week after the chain of events in Saint-Félix-de-Sébastien.

The extent of his father's knowledge of, or involvement in, the sordid affairs of The Order would never be known; a fact that Jerry found increasingly more difficult to live with. He and his brother, Yvan, decided to sell the family home in Outremont and the white Cadillac. The chalet in Venise-en-Québec became a rental property.

Ty tried to convince him otherwise, but Jerry ultimately decided not to pursue his career at CKCF Television.

On April 11, 1972, 200,000 Quebec civil servants, teachers, hospital and Social Service workers staged a general strike that would forever change the landscape of collective bargaining. The walkout that paralyzed a province had national and international ramifications. Three union leaders were later jailed for their defiance of government lawmakers.

Charles and Sarah Walkley stayed on in N.D.G. for another two weeks after Elizabeth's disturbing session with Dr. Barry Nelson. Liz gradually began to accept the concept that life is filled with the unexpected. David's untimely death and her role in the tragedy, as a ten-year-old, became a series of dream images that ultimately dissipated and dissolved altogether. She and Ty saw Dr. Nelson on three other occasions. Liz continued on a regimen of *Mianserin hydrochloride* and there were no further episodes of dissociation. On the night of Catherine's school play, she hugged Robin and whispered in Ty's ear … "I'm back."

Greg Peterson and Suzie Waldon agreed to sell the Suzie-Q photo studio in Old Montreal, the proceeds from which were split evenly between them. Marg Peterson got her wish. Greg spent his share on an engagement ring. A marriage date was yet to be determined, but Marg was optimistic that grandchildren were in the offing.

For his part, Chief Inspector Adrien Cousineau's investigation of La Corporation Énergie went nowhere. A direct connection between the kidnapping and murder of Jacqueline Morissette and cult operations around the world was circumstantial at best. Laurent Picard left Canada and was arrested on arrival in Zurich. Our Lady of Lourdes church and the adjoining rectory were a burned out ruin.

No one ever saw or heard from Yvette Comtois again. But Ty never forgot the night of the fire. When he, Greg and Réal Gendron escaped through the bedroom window into the tiny cemetery, his eyes had been streaming and he couldn't be sure of what he saw silhouetted against a setting moon in the fields beyond. A woman and three dogs bounded over those fields, and he was fairly certain that the woman … was running on all fours.

Véhicule Press